THE *Light* WE SEE

J. Lynn Bailey

Visit my website at www.jlynnbaileybooks.com
Cover Designer: Hang Le, By Hang Le,
www.byhangle.com
Editor and Interior Designer: Jovana Shirley,
Unforeseen Editing, www.unforeseenediting.com
Proofreader: Julie Deaton, Deaton Author Services

ISBN-13: 978-1-7324855-9-4

For my husband, Brandon.

Thank you for loving me the way you do.

PROLOGUE

2020

If you had asked me what it was like before I met Luke, I would have answered, *Easier.* After you read my story, you might not agree. In fact, you might get angry. You might stomp your foot. This story might break your heart, but life is full of choices we don't get to make and missed opportunities. I don't regret a single moment with Luke. Sometimes, I miss him so much that I beg myself not to pick up my phone just to hear his voice again. Make the phone call I know I'll regret come morning when the sun begins its rise again.

You might ask yourself why I did it. Sometimes, we're put in unfathomable situations, forced to make choices that eat away at us in the end. How we're able to justify the wrong, rectify the right. But this story isn't about regret; it's about living life in the present moment—at least, that's what Luke taught me. It's about forgiveness. Because in the end, when the clock begins to slow and our bodies are taken to a time that simply cannot remember, we'll know joy. Joy is the feeling we get when we set our burdens free. When we clean up our past and our souls become whole again. When we finally just let go.

Luke taught me that the benefits of loving far outweigh the price we pay to allow our hearts to give, and in return, we receive something so pure, so untainted, so beautiful in the end.

For, at the end of our days on this earth, it is love that sets us free.

Six Years Earlier
2014

"Ms. Clemens? Mr. Jenkins will see you now," the woman with the stiff bun and mauve pencil skirt says.

She says *Ms. Clemens* like I'm not the only person in the waiting room. As if there were other applicants waiting. I'm the only one on the seventh story floor in the 1970-something building—well, me, Pencil Skirt, and Mr. Jenkins.

I nod, grab my purse from my lap, and stand, following her behind the door she just came through moments ago.

"This way," she calls behind her, carrying a manila file in her left hand, tucked tightly against her side. Her heels clicking against the gray industrial-strength linoleum. Probably full of asbestos.

This isn't how I pictured the back office of *US Monthly* magazine. It's desolate and quiet. Eerily quiet. I imagined staff writers at the water cooler, discussing their stories. Laughing at jokes. The sound of nails clicking on keyboards. A dry breeze from an open window, the Los Angeles smog blowing through the room where the writers sit, working on their word counts, fulfilling their quotas.

The woman in the pencil skirt glances back, as if keeping an eye on me.

My hands tighten around my purse—or rather, my sister's purse, which she insisted I take even though I'm carrying a bottle of water, a pen, and my phone.

Is she looking back at me because she knows my background?

Is she doing that to keep her distance?

The hallway is quiet, and we pass several doors before we reach the right one.

Hello, Mr. Jenkins. I practice his name in my head.

Hello, Mr. Jenkins. My name is Catherine.

You'll need to practice interview skills, Cat, my sister, Ingrid, said to me weeks ago.

The truth is, I'm thirty-four, and I've never been to an interview before—unless of course, you count my college interview at eighteen … before everything happened.

The woman stops and opens the door on the left. "Mr. Jenkins, Miss Clemens is here."

Mr. Jenkins doesn't look up from his oversize mahogany desk, the top of his head on display, his hair sparse on top and full in the middle. Floor-to-ceiling windows sit behind him, which overlook the greater Los Angeles skyline. With only a hand and no glance, he motions me to a leather chair in front of his desk.

"Please, have a seat," Pencil Skirt says.

My heart, as if it had a new gear, has reached its limit as it pounds out of my chest.

The woman hands the manila file to Mr. Jenkins and leaves the office.

I sit. Swallow hard. My mouth dry and full of imaginary cotton.

Penny Ledbetter, who's still at Federal Correctional Institution in Dublin, California, taught me to hold my breath and count to six before I spoke when I got nervous. She said anything under five seconds was too little and anything over six seconds made her pass out. So, six was a good number for her.

She was sentenced to twenty years for setting her house on fire, her drunk husband passed out inside. She watched it burn to the ground. Others might call it murder, but Penny called it freedom from the nightmare she lived married to Bob.

Some women in prison know they're guilty. Others blame their mechanic for not fixing their engine properly when their car broke down while trying to outrun the police. Others believe while on their seventh drug charge, it was somehow their drug dealer's fault for selling out. Some choose not to blame anyone and push it off on bad luck.

I knew I was guilty, and so did Penny Ledbetter.

I do the Penny Ledbetter breath. "Hello, Mr. Jenkins. Thank you for your time," I say with far more confidence than I have. Somewhere within me, the words prove to be louder than I think when Mr. Jenkins picks up his head to look at me.

"It's a favor for Eddie. We're old friends," Mr. Jenkins says.

Eddie McGavin is—was—my attorney.

I assume my résumé is in the manila folder that was handed to Mr. Jenkins by Pencil Skirt along with the explanation of my missing in action period. And it isn't the résumé and cover letter I'm worried about. It's the application. The small box that asks if the applicant has ever been convicted of a felony.

Eddie said it wasn't his business to tell and that he'd get me the interview and I'd have to do the rest.

I really need this job. A full-time job. Consistent paycheck.

My hands sweat.

Mr. Jenkins opens the file. Scans through the pile of paperwork, which includes my explanation of why I have to mark felony on all applications.

After a few moments and what feels like an eternity, Mr. Jenkins closes the file and clasps his hands together. Stares at me intently.

My stomach twists.

The air conditioner hums to life, giving the building existence, a breath of life, and it fills the silence around us.

Finally, he asks, "Did you do it?"

His office phone rings, but Mr. Jenkins doesn't move; he just stares at me, waiting for my answer.

The ringing stops after three rings.

The silence, along with the air-conditioning, reaches into my heart, wanting to take away the memories of that morning, and all my head wants to do is keep them. Store them safely, so I'll never forget what happened. But I always answer this question with the same truth I've given for the last thirteen years. I always answer with the truth.

"Yes."

Still, Mr. Jenkins doesn't budge. His bushy eyebrows, I finally notice, are unruly and gray. What he lacks in hair on the top of his head, he makes up for with his eyebrows. Mr. Jenkins is in his late sixties, I assume. Maybe he isn't though. Maybe it's life that's given him this look, maybe his own decisions, his long hours in the office, his cocktails that have turned into seven a night, or a line of coke in the morning to counterbalance the sleeplessness.

He sighs, straightening the file with his fingertips against his desk.

The air conditioner grows louder.

It's early September in Los Angeles. It's in the mid-seventies all year long, except in the summertime when it reaches the eighties and nineties. I wonder why the air conditioner is on. Seventy isn't that warm. Perhaps it's part of the building standards, that the building must maintain a certain temperature at all times. Maybe because it reeks of age—and asbestos. Maybe the building has to be kept at a certain temperature, so the asbestos doesn't warm and crawl off the building and leak into our lungs.

Mr. Jenkins leans forward. "I'll call you tomorrow."

I get this line a lot. *We'll call you.* I need the permanency of this job. I need a consistent paycheck. I can't do freelance work any longer. It doesn't pay the bills consistently, and with my mother needing more care, I need this job. The money ran out a long time ago. The reporters stopped calling the home Mother now lives in. The offers for movies and book deals fizzled. It's a story I will never tell publicly.

It's not a story for the public.

I say something completely out of my comfort zone. "Mr. Jenkins, I'll be the best staff writer you have. I'll work longer hours. I'll give you the best stories I can."

"I'm not questioning your work ethic or your ability to write, Ms. Clemens. I'm questioning whether *US Monthly* can afford the liability of you working for us."

I feel my skin begin to tingle. My ears start to do the thing they do—fading in and out of complete silence and back to the ability to hear, as if a cover's been placed over my ears, and noise becomes muffled and distorted and quiet.

"I am worth the risk, Mr. Jenkins. What can I tell you to sway your mind about this job?" I'm persistent, and it's really uncomfortable. Honestly, I'm not sure I believe what's coming from my mouth.

Mr. Jenkins cocks his head to the right and leans back in his chair, the leather grinding against his slacks underneath him.

"What? That you graduated from Brown, top of your class? That you've written articles for national and international publications with circulation to millions?"

No, not that. About what happened that night. But I don't answer him. *I really need this job.* The desperation grows inside me as my stomach sinks to a pit of fear. *I just need one person to take a chance on me. All I need is one chance.*

"I'll need to discuss this with our legal team before I make any decisions." There's a long pause, and then he looks up at me. "Ms. Clemens, I know you can get the job done and get it done well. I just have to convince our attorneys and our public relations team of the same."

My stomach still twists, and the excitement leaves. There's no way in hell any legal team will approve this hire.

I reach across the desk to shake his hand. "I appreciate you meeting with me today, Mr. Jenkins."

He takes my hand in his and then settles back in his chair as I stand with my purse.

I turn and walk toward the door, but before I reach for the doorknob, Mr. Jenkins says, "Eddie says you're a good kid who was dealt a shitty hand."

I stare at the door in front of me, thinking about every single decision that's led me to this exact moment, all the closed doors in my face. "No, I put myself here," I whisper before opening the door. "Thank you again, Mr. Jenkins, for your time."

Ingrid, my younger sister by twelve months, is feeding Mother chicken soup. It's well after noon the next day, and I haven't heard from Mr. Jenkins yet.

"Do you think he just said that to get you out of his office?" Ingrid asks as I stare out the window of Alder Grove Assisted Living. "Besides, Cat, maybe it wasn't a good fit." Ingrid gently puts the spoon to Mother's mouth.

My cell phone rings.

"Is it him?" she asks, placing the spoon back in the bowl.

I reach in my purse and pull my phone out. The one Ingrid insisted I buy. Cell phones weren't really a thing in 2001, so it's taken some adjusting to, but it does make life a little easier. You don't have to pack change for the pay phone. You can make a call at any time. Take a call at any time. It tells you what number is calling. An 805 number flashes on my screen.

"Answer it," Ingrid says.

I nod, swallow. "Hello?" My voice is quiet, as I don't want to stir Mother, who's sensitive to loud noise.

"Hello, Catherine. This is Adrianne St. Clair, Mr. Jenkin's assistant."

Pencil Skirt.

"Hello," I say again softly, trying not to sound too eager, although Ingrid says I've never been too eager for anything my whole life.

"Mr. Jenkins asked that I call you to let you know he'd like to offer you the staff writer position on a probationary status. Please come to our downtown office on Monday morning at eight a.m. The address is 272 Wilshire Boulevard. Seventh floor. Different office than we met in the other day. Are you familiar with LA?"

"Yes."

"Great. We will see you then."

Click.

The line goes dead.

With barely a smile, I look at Ingrid and Mother. They both stare back at me.

"Well?" Ingrid asks.

Mother just stares.

"I-I got the job. Probationary."

Ingrid grins and picks the soup bowl back up. "I knew you could do it."

Mother doesn't budge, staring into space.

Ingrid smiles. Looks at Mother. "Did you hear that, Mother? Catherine got a job." Ingrid stops. Turns to me. "Maybe your first assignment will be interviewing a rock star or something like that."

Pamela, Mother's nurse, peeks around Mother's door to her one-room studio apartment, Mother's afternoon tea in hand and the monthly bill in the other. Pamela's smile is infectious and her attitude more so. She's the type of person who can look outside, see the rain for the eightieth day in a row, and say, *Well, thank you, God, for another day of living.*

Pamela sets the bill on the counter, leans to me, as if Mother can't hear, and whispers, "Rochelle combined the last six past-due months for you."

Ingrid sets the bowl back down, eyes the bill on the counter, grabs a napkin, and dabs Mother's mouth. "Tell Pamela about the job," Ingrid says to me.

It's a wonder we haven't been kicked out of Alder Grove Assisted Living for failure to pay.

"I got a job at *US Monthly*. It's a magazine."

"Well, I'll be damned. But it doesn't surprise me in the least with those beautiful letters you wrote your mama from Dublin." Pamela winks at me and walks over to Mother. "Ain't that right, Sandra?" Pamela asks Mother, not expecting her to speak.

She hasn't spoken a word since January 2, 2001.

I walk over to Mother and whisper in her ear, "I got the job, Mother."

I'm not sure she understands, but every once in a while, we'll get a low moan from her. Pamela dresses Mother every morning in a blouse and chinos even though the only place she sits is in her wheelchair. Even though the only place she stays most of the time is her studio.

Mother used to be an artist. She used a paintbrush like it was part of her. An added appendage. An existential part of who she was—is. Her art has been featured in the Musée du Louvre and the Museum of Modern Art. She's also been featured in Metropolitan Museum of Art. Her love for color and seeing things through a different lens gave both Ingrid and me access to an artist's imagination, expression. Ingrid took to it. I didn't.

Some things are.

Some things aren't.

And everything else is just bullshit.

Before
Federal Correctional Institution, Dublin

Dear Journal,

"Straighten your bow, Catherine. Your father will be home shortly," Mother said as she wiped the kitchen counter down for the tenth time.

I rolled my eyes in the most godforsaken way, reached up, and made sure the pink-colored bow was still intact. I moved it a quarter of an inch, hoping that would satisfy Mother, only so she'd get off my back.

Mother had had a six-person cleaning team at the house just hours before, who cleaned our entire house in four hours flat. All the bedrooms. All the bathrooms and everything else in between.

Ingrid and I had timed them from underneath the dining room table. From the time they'd arrived to the time they left out the side door. Of course, Mother had had them come in the service road, so no one would see.

Everybody had a cleaning service in Beverly Hills in the eighties and nineties. Mother didn't believe Ingrid and me when we told her. Mother was from the Midwest where women stayed home, cared for the children, did the laundry, cooked, cleaned the house, and made sure the chaos was balanced, and life was perfectly pieced together on the outside.

I hated dresses. Ingrid loved dresses.

She loved the lavish parties Father and Mother put on. I thought she loved the sophistication of the attendees, their scents, the way they laughed, the way they drank their champagne, the way they smoked cigars, cigarettes. I thought Ingrid was in love with the idea of the lifestyle. The easy parts.

I thought the parties were pointless and a waste.

The only time I'd see Father smile was when Hollywood poured into our house at six o'clock sharp and left way beyond our bedtime. I'd lie in bed and still hear the faint tink of the flatware, the occasional explosion of laughter. On party nights, Ingrid would sleep in her dress. Mother would blow a gasket when morning came, but Ingrid and I both knew Mother loved us most, and her anger would only last a few minutes. Ingrid thought it was worth it. We hated to make her mad, but I think Ingrid wanted to feel beautiful the morning after, and I understood that.

I peeled my dress off at the first opportunity I could. Throw my jeans and T-shirt on even if it was late.

Eventually, Ingrid and I would fall to sleep.

But it would be late when the yelling started. Father would yell at Mother. Mother would take it, as she did every time.

The yelling would fade into morning.

The sun would rise.

The birds would chirp.

Ingrid and I would get out of bed, sleepily walk downstairs.

Mother would have a silent fit when she saw Ingrid in her dress and me in my jeans.

Father would read the paper, sip coffee, nod at both Ingrid and me as we toddled into the kitchen. Eventually, he would beckon us to him, whisper, "I love you both forever." He would smell of coffee and aftershave.

"Love you, too, Father," Ingrid always said first.

"Love you, Father," I always said second.

The purple hydrangeas sat on the counter.

A night of yelling always turned into a vacation.

We went on vacations a lot. Even if it was just a day trip to Disneyland.

And Mother kept all the pieces together.

One day at Clemens Studios, Mother had to drop off something to Father. Father didn't care in the least when we explored the studios. But if the sign on the studio door read Do Not Enter, Recording In Session, Ingrid and I steered clear. A stagehand had accidentally walked into a recording session, and the director had come unglued right in front of us. Both men never returned to Clemens Studios again.

Father always said, "Keep your personal business your personal business."

Maybe that was why Father only yelled at Mother when everyone slept.

We were in Studio C when Ingrid almost died. Father had taken us to work that day, and Mother had a procedure, so as long as we stayed away from trouble, we had free rein of Clemens Studios.

We were in the dressing room—of course where Ingrid wanted to be in front of the mirror, pretending to be Jane Fonda. I had my feet kicked up on the yellow sofa they had in the dressing room, picking at fabrics on my shirt. Well, the door to the dressing room slammed shut. By itself. It was just Ingrid and me, for all we knew, in the studio. Don't get me wrong; there could have been a handyman or a lighting guy or a sound guy, but we didn't hear them.

I felt the slam of the door throughout my entire body. But the look on Ingrid's face was pure horror. She stared into the mirror, couldn't talk, couldn't move.

"Ingrid? What is it?"

But she couldn't answer.

It was when I stood and walked to her, looked into the mirror, right where she was staring.

Jason Voorhees's face was hanging on the back of the door. Obviously a costume left behind, but I couldn't convince Ingrid of it. I had to drag her out of the dressing room, out of the studio, and into the sunlight to finally get her attention.

That was the day Ingrid almost died of heart failure. Never once did she set foot back into Studio C, nor the fourth dressing room on the right. Still, we didn't know what had caused the door to slam, but it was enough to keep us out of Studio C altogether.

For the most part, Father and Mother kept our eyes hidden from the world around us. We owned one television at home and nine thousand books. We weren't allowed to watch television, except on the weekends. And when we were bored, Father would hand us each a book. Father owned a movie studio, and yet he managed to keep our minds from television-rot.

Not only did Mother and Father throw the parties, but we were also invited to vineyards and castles and spent time with prime ministers and world leaders. But I thought my most treasured experience was meeting Diana, Princess of Wales. She was bold, independent, and beautiful, but what I admired most was her beauty on the inside. The person you saw on camera was the same person as behind the camera; that was rare in our world. Secretly, I wanted to be like Princess Diana. Ingrid wanted to be like Mother. Most little girls wanted to be like their mothers, but Princess Diana was fearless, spent time in orphanages, was an AIDS advocate, helped sick children.

Mother fought for us, Ingrid and me, and I fought to escape.

I kept Princess Diana articles from magazines and newspapers hidden underneath my mattress, and I wasn't sure why. Maybe fear that someone might find them and give me pity or tell me I wasn't good enough. To Father, we could always do better, and I supposed he told the same thing to Mother when he spent the night berating her.

—Catherine

Mr. Jenkins hands me an address, his cell phone number, and a check from across his desk in the downtown office in Los Angeles. "This is the address of your first interview. I'll give you two months to do the story because I want it done right. Luke McCay is leaving Carpinteria in two hours. You have exactly two hours to get to his house and get the interview."

"Luke. Luke McCay. Where's he going?"

"I don't know. Some sort of road trip. Spoke with his publicist and said he's agreed to the interview, but he's leaving in"—Mr. Jenkins glances at his Rolex—"one hour and fifty-seven minutes." He looks down at what I have with me. Draws his eyebrow up.

I, too, look down to see if I've missed something, but my curiosity wins. "But why the interview?"

"*LA Hills* is making a comeback on Fix network this fall. I want you to find out why he's making the comeback after so many years away from television. Find out what he's been up to for all these years. And"—Mr. Jenkins pauses—"you might want to pack a bag, Ms. Clemens." Mr. Jenkins looks down at what I'm wearing again.

"Wait, what?" I say breathlessly.

LA Hills was a drama series that started back in 1990 and ran for about ten years. Luke McCay was the heart of it all. The bad boy. The man every woman wanted.

Mr. Jenkins sighs. "Did Adrianne not give you the background on all this?"

I shake my head.

"Oh, for Christ's sake." He rolls his eyes. "I'd fire her, but she's my niece."

"But my mother—I have family obligations. I can't just pick up and leave, Mr. Jenkins."

"Do you want the job or not, Ms. Clemens?" He begins typing on his computer.

I look at what he handed me. Look at all the zeros on the check.

"One hour and fifty-five minutes, Ms. Clemens. Either leave or leave the check." Mr. Jenkins still stares at his computer, typing.

Shit. I look down at the amount. I look at the address. I swallow whatever saliva sits at the back of my throat. I'd have to leave Mother again. *Will she understand?* "Can I make a call?"

"One hour and fifty-three minutes, Ms. Clemens. Time is ticking. Either take it or leave it." A vein that runs through Mr. Jenkins's forehead to the top of his bald head pulsates.

I try to swallow again, but there's nothing left. My hands are once again sweaty.

"Look, Ms. Clemens," Mr. Jenkins sighs and stops typing. Rubs the top of his face out of frustration. "You said you wanted a job. I'm giving you one that could open many doors for you. Now, shit or get off the pot. If I were you, I'd shit. Now, GO!"

I turn to leave but turn back around to see Mr. Jenkins pointing to his office door. "Go," he calls after me. "A final draft of your story needs to be submitted no later than December 1."

I get in the car, and Ingrid is waiting.

"Well?" she says.

"He's sending me on the road to do an interview."

"On the road? To interview who?"

"Luke McCay."

She's quiet.

"Ingrid? Say something."

But she's ghost white.

Finally, "Are you fucking kidding me?" She tries to contain her excitement.

"I have to be in Carpinteria in"—I look down at my watch—"one hour and forty-seven minutes."

"It takes an hour and twenty to get there, Cat! We'd better drive like hell."

"So, you want me to go?"

Silence again.

"Are you kidding me? Yes, of course I want you to go." Ingrid looks out the window, her reflection white against the sun rays.

"I need to pay Alder Grove. I talked with Eddie. We're out of money, Ingrid. The only thing we have left is the house. Listen, I received my monthly wages from Mr. Jenkins. I'm going to cash it, take some for me, and leave the rest at Alder Grove. Can you get it there for me?"

"Whatever you think is best," she says, looking back at me now.

"I think it's best."

I hear the pain in her voice when she says, "You spent thirteen years paying a price you shouldn't have had to pay."

What I want to say is, *I'd do it again, and I wouldn't change a thing*, but I don't. Instead, I say, "I'll leave the rest in the freezer at the house." Our house. The one we shared with Mother and Father. The house on North Alpine Drive in Beverly Hills.

"You could sell the house," Ingrid says.

"No."

Ingrid sighs. "Okay."

I won't sell the house because I know how much it means to Ingrid.

"Tell Mother, okay? Tell her I'll be back, this time quicker than the last time."

These words make me think about the eleven years I spent in the Federal Correctional Institution in Dublin, California. Ingrid came down every weekend to see me. Every single weekend without fail. How she made it work still baffles me.

I pull up to a beachside house and double-check the address that Mr. Jenkins wrote down. The house is simple but big. A large front window overlooks the Pacific Ocean. The beach is somehow quiet—without people, without wave-catchers and watchers. Houses line the shore, each having their own architect, their own set of plans. Nothing is the same, and each house is unique. Some are beach cottages, others are more modern with browns and tans and creams, and others are far more extravagant with several floors and several decks that overlook the ocean.

The sky is blue, not the light blue when the sun is high in the sky, but a deep blue as if, somehow, God gave the sky a higher setting of vibrance and smiled.

I get out of my 1997 Volvo, lean in, and grab my backpack full of clothes, my purse with my wallet, and several notebooks, sharp pencils, and a few pens.

A 1965 Ford Mustang sits in the driveway. It's midnight black. One sits in one of our garages at home. Undriven and unloved for years.

What the hell am I doing? I look at the staircase that leads up to the front door, which is open.

I push my hands against my pants to dry them as the sweat begins. I throw my backpack on my back and my purse on my shoulder, and I manually lock the Volvo and look up at the house.

I see him.

I swallow and pull my fingers through my naturally curly brown hair that oftentimes gets unruly while driving the coast with my windows down.

A feeling I missed for eleven years.

Luke's back is to me, and I somehow feel as though I have a leg up. As if I've seen him first and I can buy some time in taking down his features.

But he turns and starts down the stairs, watching his steps, but then he looks up and sees me standing below.

He slows, staring at me, and makes his way to the bottom of the steps.

I can't help but stare at the creases on his forehead, the lasting grooves that sit and wait for his smile. His perfectly shaped chiseled face, high cheekbones that narrow out his face. I wonder if Luke was created just for the woman's eye, and for those who see him, do they know that perfection was produced just so they had something beautiful to look at? His lips, thin yet perfect, create a mythical illusion that they might be fuller on some days when the sky is this blue. On days like this, he looks like he just finished filming on a set. His confidence displayed in the set of his shoulders.

Seagulls call, breaking me free of my thoughts.

"You that reporter?" Luke calls out, his tone salty like the ocean, rough and gritty. He throws on a baseball cap. The button-up shirt he wears exposes his chest; a light dusting of chest hair is exposed. Cargo shorts hang loosely from his hips.

"Staff writer for *US Monthly*," I correct him. The word *reporter* sounds too demanding, too untrustworthy.

I take a few steps forward, and when I get closer to him, something happens. It isn't about his face or the creases in his forehead; it's the worry I see in his dark brown eyes. I know the worry because I've seen it in so many. A worry I feel almost every day I walk the free earth. Because life on the inside of prison walls seems easier than life on the outside.

"I'm here to do the interview."

I saw the worried look in Eddie's eyes at my sentencing hearing.

I saw it in Paula's eyes as we sat in cell three, and she talked about accidentally killing her six-year-old daughter while driving drunk.

And mostly, I see it in Mother's eyes.

"You missed your window. I'm leaving." He walks past me. The scent trailing behind him is woodsy and fresh, leaving me no other option but to turn toward him.

Luke opens the trunk of the Mustang and throws an overnight bag in.

Do something, Cat. You need the money. You have to get the interview.

I throw my shoulders back, walk to his trunk, and throw my backpack in, too.

Luke turns to me. His eyebrows narrow.

"I need the interview," is all I say, keeping my purse tucked in tight beneath my arm, praying to God he'll give me a chance. I try to act casual as I make my way to the passenger side of the car, pull open the door , sit down, and shut the door behind me. In the back seat, I notice a guitar case.

After what seems like an eternity, the driver's door opens. Luke gets in and starts the Mustang with a loud roar.

He side-eyes me as he pulls out of the driveway.

I want to ask where we're going.

I want to tell him that I think this might be a bad idea and that I've made a mistake.

But something deep inside me won't bring the words to my mouth, the ones floating in my brain.

I breathe.

My heart pounds.

And Luke hits the gas.

The Carpinteria air seems cleaner. The city seems less populated. But anyplace is less populated compared to Los Angeles. I wonder why Luke chose this town to live in. Does he have houses in other cities? I grab my notebook from my purse and begin to write these questions down. I didn't have time to prepare any questions. He's probably thinking I'm this unprepared, new staff writer, that I'm green, like a new pair of tennis shoes waiting for the big game. And maybe I am. My last interview was in college at Brown. We had to do one—no, several, for *The Brown Daily Herald*. So, it's been a long time.

I try to visualize his face without stealing a glance.

"You from Carpinteria?" he asks, his tone cool and deep, as if he should have a cigarette hanging loosely from his lips and have a drink in the other. Wear a leather jacket that says *Killer* on the back. One hand on the top part of the wheel as he stares straight ahead.

"No. Los Angeles." I don't say Beverly Hills because I don't want him to get the wrong impression. I don't tell him that Ingrid and I grew up playing on movie sets or spent time under tables at lavish parities, pretending to be The Goonies on the search for lost treasure.

"What about you?"

"Kentucky." Luke keeps his eyes on the road but reaches into a compartment and grabs his sunglasses. Puts them on. "What's your name?"

"Catherine."

He nods. "Look, Catherine," he sighs. "Maybe this was a bad idea. Maybe I should take you home."

We're going back toward Los Angeles. My car is back in Carpinteria.

Build a rapport.

"Maybe you should." I shrug. I grab my sunglasses from my purse and slide them on, roll down my window, and allow for the September air to blow through my hair.

I stare out at the Pacific that guides us. Oceans could be famous. There are only a few, and yet everyone knows them by name. People have traveled them. Swam in their water. Watched them from afar. Flew over them. They've been in movies. Hosted celebrities. And yet there they are—steady, mighty, and breathtaking.

"You surfed on *LA Hills* as the character Dylan Klein. Do you surf as Luke McCay?" I ask, embracing the wind that blows, the wind I didn't get to feel for an awfully long time.

"Every chance I get."

"Don't see any surfboards on top of the Mustang." I look at him and watch how the lines that are drawn from his eyes move, indicating a smirk.

I realize I like his smirk—and not in the way you might think. I like his smirk because I don't think Luke is the type of guy who smiles often.

"Going east. Not many oceans that way."

"So, you'll let me come along?"

"Suit yourself."

Before

Federal Correctional Institution, Dublin

Dear Journal,

One night, I crept down the stairs to listen while Ingrid snored in her purple lacy dress, one foot hanging off her mattress.

We'd always shared a room. With all the rooms in the house, Ingrid and I needed each other—as much as I hated to admit I needed anyone.

Father had a way of manipulating Mother without insulting her directly. I noticed it even if nobody else did.

"The meatballs were cold. The coffee was weak. Sharon Sunberg was insulted by the crackers. She's Jewish, Sandra. Truly, I wish you'd take more care in planning these parties for our friends," he said. "I wonder what you'd do without me," he said rhetorically.

Mother didn't say a word.

And she took it all.

Then, when she was sure he was done, she said, "I'll try to do better next time, Jonas."

"I hope so. I'm going to bed. Clean this mess up."

And when Father went to bed, I listened to Mother weep as she cleaned every last glass and fill the Tupperware with leftovers that we wouldn't eat this week because Father didn't like leftovers. Mother believed in leftovers and family dinners and cooking for families that weren't well and church on Sundays and bake sales and fundraisers for good causes.

Father worked many hours, so our family dinners consisted of Ingrid, Mother, me, and Eugene, the stray dog Mother had picked up one day down on Sunset Boulevard on her way home from the grocery store.

While Mother cooked meals for families that didn't have what we had, Ingrid and I helped. Father didn't know. It was better that way. Father worked hard, very hard, for what we had. He hadn't been given anything when he grew up.

He always ingrained in our heads, "Nothing is a free ride. Work hard for what you want, and eventually, you'll make something of yourself."

Mother, Ingrid, and I drove sixty-eight-point-two miles every Sunday to attend Saddleback Church. Father never attended. Sunday was usually his only day off, so instead of going to church with his family, he would stay home and read the newspaper or do what busy men do on their days off.

Bake sales, fundraisers, and good causes at the church were big on Mother's list, and it always included Ingrid and me. Mother had us giving back even if she asked us to lie to Father about it. When Mother made sizable donations to a charity or a cause, she'd make sure it was listed as anonymous. It was often enough that we continuously received charitable letters in the mail, asking for money. Mother hid those, too.

There was a fire in Glendale, a suburb of Los Angeles, in June 1990. I remember watching it on the television. Mother called her friend Sally, who called Linda, who called Brenda, who called Nancy, and within an hour's time, Mother had Ingrid and me in the kitchen, cooking for four hundred people who'd lost their homes.

"If your father asks what we did today, you'll tell him we went grocery shopping, cleaned the house, and washed the cars, understand?"

We nodded.

I'm not sure Father cared too much about what we'd done that day, but Mother constantly played it cautious, as if she wasn't sure what storm she'd be stepping into when he walked through the door in the evening.

One thing she constantly said was, "It's better to prepare for the storm than be caught in the eye."

Ingrid and I went along with it, but I'm fairly certain we didn't understand what she meant until we got older.

Truly, I thought Father did care for others. He had an odd way of showing it. Mother bought us the gifts for our birthdays, Christmases, and Easters. Father put money into our savings accounts instead.

One day, Mother sent me into Father's home office to get his cocktail glass he'd left in there the night before. We were never allowed in Father's office unless he was in there, and there had to be a reason we were in there. But Mother was in a rush. Father liked everything pristine, neat, organized. A leftover cocktail glass wouldn't go over well, and Mother knew this. So, when she sent me in, I made sure to run my fingers along the giant mahogany desk. Touch the expensive pen that he had sitting next to the lamp. I made sure to take in the shelves of bookcases that lined the walls. I made sure to touch the leather chair, sit in it, slowly spin in it, stare up at the carefully designed ceiling made of ivory. Father had had this office specially designed for him to include the handcrafted ivory ceiling and the bookcases and shelves that held forty-two books each—because forty-two was his favorite number. The clear, glass paperweights engraved with JLC—Jonas Lee Clemens. Another with CIC—Catherine and Ingrid Clemens. I picked up the paperweight and looked through them, my best attempt to view the world through Father's eyes.

Magnified.

Tainted.

Distorted.

Rubik Cubes made for Father from Ern Rubik himself. Solved, they sat on a shelf, all three of them—one for Father, one for me, and one for Ingrid.

But it was the dull orange envelope that caught my eye that afternoon in the bottom drawer, which had been left open only a smidgen. I knew it wasn't a good idea to go through Father's things, especially in his office, but I couldn't help myself. After checking the doorway to see if it was clear, I carefully slid open the drawer, and in there, I found an opened St. Jude envelope. As quietly as possible, I took out the white piece of paper inside. My eyes saw the number amount, but my brain just couldn't register it. My father had donated over one million dollars. A thank-you note from Danny Thomas himself.

I slipped the contents back into the envelope as my heart pounded. I put the drawer back just so, took the crystal cocktail glass, and left no trace behind.

I never asked Father about it even though I was curious. I wondered why he'd donated all that money to sick children when he wouldn't spare any change for catastrophic disasters both in the Untied States and worldwide. I wondered why his heart seemed so tainted on the outside. I wondered why he acted as though he didn't care about other people—aside from his family. But maybe he did, and we just didn't see it.

When I returned to the kitchen with Father's glass, Mother didn't ask why it had taken me so long. I didn't think she cared. Ingrid eyed me like a hawk. She knew something was up.

That night, when we went to bed, Ingrid in normal pajamas this time, I told her what I'd found.

She was quiet for a long moment. Then, she said, "I saw Father with another woman."

I didn't respond. I waited for words to settle inside me. This was a broad statement. It was filled with different scenarios. Different justifications, reasons that Father would be with another woman, and yet my heart didn't allow me to ask what it meant.

What do you mean, Ingrid?

Instead, I ignored the statement as if she'd never said it.

And she ignored the St. Jude donation.

That night, we fell to sleep full of questions, and that was just how our life continued.

In plain sight, our family seemed pleasant, as if we were well put together with God on Sundays, wealth, beautiful clothes, nice cars, family vacations, and if you looked in our family photo album, you'd probably agree that the Clemens family was quite perfect. But behind closed doors, that was when the skeletons came out and danced, and the elephants ran from one side of the house to the other. Ingrid and I soaked it in like a sponge.

The only way to function in life is:

Chaos.

Lies.

Repeat.

Sometimes, the chaos got so loud that it was hard to see the truth, especially as Ingrid and I got older.

It was my senior year of high school and Ingrid's junior year. Neither of us drank or went to parties; Father wouldn't have it. He'd have our asses if we were downwind of that noise. Both of us maintained a 4.0 grade point average. Did what our parents told us to do. Never stayed out late.

But Ingrid had trouble with boys. One night, she came home from the "library"—that was our code word for breaking rules.

She sat down on her bed, on her side of the room, with a look I hadn't ever seen before.

I sat on my side of the room, staring down at my acceptance letter from Brown University, and thought, I can't leave her, not in this house, not with Mother and Father.

"I'm pregnant," she said calmly. "And I don't know what to do, Cat." She twisted her fingers in her lap, stared down at her slender thighs. "Mother is too overwhelmed to deal with my mistake. And Father ..." Her voice trailed off. "He'd most likely disown me." A nervous laugh escaped her lips. "Or write me out of the will."

Ingrid had never appeared more fragile to me than she did in that moment. Her heart wasn't her own anymore, and I could see that. It belonged to what grew inside her. But I knew in my own heart that she'd make the right decision for herself. Most of the time she did anyway.

"Is Donald the father?"

"No."

At first, I heard yes, but after a moment, I realize what she'd said. Donald Martin had been her boyfriend since freshman year.

"Then, who?" I whispered into the night.

"Jake."

"How do you know? That you're pregnant, I mean."

"It was one night a month ago. I-I don't know. We were at the library, grabbed a bite to eat, and ... then he kissed me." She closed her eyes with a tight squeeze, maybe remembering her mistake, or her love for him, or something in between. "Maybe it was the spring flowers or George Michael's 'Faith' that played on the radio in the restaurant. Or the way Jake told me that he'd always had a crush on me. Maybe it was something new, Cat." She blew out a mouthful of air. From her bag, she pulled out a pregnancy test and showed me.

I knew enough about pregnancy tests to know that two pink lines meant pregnant.

"What am I going to do, Cat?" she asked.

"I got accepted to Brown," I said, my best attempt to alleviate her shock, maybe some sadness.

The corners of her mouth spread, which created the beautiful smile God had given her.

"You'll make the right decision, Ingrid."

She shook her head. "I don't know, Cat." Ingrid covered her mouth to hide the frown. "I'm really happy for you."

That fall, Ingrid didn't have Jake's baby in her belly anymore. She broke it off with Donald, saying she was going away to college, said she needed time, but I think the truth was somewhere in between. Ingrid, nor I, knew anything about love. We knew nothing about intimacy, but we knew how to survive in chaos. We knew how to survive, period. We'd watched Mother serve Father for years. We'd watched Mother take his words. His manipulation. His lack of acceptance. We'd learned well. We'd learned that to survive, love was earned. Love was only for pretty, perfect things, and maybe Ingrid was searching for a man's acceptance that night with Jake. And even though she'd had all the acceptance from Donald, maybe it just wasn't enough or what she thought she needed.

What we saw was our father pushing Mother to do more, to be more, and yet the only time we saw him touch her was when they danced to "Fading Away" by James Taylor. The words were so simple yet so raw, so telling.

The truth is, I think Ingrid needed a man's acceptance instead of her own acceptance.

And where did I stand in all of this? Well, I stood on the other side. I kept men at a distance. And if it was sex, it was just sex, and that was all it was. I wouldn't let my heart fall for anyone. I wouldn't become Mother or Ingrid. I was going to blaze my own path and never allow myself to get trapped into the perception of love.

—Catherine

"Where are we headed?" I ask, praying for a rest stop soon.

If we hit another bump, I'm sure I'll pee my pants, which wouldn't make for a good first impression. Somehow, I convinced him in a not-so-convincing way that I should come along, and I'm not about to start asking for things.

"You hop in a car with a man you don't know, drive for five hours, and then ask that question?"

With my eyes on the road, I say, "Seems to me if you tried any funny business, all fingers would point to you. My car is parked at your house. My fingerprints are in your car." I run my fingers alongside the doorframe. "And if it makes you feel better, I'll leave a trail behind us that will lead to my whereabouts."

He does this thing with his lip, as if he's trying to stifle a smile, but it turns out to be a lip quiver instead.

Luke says, "Funny business. I haven't heard that term in a long time."

A blue sign appears up ahead.

"Rest stop. You have to pee?" he asks.

Yes. I shrug. "Sure, if there's one up ahead."

We pull into the rest stop, and I jump out and try to casually stroll to the restroom marked *Women.*

I hear Luke's door shut behind me, but I don't look back because if I don't stay focused, I'll have to ask Luke to find a washer and dryer.

I'm walking out of the restroom when I notice a man and a woman talking to Luke. Slowly, I make my way toward them. He signs something, nods, listens. From the woman's animation when she speaks, I can tell she's excited. The man, arms crossed, listens to his wife, smiles, and then takes off his hat and points to a place.

Luke signs the man's hat.

But I stay back and watch it happen.

The woman hands her phone to her husband, and he snaps a picture.

They wave.

They leave.

Luke turns and sees me walking toward him. Crosses his arms. "Either you really had to pee or you walk really funny when you walk fast."

"I'm a dancer." I nod. "Working on a few new moves." I pull the door handle of his Mustang. I don't say anything about the fans because it seems like that isn't a comfortable place for him to be.

Luke gets in, shuts the door, and starts the engine. "You asked earlier where we're going." He puts on his blinker, and we get back on the highway. "New York. Make some stops along the way."

New York? I pull out my phone. "I'm going to make a call to law enforcement—you know, so they can track my whereabouts—and hopefully, I'll be home in time for Christmas."

Luke shakes his head, again with the lip quiver.

I'm kidding. He knows it, but neither of us smiles as I slip my phone into my backpack.

"Figure we'll drive for another three hours or so and then find a place to sleep."

I nod, wondering how in the hell I'm going to afford to sleep where he sleeps. Shower where he showers. Eat where he eats.

Luke turns on the satellite radio. James Taylor starts to play.

The tail end of "Fading Away" plays. It's the song Mother and Father used to dance to. Still, after all that happened between them, watching them dance, the memories I have when Ingrid and I used to sit under the dining room table and watch them move so effortlessly, it still brings me a sense of hope. And all of this is way too close to home, and we haven't even reached the Arizona state line from California.

"Fire and Rain" begins.

Luke drives.

The engine quietly roars beneath us.

The wind blows in my hair.

And James is on the mic.

I close my eyes and lean my head against the headrest.

It's a sad song, and when he sings the part about not being sure where to send this song he's written, my heart breaks a little more than the first hundred times I listened to it.

The confusion of death. The complacency, the displacement, the lack of what to do and where to go and who to call. How to do laundry and make a grilled cheese. The simplicity of mundane tasks seems so much more difficult, and it's not that one can't do it, but because it just doesn't seem that important anymore.

Luke doesn't ask my last name until the song is over.

"Clemens."

"Catherine Clemens," he says. His eyes search the surrounding area that's slowly fading to black as the sun bids its last farewell before setting.

"Luke McCay," I say. "What part of Kentucky are you from?"

"Bardstown. You familiar?"

"No. Do you go back to visit?"

"My parents."

"Siblings?"

"No."

"Ah, that explains it."

"Explains what?" Luke looks over at me and then back at the road.

When he looks over this time, I notice his eyes are an earth brown with flecks of green that could also be seen as hazel, maybe, depending on the light and the mood and goodness of the world.

"Your love for James Taylor."

"What?"

"Statistically speaking, seventy-one percent of James Taylor fans come from single-children homes."

Luke looks over at me again. Shakes his head. "Seems to me you like him, too. Are you an only child?"

"No. One sister. Ingrid. I'm of the twenty-nine percent of multiple-children households who love James Taylor."

Then, I see his smile crack, and it's beautiful. "You're lying."

There's a long silence as the road hums under us.

"Maybe."

It's just after nine p.m. when we pull into a Best Western in Mesa, Arizona.

"Can never go wrong with a Best Western," Luke says. "Are you hungry?"

"Sure."

"We'll get checked in and see what we can find." He looks at his watch that looks like it's worth a million dollars.

We grab our bags from the back and walk to the front door of the hotel. I go to reach for the door handle, but Luke grabs it instead.

"My father wouldn't be too happy with me if he knew I didn't open the door for a woman."

"Hello. Welcome to the Best Western in Mesa. One room?" a man says from behind the counter.

"Two," Luke and I say at the same time.

Edwardo, his name tag reads, says, "Wonderful." His fingers slide across the computer keyboard. "You're in luck. We have two rooms right next door to each other."

Luke grabs a card from his wallet. "Put both on here, please."

"No. I've got mine." I touch Luke's arm, not out of attraction, but out of surprise.

When our eyes connect, he knows I mean business.

"I didn't take this interview for a free ride," I whisper.

Luke's eyes linger on mine.

"Then, one room on the card?" Edwardo asks.

Luke looks back to Edwardo. "Guess so."

Edwardo looks at the name on the card, looks back at Luke, and back to the card. "You look so familiar. Are you from the area?"

"Just traveling through."

Edwardo slides the card through the machine. Shakes his head. "I feel like I've seen you before."

"Familiar face probably." Luke looks back at me. Then to the clock. Then back to Edwardo.

"You're all set, Mr. McCay. Room 236." He hands Luke a key card, a map of the hotel, and his receipt.

Luke steps aside.

"Room 237, and that will be one hundred fifty-two dollars and sixty-three cents. Cash or card?"

"Cash," I say and pull out the money from my wallet before handing it to him.

He hands me my change, my receipt, a key card, and a map.

"Thank you."

"You're welcome. Upstairs to my right. Have a nice rest," Edwardo says.

Luke walks back to the counter. "Places to eat in the area?"

"Which do you prefer, Mr. McCay—American, Mexican, Italian?"

Luke looks over at me.

"I'm easy. Food-wise."

"Mexican," Luke says.

"La Costa. Down this frontage road, about half a mile on your left. They're open for another hour."

"Thank you, Edwardo," Luke says.

We exit the lobby and walk upstairs to find our rooms.

I get a bean-and-cheese burrito because it's the cheapest thing on the menu, and Luke gets the enchiladas. We eat in silence. The restaurant is nearly closing, and the employees are beginning to quietly shut down the place.

I chew through the tortilla, and the bean-and-cheese combination is flavorful. Not like any bean-and-cheese burrito I've had before.

"How is the food?" our waitress, Tami, a washout blonde with blue eyeshadow, asks.

Luke nods, his mouth full.

I take a sip of my water, too cheap to get anything else. "Good, thank you."

Tami walks away and comes back with the bill, a subtle hint maybe that our time here is up.

Luke grabs the bill quicker than I can.

"How much do I owe you?" I grab my wallet from my purse, waiting for his response.

He grabs his card from his wallet and sets them down on the table. Waits for Tami.

"You got a water and a bean-and-cheese burrito. It was five dollars and thirty-six cents. I can cover it." Luke takes down the rest of his beer.

I watch as his Adam's apple moves with each swallow.

His stare stays on me until he sets the bottle down, and I throw a ten-dollar bill down.

Luke shrugs. "That's a big tip for a bill that was no more than twenty bucks."

Tami walks back to the table, takes the bill, and Luke's card. "I'll be right back."

She leaves and comes back, sets the bill and his card on our table, and hesitates before she leaves. "You look a lot like a heartthrob on a show I used to watch in the 1990s—I can't remember the name of it. I was doing a lot of drugs back then." Shakes her head and laughs. "Clean and sober now."

Luke says, "Congratulations."

Tami wipes her hands on her apron and studies Luke. "Yeah, yeah, thank you." Still trying to place his face. "Anyhow, you two have a great night."

Luke fills out the tag and includes a tip.

I see him scribble the number one hundred where it says *total.*

I shake my head, stand, and grab my ten-dollar bill back, shoving it in the front pocket of my jeans.

We drive back to the hotel in silence.

We walk up to our rooms, and we're standing at our doors. He waits for me to slide my key card first.

"Thanks for dinner," I say as my lock pings, indicating it's unlocked.

"You're welcome." Luke slides his card and receives the same ping.

His eyes linger on me too long, and I like the way this makes me feel, as if he's searching for answers without asking, attempting to respect my privacy. I hold all my questions back until I can build the trust and do an extensive Google search.

"Good night, Luke," I say.

"Good night, Catherine."

I walk in and quietly shut the door behind me, resting my back on the door.

There's a soft knock.

I push myself off the door and open it; my stomach begins to explode with butterflies.

Luke is standing there. "You shouldn't open the door this late when someone knocks. You should ask who it is first."

"Thank you, Officer McCay. I'll be sure to do that next time."

"Good. Thank you." And he walks back over to his door.

I shut mine again. Try not to smile as my back falls against the door this time, and the knots in my stomach grow.

Before
Federal Correctional Institution, Dublin

Dear Journal,

It was the end of my sophomore year at Brown. After Peter, my high school boyfriend, and before Michael, my college boyfriend.

Sex.

Just two humans consenting to a decision that allows them to feel good about themselves, about the world, about their good decisions, bad decisions, and everything in between.

I didn't know his name, but it felt really good when he pushed my body against the wall with his own, when he put himself inside me and moaned.

Although I knew it wasn't my best decision, sex with strange men began to cure whatever hurt I had inside me. It cured every insecurity, every broken piece of me. It helped the deep hurt. I knew it was a bandage for old wounds, wounds unseen by the naked eye. And I also knew how dangerous it was. How addicting it could be.

After all, it was just a short-term solution.

Then, it was sex in unsavory places. Sex in strange places with men I didn't know. That's why there were only nine men between Michael and Peter. Deep down, I knew it wasn't right. Somewhere within me, every time it happened, something mended and something broke, but it was the broke that far outweighed the mend. Because, really, the mend was only like a bandage to the broken pieces of me. Through those nine men, every morning when I awoke, I'd promise myself it wouldn't happen again. But the urge to fix me would return, and I always found the easier way.

Man number one: sex in a public restroom in a stall.

Man number two: sex in the park at night on the slide.

Man number three: sex in a car with one of my professors.

Man number four: sex with number fifty-two from the football team in the stadium after the game.

Man number five: sex in his house after a house party.

Man number six: sex at McPhail's, a college bar, in a dark corner.

Man number seven: sex at the Four Seasons when I was home from college.

Man number eight: sex in my dorm room while my roommate slept.

Man number nine: sex in an airplane on a red-eye home to the West Coast.

I wouldn't exchange numbers, even when the men asked. I'd stop them or leave before they told me their name.

It wasn't important.

I know that sounds selfish, as if their feelings didn't matter. But if I knew their name, shame and guilt would burrow itself deep inside me, and I'd have trouble finding air again.

When the fear of what I was becoming became too much, I knew I had to stop.

When Ingrid had explained that evening with Jake, when the wind had been warm, the music had been right, I understood. Though, deep down inside, I knew it wasn't that. I knew it had everything to do with our father and what Ingrid and I could piece together about love.

Michael approached me in the bakery, just off-campus, that cold, wintery morning. He asked if my coffee needed to be refilled.

I told him, "No, thank you."

He didn't insist. He didn't make small talk. He just sat down and explained to me all the reasons he'd asked about the coffee. Never used the old pick-up lines, instead giving me some truth.

Nerves built up inside me, freezing panic. Michael wasn't the type of man I'd sleep with and run. Michael was the type of man who wouldn't let me leave, wouldn't let me walk away without knowing my name.

I knew my parents would love him.

He volunteered at the animal shelter and was studying pre-veterinary science. Planned to transfer to Tufts University for veterinary school. He was German, a plus to Father's side. Said he cooked on Christmas at the local food bank. I knew Mother would love him.

I called Ingrid when Michael and I made it official, that I agreed to be his girlfriend.

She was now at Stanford, getting her prerequisites done for nursing school. Ingrid was the smart one. I was the logical one. School, particularly science and math, just came easy to her. For me, school was a lot of work. I had to work hard for good grades while Ingrid breezed right through.

I brought Michael home that Christmas to meet my family, though I didn't want to. It wasn't that I didn't want Michael to meet my family; I just wanted to keep things separate. Michael was a safe place to land while my family and home life had deeper levels of chaos, ones that loomed in the background, festered, twisted, turned, shifted, moved. And now, my memories and Michael were tainted. Mixed together like dough and water.

Every time I came home from college, it felt like I was stepping into a guessing game. When Ingrid and I had lived at home, I could gauge the situation. See where my place was. Fit in, mold myself around the situation or situations. I knew where I stood and what to prepare for. When I came home from college, it was a true Dr. Jekyll and Mr. Hyde. Things had seemed to get worse between Mother and Father after we both left home.

Father seemed more removed.

Mother seemed distant, even from Ingrid and me. Maybe trying to protect us from what happened behind closed doors. Mother believed in protecting her children, us, from anything that might harm us, which included the truth.

Father drank a lot more. When he came home from work, Mother would have his cocktail ready, and he'd retreat to his office. He wouldn't come out until his movements were just a step behind normal. Until the smile he bore was on the brink of realistic.

Mother's left eye would twitch when she cleaned the kitchen even though the kitchen had been cleaned ten minutes earlier. She'd busy herself by baking bread at ten o'clock at night.

One night, I came down, unable to sleep, and Mother was at the stove. Father had a handful of her hair and wore a look I'd never seen before. Father was never physically violent with Mother; he was far too smart for that. But his words were like the sharp end of broken glass—they could cut through anything.

But in the darkness of the hallway, I stood, watched, just as I had as a child, too scared to move. In one quick movement, he shoved her head down, and her forehead knocked against one of the burners.

Please stop, I begged Father through my unspoken words. *Please.*

Mother pulled her head back up, blood dripping, and seconds passed.

"Clean yourself up," he slurred. "We have dinner guests tomorrow."

The next morning, Father was reading the newspaper, sipping his coffee just like nothing had happened.

Mother stood at the stove again, preparing breakfast.

Purple hydrangeas sat on the counter.

I wanted so badly to believe this scene. I wanted so badly to live with this family, not the family from last night.

"Look what your father bought me this morning," Mother said, looking at the purple flower arrangement.

"What happened to your forehead, Mother?" I asked.

Please, I begged myself, *believe what she tells you, not what you saw last night. Not the truth. Believe whatever comes from her lips.*

"You know me," she said. "Bumped it on the shower door when I slipped."

Father turned the page of the newspaper and then took another sip of his coffee.

"Good morning, Catherine. How did you sleep?" he asked without looking up from the newspaper, without looking me in the eyes.

Maybe he'd see the hurt, the dismay, and maybe I would see his guilt. Maybe in that guilt, I'd be able to give him pity, but it didn't happen.

"Not well," I said. *Because I couldn't get the scene out of my head—of you smashing Mother's face against the stove,* I wanted to say but held my tongue.

"I'm sorry to hear that," he said as he continued to read the newspaper.

Mother cooked.

And I sat in silence and made my best attempt to unsee the truth.

I called Ingrid later that night after the dinner company left. After we'd put on The Clemens Show, one of illusion, one of make-believe, a night full of smoke and mirrors. I wanted to tell her what I'd seen, partly because I wanted to get the ugliness out from my heart, but also to alleviate the loneliness of keeping the secret of what I'd seen the night before.

But I couldn't tell her. I didn't want Ingrid to feel the same feelings I did. I wanted to protect her. So, I kept it to myself, tucked it into my heart, and allowed room for the bruise it would make. Instead, we talked about the new boy she was dating and Michael and school.

"Is something wrong?" Ingrid asked at the end of our conversation.

"No, just tired. Had some champagne that made my head ache," I lied once more.

But then, after we hung up, it dawned on me. *What happened in my first year of college while Ingrid was home with Mother and Father?*

Ingrid never said a word, maybe for the same reason I hadn't.

It seems we spent many years trying to survive, to protect each other from things that were out of our control. Hang on to the good memories and the lies in between. The lies we told ourselves when our reality seemed so good on the outside, but on the inside, we were fading away.

What seemed to redeem Father's indiscretions and Mother's will to make their relationship work came down to two things, I think—love and faith. Love that Father had for Mother even if it was tainted and ugly. Faith that everything would inevitably be all right someday.

On January 2, 2001, all of that went away even if it was just for a few moments. But there were decisions we made that night that we can never take back. Decisions that we have to live with for a lifetime.

—Catherine

I shower first and then grab my laptop from my overnight bag. Pull the bedspread all the way off of the bed and set it in the corner of the room. Who knows what happens on those things? They aren't washed every day, and I'm quite sure at least fifteen percent of the US population has left their DNA behind on a bedspread in a hotel room.

I open up my laptop and grab the Wi-Fi code from the map Edwardo gave us. I Google Luke McCay.

Many of his pictures come up. A few of them of him smiling with his costars—Jennie Gait, Steve Weatherby, and Brandon Pace. Birthplace is Bardstown, Kentucky. Born on October 8, 1970. I'm certain that Luke is a man who was graced with a face that doesn't age.

Maybe, I think, *it's the salt water from all the surfing. Maybe it's the salt water that keeps his skin so perfect.*

After two hours of searching, I conclude that Luke doesn't have any social media sites—because he hates social media, one article said. That he loves animals. That he's a private person. That *LA Hills* was the last television show he did. That he hasn't done an interview since the show ended on May 17, 2000. He's done cameos for certain shows that his costars have gone on to make.

That he's been off the radar for quite some time.

I did come across a picture taken back in 2002 of Luke and his father, James, at a junkyard just outside of Bardstown with a beat-up, old 1965 Mustang. I can't find any traces of why he walked away from acting or any traces of family other than his mother, Beth, and his father, James. One article, published in 1995, said that he had his eye on a certain someone and that they'd married, but that was it.

There's another knock at the door.

I walk over and open it up.

Luke's standing there, his hair wet, in a white T-shirt and worn jeans that hang loosely around his lean hips. From this angle, and many other angles, I see how women fawn over him. Men want to be him. But what I see in him and what others see from him are different. I see a man who carries a burden. A beautiful man who carries a heart too big for his body. But I've always been told I look at people differently than most.

"You didn't ask who it was." He puts his hands on his hips.

I shut the door. "Knock again," I say through the door.

My words are met with silence.

Silence still.

Luke finally knocks, but it's slow and paced.

"Who is it?"

Again silence.

Finally, "Luke."

I open the door. "Oh, hello." I smile coyly.

Luke shakes his head. "I need your cell phone number. Just in case." He's got his phone in his hand.

I give him my number. No other comments or banter. I just give my number because I know it will ease his mind.

My phone pings, indicating a text, but my eyes don't leave his.

"Good night, Catherine," he says as he retreats back to his room.

"Good night, Luke," I whisper.

I shut the door and grab my phone in my purse.

Unknown: It's Luke.

I program his number in my phone.

Me: It's Catherine, but you can call me Cat.

There's no text back, so I put my phone on the nightstand, close my laptop, and turn off the light.

After I've showered and packed up my stuff, I head down to the lobby for coffee to find Luke sipping from a glass mug, reading the newspaper. It's just after eight in the morning.

Lisa, not Edwardo, is on staff today.

I walk to the coffeemaker and pour a cup of coffee. Luke doesn't look up from his newspaper until I sit down across the table from him.

"Sleep well?" I ask.

"I don't really ever, no," he says. "You?"

I average probably four interrupted hours of sleep a night. "As good as I can." Take a sip of coffee, peek in his cup. "Just black?"

"Yeah."

I nod.

Luke looks at his watch. "Say we head out around eight thirty this morning." It's not a question.

Truthfully, I didn't sleep that well at all. I tossed and turned and debated on asking Luke this question at one thirty in the morning. Two thirty in the morning and three forty-five in the morning. Finally, my eyelids and brain gave up. But now, he's here, reading the newspaper, as if we'd somehow stepped back in time. Where people read the morning newspaper. Back to a time when things were simple.

I left for the Federal Correctional Institution, Dublin, when I was twenty-one years old on July 15, 2001. I served thirteen years exactly. I was released back into a world that's driven by technology. No more Saturday morning cartoons or newspaper readers. Pictures aren't developed at photo shops anymore; they're taken with phones where online albums are created. CDs are almost nonexistent. I'm almost certain a VHS player is probably on display in a museum somewhere along with pagers. There's no more waiting for anything. All the gratification we think we need is at our fingertips.

Everything has changed.

I'm almost certain Luke Googled me just the way I Googled him. I'm also certain a background check on me was done by his publicist before he even took the interview. Googled my freelance stuff. He pretended not to know my name, but he knew it.

So, I ask him the same question that's been burning me up since last night, "Why'd you take the interview?"

Luke isn't surprised by this question. He doesn't ask me the only question I seem to get when my track record is exposed.

Did you do it?

He doesn't lie to me or make excuses or fumble over his words. He doesn't give me remorse or pity or any of the bullshit.

Luke simply stares back. "I know your heart can handle it."

But behind his stare is a flicker of guilt. I see it, and it's only momentary. It disappears as quickly as it appeared.

He says this like he knows the end of the story, how this will all play out.

As if he knows my heart.

I take my finger and trace a natural groove in the table. Watch as a piece of my vulnerability is seen, exposed, floats across the table and is given to Luke like a gift. *Why would these seven little words open up my guts?*

My heart can handle a story, Luke, just not my own. My stomach clenches. A quick and faint memory from the morning of January 2nd, reaches inside me.

Luke interrupts my thoughts. "Let's go." But his tone is soft and sincere and commanding, all at the same time.

I can't produce my usual wit, stuck in the moment, so I stand. "I'm going to go grab my stuff."

"I'll meet you at the car," Luke says from his sitting position.

Arizona is quiet and desolate in some places. My eyes are transfixed on the red sand, as I wait for a snake to bid farewell while it maneuvers across the desert floor with speed.

I take my notebook out.

"When did you know you wanted to be an actor?" I ask.

James Taylor's "Shower the People" comes over the satellite radio.

"I didn't." He leans on his left arm as it sits on the windowsill.

The air conditioner blows soundlessly.

"I came out to Los Angeles to play music."

This makes me think of Mother, who moved to California to study art when she met my father.

"It was 1988. I was eighteen and wanted to play the guitar like Taylor and Cat Stevens and Carole King and Lynyrd Skynyrd. I just didn't want all the bullshit that came with it."

"Bullshit?"

"The fame. I just wanted to play music and make a living at it." Luke shrugs.

"So, you became an actor?" I pause. "And all the bullshit came anyway?"

He continues and doesn't look my way, "I had this opportunity with Epic Records in LA in 1989. They were ready to sign, and I was ready to sign. When I picked up the pen, Clovis, the vice president of the company, started talking about selling out to millions and international travel. The next so-and-so. I panicked. I walked away. I didn't want all that."

"So, you walked away." From the depths of me, I understand this.

Luke nods. Looks out his window and back to the road. "So, I spent the next year scraping by working construction and doing late-night gigs after work to pay the bills. And I kicked my own ass for not signing the contract. But my ego wouldn't let me go back into Epic Records and ask for the record deal. Besides, it was a year later, and they'd probably already found someone else. I let it go."

I jot this down.

"A buddy of mine told me about an audition for a part in some drama series, and I thought, *What the hell?* I needed a bit more income to meet the music needs and because the construction gig wasn't covering it all."

"And you'd never acted before?"

Luke shakes his head. "Nope, and needless to say, I didn't get the part I'd auditioned for—but I got the part of Dylan Klein."

I jot this down, too, and wait for him to continue, but he doesn't.

"So, *LA Hills* takes off. Blows up. Then what?" I ask, looking out the window, waiting for his answer, doing my best to appreciate the red clay and rock formations and cacti.

"No, actually, it was after the first season. It was a bumpy start. Some of us were just finding our acting legs. Some of us were veterans to it. Some of us couldn't lay off the coke or the booze. Some of us just didn't want to be sober. And some of us thought we could rule the world so as long as egos could withstand criticism."

I don't ask who, but I write down the quote, knowing full well I won't use it. Somehow, I know this story isn't meant to be a piece on sex or drugs or sobriety. This story is about Luke, and I feel as though I'm missing the angle.

"After the first season ended, that's when everything exploded."

Luke stalls. "Yeah."

I take in his profile as he drives. The crow's-feet that stream from his eyes are more pronounced and better seen when his sunglasses are on—the black frame attracting attention, I suppose. His lips are firm and sensual, and I wonder what it would be like to kiss them. *How many women have his lips touched?*

But more importantly, I see the worry once again.

"You're staring at me, Catherine." His lips curve. And he says this not in a weird way, but in a way of concern. "What are you thinking about?" His narrow eyes meet mine.

"I wonder if your shoulders ever tire from the burden you carry." It isn't a question.

Taylor's next song comes over the airwaves—"Something in the Way She Moves."

Luke's eyes meet mine. He leans down, turns up the radio, and James transports me to 1968 where miniskirts and go-go boots and printed tights are things of importance, of beauty. The lyrics attach themselves to my insides, and I can't help but wonder if fate decided to show its first round of cards.

We allow James to carry us through Arizona for the next several hours, and the exchange we last had hours ago has left us wordless. Cat Stevens's "Landslide" comes on. This reminds me of my first real boyfriend in high school my senior year. The first man I'd ever let touch me, slip inside me. Sex was just something I did to pass the time. I think it meant more to Peter than to me. I allowed it to happen because that was what kids our age were doing. In hindsight, I wish I had waited. I wish I would had known a man like Luke. Instead, I watched him on television, romancing with beautiful blondes who were thin and had breasts like grapefruits.

College at Brown University came, and Peter and I didn't last. My relationship with Peter was the starter relationship. It was as if I'd used the relationship to figure out how to navigate love and touching and what everything felt like. The relationship that had broken through all the firsts.

First kiss.

First base.

Sex for the first time.

Then, Michael came along. It felt more like love. More intimate. More connectedness. I could have spent the rest of my life with Michael, I suppose. He liked sports and movies and poetry. I liked sports enough to know they usually involved some sort of ball and poetry enough to appreciate a beautiful line when I read it. It was the movie choices we couldn't agree on. While I enjoyed drama and comedy, Michael enjoyed suspense and good guys versus bad guys.

But it wasn't the time together that pushed us apart; it was the time apart that eventually ended our relationship. Really, it was everything that happened on January 2, 2001. It was all such a blur, and according to my therapist in prison, post-traumatic stress disorder can change the way we see things, feel things, associate things.

Before we reach Arizona and New Mexico state line, Luke asks if I'm hungry. "I lost track of time," he says.

There's a long pause between us because I don't notice that I'm hungry, starving, until now. "I could eat."

It's late afternoon, and the sky over Arizona fades from a deep blue to a light blue, like the varying depths of the ocean. We pull off at a Dairy Queen.

"I cannot believe you grew up in Southern California and have never had a bacon double cheeseburger from Dairy Queen," Luke says.

I shove another French fry in my mouth and take a drink of Coke. "I think it's an injustice to add bacon to anything. And to ruin a burger like that?" I shake my head. "Cruel."

Luke tries not to smile, but I see it peek out from the corners of his mouth.

Try not to smile. I shove another French fry in my mouth.

"I don't think I've ever met a woman who didn't like bacon." Luke takes another bite of his burger.

I shrug. "It's not that I don't like bacon. I just think bacon should be enjoyed and savored as one food entity. I think it's a disservice to bacon lovers alike to mix it with something else. That's all."

"But wouldn't you agree that bacon adds flavor to everything?"

"I don't know. I haven't tried it with anything else."

Luke looks at me. Sets his burger down. Takes a napkin and wipes his hands. "You mean to tell me that your whole life has been spent eating bacon by itself, and you've never once felt tempted to slip it into a burger or wrap it around a hunk of meat?"

"I don't like change," I counter.

"That's it." Luke shakes his head, rubs his hands together, and then picks up his burger. "Open up."

I lean back, cross my arms, shake my head. "No way."

Luke holds the burger with two hands across the table. "Come on. Open up. If you don't like it, I'll gladly refund you the experience."

Curiosity piques my interest. "How would you refund the experience?"

"What's your favorite dessert?" he asks, still holding out the burger.

"Starbursts."

Luke nods. "Starbursts then. If you don't like the bacon on the burger and it doesn't change your view, I'll buy you Starbursts for a lifetime."

I laugh out loud, and it feels so good. Cover my mouth and realize how loud it must have been.

Luke's mouth changes, and his look does, too. The worry I see in his eyes has somehow shifted just slightly.

"Starbursts for life?" I lean forward, look into his eyes. "The orange ones."

"Orange Starbursts for life," he whispers.

I open my mouth and take a bite of his burger. I think about the way his mouth touched the same spot when the tomato explodes in my mouth. The onion gives off the crunch, the cheese and meat patty run my taste buds on overdrive, but it's the bacon that pulls everything together.

He's right.

I chew.

Nod my head.

Stare at the ceiling.

My mouth is full of heaven.

Chew again.

Nod.

Finally, I find his eyes as I swallow the last bit of the bacon double cheeseburger, the slice of heaven that Dairy Queen offers.

I try to gather my thoughts, find a way to explain what this has done to my overall eating experience at thirty-four years old.

Luke sets the burger down.

Attempting to act casual, I lean forward.

"Well?" he asks.

"You're right. The bacon just does something to the experience."

Luke smiles, and my heart doubles over itself. I swear, if a heart could move from place to place, it would leap right out of my chest and demonstrate what I feel inside when I see Luke smile. It's as if the tips of the corners touch his ears. Watching Luke smile is something that every woman needs to experience—not the smile from Dylan Klein, but the genuineness, the quiet confidence, the humility of a man I've never had the pleasure of knowing until this moment right here.

His smile lights up the world and all the dark corners where sadness festers.

"What?" he asks.

I try to control the chills that have taken over my skin and put my heart back into my chest. "You have ketchup"—I touch the corner of my mouth—"right here."

Luke rubs the napkin over his mouth. He doesn't have ketchup on his face, but I needed to buy just a few moments of clarity to remind myself that this is just a story, and I'm just the staff writer.

The chills finally leave.

"We should go," I say, "get back on the road." I'm eager to step away from what I'm feeling because it's way too close for comfort.

Luke stands, takes both of our trays, walks to the trash, but not before three young women in Dairy Queen uniforms nervously approach Luke.

Two of the workers push their friend forward. "Are you the dad from the show *River's Lounge*?"

He did a few cameos on the show. I remember.

Luke looks at the three young women, back to me, and back to the young women.

It's truly very sad that these women will never understand what Dylan Klein did for women in the 1990s. These girls weren't even born yet. It's sad that they will never understand the importance of the coy smile, the surfboard, and the bad-boy image. It's equally just as sad to see that the heartbreaker of an era will not be known to women born beyond the eighties. It's a travesty.

He's resolved to being a dad on a current hit show.

"He's Dylan Klein. Grab your phones and look that shit up," I say as I roll my eyes and walk past the three young women and out the door.

As we make our way into New Mexico, the incident with the young women doesn't seem to bother him. He's back to his normal, pensive self.

The beginning of New Mexico, coming in at the south end of the state, is barren and flat. The green I see isn't a true green; it's a tired green, washed out, faded, not the type of green found, say, in Northern California. Mother and Father used to have a place in Myers Flat, California, where Ingrid and I would spend hours getting lost in the redwood forest. The green in the trees, from what I remember, was bright, vibrant, and full of life.

A mountain range off in the distance is a sharp, jagged line where peaks and valleys sit a short distance away from each other.

No music plays from the radio. It's just me, Luke, and the warm New Mexico breeze that billows through our windows.

"For the record, Dylan Klein is still the love of many hearts," I say, not in any effort to help him feel better, but to give him a dose of true reality.

He side-eyes me and then looks back to the road with one hand on the steering wheel. "When I first got the job for *LA Hills*, the producer asked if I'd be wiling to get a nose job."

"What?" I ask—not because I didn't hear what he'd said, but because I don't believe his nose needs fixing. That it might somehow be defective. It works fine, which is key, and besides, it isn't abnormally big or too small. It is narrow, comes to a point, as it should, and sits perfectly on his face.

"Somehow, my nose didn't fit the bill for the Dylan Klein they had in mind. But after a day or so, after a lot of thought, I realized I wasn't willing to change who I was for such a small part of life, you know? That if they didn't like me for me, then I wasn't the right man for the job."

"I'm glad you didn't get the nose job," I say into the wind, halfway hoping he doesn't hear me because I don't want things to get weird between us and I don't want what I say to be the reason things get weird.

Luke looks down the road we travel. Barren desert on each side of us.

I look back down at my notebook. "You have no social media accounts, according to the internet."

Luke shakes his head.

"Why?"

"Why have them?" Luke looks over at me.

Social media didn't exist before I went to Dublin. Neither did smartphones. Bag phones were all the rage.

"From what I've seen with social media, it's just a big, fat lie. All of it. A fake facade that users put out there to compare lives. Who's prettier. Who's skinnier. Who's richer. Nobody tells the truth. It's all bullshit. And we're making the rich richer by using it."

I look straight ahead and feel Luke's eyes burning a hole on the side of my face.

I turn to face him. "What?"

A small smile touches his lips. "I like you, Catherine Clemens."

I try not to enjoy the way my name sounds from his mouth.

"I take it, you don't have any social media accounts?" he asks, adjusting so he's got one hand on the wheel.

Immediately, I feel guilty. "I'm sorry. The question was for you. My personal opinion seemed to jump in here somehow. I'm supposed to be interviewing you, not the other way around."

"Why are you sorry? Catherine, I see this as a two-way conversation. Not a fucking press conference. Besides, I asked you the question back."

Luke gives me a quick smile that makes my pulse race. There's an inherent strength in his face. One that tells me he's had to overcome a lot to get where he is now. I guess we'll have to cross that bridge when we get to it.

Don't smile, Cat. Just get along with it.

"Let's start over. You don't have any social media accounts, according to the internet."

"I do not."

"Why not?"

Luke looks over at me. "I just don't like people knowing my business."

I jot down his answer even though I'll probably be able to remember every answer he gives me because this is starting to become an unforgettable trip.

"What was it like, growing up in Bardstown?"

"Simple. Slower. Sunday dinners. Town chili cookouts. Playing in the woods. Church Sundays. Coming home from a day of play at dark when the neighborhood streetlights came on. Collecting cans for money and trading it in for baseball cards. Sitting on the front porch and reading the newspaper. Listening to the radio, waiting for your one favorite Taylor song to come on. Helping others. Putting cards in our tire spokes to make them sound like motorcycles. Building tree forts. Knowing you'd better not break any rules in town because everybody's known you since birth and they'd report it back to Mom and Dad before the deed was done." He pauses. Pulls his lip through his teeth. "That Laura Knettles would be at church, school, and Sunday dinner, and if I had just enough courage, I might kiss her. Where Mr. Reeves was not only the town barber, but also the mayor." He exhales, maybe asking himself why he moved from something so sweet. So comfortable. So simple. "Nothing like LA."

I'm strangely attracted to this lifestyle. A lifestyle I'm so unfamiliar with but might have experienced just a touch of it with our summer trips to Myers Flat.

"Tell me more," I say as I ease back in my seat and watch his mouth move.

"My buddy Benny and I would sneak into the movie house on Friday nights to see R-rated movies like *Sudden Impact*, *Scarface*, *Blue Thunder*." Luke stops, almost trying to find the right words. "Benny always wanted to be a helicopter pilot for the Army," he says the words tentatively as if testing the idea. He bites his lower lip.

Luke pulls out his phone and does a quick search on his Maps app while I try to figure out how to ask more about Benny.

"I need to make a stop in Las Cruces," Luke says, pushing his phone back in his pocket.

"Okay."

We drive for a few more hours, and I realize New Mexico isn't a place I'd ever want to live. I'm sure it's beautiful to some, but I can't get the hang of it. The barren land. The occasional rock formation. The flatness of it all. It's a place I never want to come back to.

But my heart isn't in Los Angeles either and certainly not in Beverly Hills where I grew up.

I've always felt like I lived on the outskirts of the city, never quite fitting the mold like Ingrid. The city life grew around her and inside of her, like she was a piece of it. It wasn't until our first tip up to Myers Flat that I knew my heart was meant to be there. That the gigantic redwood trees beckoned me, called me by name, spoke to me as I walked among them. And under the canopy of trees existed banana slugs bigger than snakes, trillium, and the biggest ferns in the world blanketed along the forest floor. Myers Flat, in a lot of ways, reminded me of *The Goonies*, maybe because Astoria, Oregon, seemed a lot like Myers Flat with its rain, small-town feel, and giant trees.

In prison in Dublin though, I felt like I belonged, oddly enough. I had a cell, a number that told you who I was. The manila folder that told you what I had done to earn my spot there. I lived thirteen years in one place. I'd lived only twenty-one on the outside.

Before I'm aware of it, Luke has already turned off the highway, and we're in a neighborhood. He double-checks his phone, slides it back into his pocket, looks past me to his right, and pulls in front of a house.

"I'll leave the car running. I just need to run inside real quick." Luke almost leans across my lap to see the house.

With the proximity of his body to mine, I remind myself that he's an attractive man with a nose not fit for LA. "I still can't believe they wanted you to get a nose job," I whisper as he eases back from my lap.

Did I say that out loud?

I swallow. "What I meant to say was, your nose is perfectly symmetrical. Your nostrils are of normal size. Clearly, it's textbook size." *Christ. That's also not what I meant to say.* "I'll wait in the car," I say, clearly unfit to speak words that don't embarrass myself.

But something in his manner soothes me, something about the look he's giving me from the driver's seat, a sense of urgency and tenderness. "I'll be right back," falls from his lips.

Luke keeps the car running and gets out. Walks to the front door and hesitates before he knocks.

A woman with dark hair wearing an apron opens the front door. She nods as Luke speaks, though I can't hear what he's saying. The woman retreats from the door, only for a man in a motorized wheelchair to come to the door. A grin spreads across the man's face as his arms reach out to Luke for a hug. The man smiles broadly and looks at me in the car.

Luke looks back at me and runs back toward the car. He opens the door. "Please, come with me."

Luke puts out his hand to help me out of the car. Before I take it, I shut off the car and grab the keys from the ignition.

I take his hand.

And I cannot remember a time when my body has ever responded to a man's touch in this way.

It feels like …

A warm breeze.

A clear conscience.

After love has been made.

Relief.

A hard day's work.

Home.

As if all of the things gone wrong up to this point suddenly make sense.

Our hands linger in each other's just for a moment.

"Come with me, Catherine," he says.

Ten years ago, I've just learned, Benny was hit by a drunk driver and paralyzed from the middle of his chest down. He'd become the helicopter pilot he always wanted to be and was stationed in Las Cruces. Since then, he's been medically discharged.

Alberta, the woman with the dark hair and the apron, is Benny's caretaker. Ben, he goes by now.

"Catherine, would you like something to drink?" Ben asks.

"No, I'm okay for now. Thank you." I sit across from Ben as Luke sits next to me.

"McCay, you know where the drinks are. Get it yourself." Ben laughs. "Have you heard this guy play the guitar, Catherine?" Ben asks. "It's like silk."

"Shut up, man. How are you?" Luke asks.

"Good. You know, just keeping in shape." Ben looks at me. "It's a joke. Ten years in a chair, you have to find humor somewhere, right?" Ben looks at me. "So, Luke says you're a magazine writer?"

Among other things, I think to myself.

Ex-con.

Parolee.

"I am."

Alberta brings us water anyway. Luke and I thank her.

"Man, do I have some stories for you."

Ben tells a story about the time he and Luke were finally caught sneaking into the movie house. "McCay knew how bad I wanted to see *Blue Thunder*. See, McCay had finally grown a pair and asked Laura Knettles on a date. But, shit, we were, like, sixteen at the time. But she could only go on a date the exact day *Blue Thunder* released. Man, he knew how much that movie meant to me. So, he ended up telling her that he was sick and couldn't make it. I told him he was crazy and that he should take Laura out because he'd waited so long to ask her out. He refused. So, we did our usual back-door sneak-in. Took our normal spot in the back. Right when the movie started, two kids sat a few rows in front of us. Thought nothing of it. But when the projector broke and the lights came on, two things happened. One, Laura found out that Luke wasn't sick, and two, we were never able to sneak into an R-rated movie again. The two kids who had come in late were Laura and her older brother, Nick. At that time, you could go to an R-rated movie as long as you were eighteen."

Ben laughs.

Luke smiles, rubbing his lips with his fingers. It's the second time I see the smile that's genuine, pure. He looks at me. The earth-brown eyes have traded themselves for a deep hazel.

"Don't include that in the story, okay?" Luke starts to cough, grabs his water, and takes a few swallows.

We visit for an hour or so when Luke explains to Ben that we have to get back on the road.

I stick out my hand to Ben. "It was so nice to meet you, Ben."

Ben looks at my hand. Laughs. "Nah, friends don't shake hands." And he reaches up from his chair and wraps his arms around my neck in the softest way possible. "It was my pleasure, Catherine. Watch out for him, would you?"

I don't answer Ben because I don't know how to. I don't know what he's asking me to do, so instead, I turn on my heel and toy with the words in my head as I walk to the car to give Luke and Ben a moment for their good-byes.

"Watch out for him, would you?" As in don't let him make a bad choice?

"Watch out for him, would you?" As in he's fragile, and he needs you?

"Watch out for him, would you?" As in watch his back?

I lean against the Mustang, out of earshot.

Luke is hesitant. His hands in his pockets of his cargo shorts, he kicks the lip of a brick and then looks at Ben.

I can't hear what they're saying, but Ben listens to what Luke is saying. Ben is quiet, and one thing I've noticed about him is he doesn't like silence. He likes to keep the conversation moving. Perhaps it's his own insecurity; maybe it's not. Maybe it's just the way he was made.

They both wait for the other to speak.

Luke reaches into his back pocket and hands Ben a white envelope. I try not to stare, but I can't help it. I feel as though I'm eavesdropping, watching a conversation that isn't my business.

But I can't look away. I remember watching *LA Hills* and thinking about Dylan Klein. I wondered back then if his voice really sounded that smooth. I wondered if he drove his sports car that fast on Highway 1. I wondered if he really smoked cigarettes and made up for lost time with women he didn't know. I wondered if he was really that handsome in real life or if the cameras somehow managed to catch the good angles all the time. I wondered if he kissed women with want and need and passion—because the man who's coming toward me is older, somehow softer, and still just as beautiful.

"You ready?" he asks.

Without answering, I open the car door and get in.

Luke goes around to the driver's door, and I look back at Ben, who's still on the porch, waiting for us to pull away.

Luke starts the Mustang, and the motor comes alive with a roar.

Is Ben really all right with being in the chair for the rest of his life?

Is Ben really all right with the person who did this?

My grandfather, Elias, used to say, "Acceptance is the key, Catherine," in his thick German accent. "No matter what happens in life, if we cannot accept it, it will ruin us."

We pull away from the curb of Ben's house, and I wave at him.

But I have a hunch that Ben is far beyond acceptance.

We take a left and then a right that leads us back to the freeway. I don't ask what Luke handed Ben, nor do I ask what they talked about, I just stare at his right hand on the gearshift, his knuckles big and white.

"Your hands are dry," I say. "Do you work a lot with your hands?"

"Fixing up my place," he says from somewhere a million miles away.

I grab a lotion bottle from my purse. "May I?" I hold up the lotion bottle. When I was in prison, I'd receive a bottle of this lotion every month without fail. I still haven't figured out who sent it to me, but it works. When I got out, I found it at some voodoo shop in LA. I squeeze a dime size on my fingers. With my other hand, I take a dab and gently put my fingertip to each of his knuckles and carefully massage it in.

He watches me as I do this.

His hands are not the hands of an actor, but a carpenter. Working man hands. Not soft. Not gentle.

"Do me a favor," I whisper.

"Yeah?" he says.

"If the acting gig doesn't work out, don't be a hand model. I don't think things would work out in your favor." I smile, look up at him.

"Dream crusher." He gently pulls his lips to a half-smirk and then pulls his hand away, placing it on the steering wheel in a way that says, *I can't go any further. You touching my hand isn't something that should be happening.*

I put the lotion in the glove compartment, so he has it. I want to explain that I didn't mean anything by the lotion on his hands. That it's just something in my nature. To help. If he hadn't been driving, I'd most likely have just handed him the bottle instead. But I don't say any of this.

"Remember when Michael Jordan came out of retirement for the second time?" I take a different approach.

"Of course."

"Do you remember watching Jordan play the game of basketball? It … it was like watching all the pieces of life fall into place. Like eating the world's best burger—with bacon." I smile. "Like touching silk. Like smelling a bouquet of red roses. Like listening to 'Pas de Deux' from *The Nutcracker*. Like watching the defining moment in *What's Eating Gilbert Grape*—when they burn the house to the ground." I continue, "So, anyway, when Jordan came back to play for the Washington Wizards and failed miserably, it was heartbreaking to watch." I look out the window to a three-toned rock formation. "We had one television at Dublin, and when the game was on, Lucinda, one of the correctional officers, let me watch it in the dining hall."

"What's your point?" Luke asks.

"If you become a hand model, you'll fail miserably."

Luke gives a feeble attempt at forcing himself not to smile. "Noted."

I grab my notebook from the floorboard and look at my list of questions. "Why'd you stop acting?"

Luke's sunglasses protect him, keeping me from seeing what his eyes say that his mouth can't. "I didn't." He shrugs. "People just couldn't look past Dylan. They couldn't see me as someone else. Couldn't see me as their leading man in a thriller. Couldn't see me as their leading man in a comedy. Producers, directors couldn't see past the one defining role in my career."

"So, you just stopped?"

Luke looks at me, his eyebrows rising above his sunglasses. "It wasn't my first love anyway, Cat."

My heart stumbles over itself, tries to find its rightful pace again. The way he says my nickname is like it's casual, like we're old friends, like we've somehow reached an agreement of trust.

It's music. Music is his first love.

"Besides," he continues, "I have enough." He takes his left hand and rubs the back of his neck.

"Do you want me to drive?"

"No, I got it. Slept wrong last night, I guess."

I nod, looking out the window again. "Do you ever feel cheated? Like maybe if you hadn't gotten that role, things would have been different?"

Silence sits in the air for several seconds before Luke breaks it with hoarseness. "My dad used to say, 'Luke, we're all put on this earth to do several things, not just one. So, take the good shit, the bad shit, and everything in between." He coughs, clearing his throat.

"Do you think everything is forgivable?" I stop. Hold my tongue. Surprised at myself for allowing this to slip out.

He coughs once more, recovers quicker than last time. "No."

I let the small grooves of the dashboard take away my ability to allow fear drive my imagination.

"Do you?" he asks.

"No." My own word rests shallowly on my lips, as if waiting for me to take it back. "But sometimes, we just have to take the bad, right?"

"Something like that," he says.

The road is flat and surrounded by desert. Cacti follow us for miles.

Since that awful night and all these years later, I question every single thing I did that night and question if I had been put in the wrong place at the wrong time. Did I put myself there? Did I make the wrong decision at the right time or the right decision at the wrong time?

I've played the scenario, the series of events that led up to it, in my head a million times, and no matter what, I keep coming up with, it had to happen.

"Promise me something," Luke says.

I don't answer at first. "I can't promise you something if I don't know if I'm capable of keeping it."

He ignores me. "When you look back on this life, when you're old and gray, you'll give yourself the gift of forgiveness."

His words are like a direct hit on my chest, leaving a smattering of red, like Luke has exposed a piece of who I am, the demons that I keep.

"I thought you said not everything is forgivable?"

Luke's manly hands sit on the steering wheel. "Not everything is forgivable, but the truth of forgiveness lies in the eyes of the keeper."

Both sadness and truth come over me. *In other words, what I think isn't forgivable, someone else might.*

"Promise me," he says, showing no signs of relenting.

I let the sun find my arm, and I move it in its rays, feeling the warmth. *I don't make promises I can't keep*, I want to say. I want to tell him what happened on the morning of January 2, 2001, so he'll know what I'm up against.

"I promise."

An unkept promise full of good intentions is no better than one lie among truths. The only difference is the person behind them.

Luke turns on the radio. Jimmy Buffett plays.

"Tell me two truths, Luke," I say, allowing myself to get lost in Buffett's tone of good days.

Luke taps his fingers on the steering wheel to an unheard beat. "One, Nutella on bread with milk at one in the morning is a guilty pleasure. And two, I still haven't found the perfect wave."

"You couldn't surf in Kentucky, so you learned to surf when you came out to California?"

"Best money paid was to a guy named Kane who lived in a shack just off of Venice Beach. This was back in the eighties, of course. Took two days with me. I've been hooked since." He looks over at me. "And you?"

"I don't know how to surf."

"I assumed you didn't. But what I meant was, what are your two truths?"

I take in a deep breath and let it out through my nose. Look over at Luke. "One, I grew up wealthy and didn't have a thing. Two, sometimes, when I'm alone, I wonder if I'll ever make it out of my own head."

Luke hits the gas pedal as I fall deeper into the seat, melding myself to it, wanting the fear and thrill to live forever.

I can barely hear the radio over the roar of engine.

Luke goes faster and faster.

I sink deeper and deeper.

Before
Federal Correctional Institution, Dublin

Dear Journal,

The only time Mother made me wear a dress was in Minnesota in April 1993. My maternal grandmother had passed away. We were there for the funeral.

"Catherine Jane, don't you dare put a run in those tights," Mother called from the house as Ingrid, me, and a few of the kids played in the front yard.

I rolled my eyes, and Ingrid smiled.

"Where's your dad?" one of our cousins asked.

"Working," was our simultaneous response.

Father didn't go many places with us, and secretly, I always felt it was just easier without him. Mother was more relaxed, and Ingrid and I didn't try so hard to impress him.

"But shouldn't your father want to be with his family at this time? His wife at least, in her time of need?" a woman said from the sidewalk.

Ingrid and I stopped. Shielded our eyes from the sun's light, stared at the woman who'd asked the question.

I didn't know what to say to the woman I'd never seen before, and I wasn't quite sure what she was asking. So, instead, Ingrid and I just stared. Eventually, she walked away.

But her question rummaged around in my head into the evening, the next day, even when we flew back home to California on Father's private jet.

I didn't ask Ingrid what she thought until Mother's eyelids closed for a minute on the flight home.

"Do you wonder why Father didn't come with us?"

Ingrid looked up from her book. "No. He had to work."

That was when the realization of our chaos hit me.

Why would we know anything different when this life was the only life we'd known? Just like flying on a private jet rather than the big aircrafts with loads of people we didn't know. Just like holidays with strange people in beautiful places. Lavish dinner parties with famous actors and actresses. Walking the red carpet at the Oscars with Father. Cameras being shoved in our faces—which only happened once, as Father put a stop to it. Beautiful homes and Olympic-size swimming pools. Our house was made up of seventeen bedrooms, thirteen bathrooms, and a lot of space between them. It had so much space that the chaos lay quietly in the grout of the marble floors until it was time for the madness to awaken.

Every single day, Mother paid the cleaning service to come. Ingrid and I knew that Mother feared Father's backlash if the sink had leftover toothpaste or the marble counters had a smudge or anything was out of place. Because Father always knew when something was out of place or something hadn't been cleaned to his specifications.

Mother knew she'd take the brunt of it. She didn't know we knew, but we did. So, Ingrid and I became obsessive about keeping our rooms immaculate, cleaning up behind ourselves.

Father never really talked about his childhood. Though I remember one time, we came across some pictures of his childhood home. In the background of the images, there were things everywhere. Stacks of books. Stacks of dishes. New things. Old things. Used cat litter boxes. And in every picture, Father wore only a diaper and a filthy face. He never once talked about his mother. But sometimes, he'd talk about Grandfather.

One day, hesitantly, I asked Father if I could look through his childhood photos.

He responded with, "They're all gone, Catherine. They're all gone."

More later.

—Catherine

Dear Journal,

One night, I heard Ingrid get out of bed.

"What are you doing, Ingrid?" I asked. "It's late."

She put her slippers on. "The top shelf of the refrigerator had a little spilled milk. I want to make sure it's clean before morning."

I understood. We didn't want Mother to get into trouble because Father never laid a finger on us—no matter the circumstance.

"I'll help you."

And we both made our way down the forty-two stairs it took to get to the kitchen on the first floor.

Sometimes, I felt like a stranger in my own home. I'd watch reruns of *Leave It To Beaver* and feel the sensation of need. If only Father could smile like Ward Cleaver, I knew that would make things easier. If only he didn't work so much, he wouldn't be so stressed. The Cleavers had a normal house in the suburbs. Ward worked, and June stayed home. They didn't have a lot of money, nor were they poor by any means. From the knotting pit in my belly, I knew the Cleavers were a happy family. Genuinely happy. And all I wanted as a child was to be a Cleaver. Molly Cleaver. Molly because of Molly Ringwald.

Ingrid and I had all this space, all this time, beautiful things, all the material things you could ask for, and yet all I wanted was a happy family. A home where we didn't have to tiptoe around like we were on eggshells. Where Father was happy and smiled and gave love. Where he showered Mother with affection instead of purple flowers that resembled the color of bruises he left on her heart and, later, on her body.

Mother always sent us away to summer camp for at least four weeks in the summer. Space camp. Girl Scout camp. Horse-riding camp. Sports camps. Dance camp. Zoo camp. German language camp. Cooking camp. Music camp. Drama and acting camp. Film camp. Math camp. Writing camp. It wasn't that she wanted to get rid of us. I knew Mother wished Ingrid and I would find some normalcy; she was giving us a break. And I knew Father would never argue to get us out of the house.

I think, in some ways, it allowed him to be someone he really was. I think he kept a filter on what he said and did when Ingrid and I were home. Which scared us for Mother when we left. We'd beg her, plead with her not to make us go—and not because we didn't want to, but because we were terrified Father would do something to her while we were away. Of course, in true Clemens fashion, Ingrid and I never told her this. We just used the excuse of homesickness, which wasn't entirely a lie either.

But Ingrid and I both knew that death would be the only thing to separate her and Father. And divorce, back in the 1980s, was looked down upon. And let's not forget that Mother was—and still is, I suppose—a Midwesterner, and in the Midwest, you stay married—even in the afterlife. Divorce just wasn't an option.

Besides, on the outside, the Clemens family kept all the pretty pieces together. Nurtured them, polished their outsides, but on the inside, the decay began to spread like a venomous poison.

—Catherine

"Thank you, Officer," Luke says to the patrolman who clocked him at ninety-two miles an hour, only giving him a ticket for ten miles over the speed limit, not seventeen, because Luke posed for a picture with the officer for his wife and signed a patrol shirt the officer had had in the back of his cruiser.

I hadn't minded the speed or the car or the heat. As the car had gone faster, I'd felt the speed trailing through my veins like a drug. Like sex used to be when I allowed it to be.

Looking over at Luke as he takes to the roads of New Mexico again, I want to ask him more personal questions, so I do.

"What was your first memory as a child?" I tie my hair up so that it doesn't blow in my face. I want to see his mouth move when he gives me this answer. Watch how the answer falls against his lips, see if there's trepidation or fear or love or commitment.

"I was about five," he starts. A cool, calm look sets in his eyes, his sunglasses on the dash, where Luke set them when the officer asked for his license and registration.

"My father told me not to do it. An electric fence could hold up to ten thousand volts of electricity. The fence was there, and I was there. Curiosity always seemed to get me into trouble, even to this day. Maybe I wanted to see what it felt like—the wire, the power, what my body would do when the electricity took hold of it. My father always said that I was too smart for my own good. I knew it would hurt, but I couldn't help myself," Luke says, resting his forearm on his leg, his fingers still lingering on the wheel. "So, when my dad turned around, I took ahold of the fence." Luke smiles as if his conscience is clear, as if air is a drug and to breathe it is a miracle. "I fell facedown in the hard dirt. Felt like my entire body was one big muscle, stuck and cramped. It lasted for a few seconds maybe. My dad turned around, shook his head, and said, 'I hope you live your life with a little more care, Luke,' and then walked away." Luke laughs. "I never touched an electric fence again."

He looks over at me, drapes his eyes over my body. It's the first time I see any emotion from Luke, and I'm stuck, staring at him, almost afraid to look away.

"What about you?" he asks, turning his attention back to the road.

I think on it. I want to buffer, filter the bad stuff. Because my first memory isn't one I want Luke to know. So, I tell him what I want him to know, what I want him to remember, though lying might be easier. But I've learned, in the long run, the debts for lying are paid tenfold.

"I was seven, and Ingrid was six. My father came home from work early with a new Corvette and … purple flowers for my mother. Surprised us with a trip to Myers Flat. He'd purchased a cabin." I feel the memory settle over me like the breeze on a warm summer day when it's not too warm. The corners of my mouth turn up into a smile.

"You should smile more often, Catherine." I hear Luke whisper. "You have a beautiful smile."

A smile, a genuine smile, can be felt, understood, I believe.

"You should, too," I say.

The Texas flag is larger than the state of Texas it seems. As it waves its glory across the state line, a light illuminates the red, white, and blue. The sun has set now, and other than the flag, we can only see whatever the headlights unfold.

"Are you hungry?" Luke asks.

"Yeah. You?"

"I can eat. Maybe we'll find somewhere to crash and then find a place to eat."

We pull into a motel. It's the first one we see, and by our outward assessment, it seems safe, clean. Luke pulls under the covered awning. The Vista is dated, reflecting a time back when milkshakes were a dime and hamburgers were fifty cents. Luke opens the door for me when I attempt to walk past him, but a man storms out of the doorway, and in my best attempt to move out of the way, I fall against Luke's chest.

The man turns around swiftly, looks back at the two of us. "My apologies," he says and walks to his car.

With my back against Luke's chest, my head tells me to move, but my heart won't allow it. He smells like Polo, and all I want in this moment is to remain like this, his heart thumping against my back. His mouth next to my ear.

I hear a sharp breath from Luke, and somewhere deep inside me, I feel as though I've burdened him.

I pull myself from his chest and go to speak, but he asks, "Are you all right?" and he says it in a tone I'm unfamiliar with. In a tone I haven't heard him speak from. It's low and breathy and quiet.

I nod.

"Welcome to The Vista, friends. I'm sorry. If you're looking for a room, we're at full capacity tonight," the man from behind the counter drawls, pulling his fingers across his handlebar mustache. "Y'all, we're having a new country festival, and it seems from here to Odessa, all hotels full. Plus, there isn't much out here." A slow chuckle escapes his mouth. "Y'all can try The Sandman though."

"And where is that?" Luke asks.

"There might be some availability just down the road, about a quarter mile. It'll be slim pickins' though."

"Thank you," Luke says from his position at the door, still holding it open, and I'm now a safe distance away.

We're a quarter mile down the road, and The Sandman isn't much different from The Vista. Same dated look but no overhead awning to speak of. The parking lot looks to be at maximum capacity.

"You stay in the car. I'll go in," Luke says.

"Okay." I need some distance. I need time to get my brain straight and my heart right.

When Luke shuts the door to the car, I give myself a pep talk.

This is professional, Cat. Prison changed you. Sex can't be a free-for-all anymore. You've grown out of that. You know it can't cure you. You're no longer a college student; you can't use sex to fix your issues.

Luke returns. "Full capacity, but Larry, the guy inside, recommended the Kampground of America just a quarter mile down the road." He looks at me. Smiles.

"I suppose everything in Texas is a quarter mile away?"

We both chuckle.

"I got a tent in the back and a sleeping bag," Luke says.

He starts up the car, and I feel the power in the engine again.

Our last stop for the evening is the KOA. There's a mini grocery store attached to the KOA, so when we walk in, Luke says he's going to talk to the woman about availability and I peruse the food.

Nothing nutritious, just premade food that's as healthy as prison food. But at least with prison food, we had representation from each food group.

I grab two beef cup of noodles, two breakfast bars, two bottles of water, and I'm about to go pay for them when

Luke walks over to me and stands a little too close. Too close for any good thing to come of this, only because I know myself.

But if we're two consenting adults, by law, it's all right, right?

You're working, my conscience chimes in.

You can't do this, Cat. Stupid idea.

My face starts to burn, as do the tips of my ears.

"Looks good," Luke says.

I swallow any saliva that I have, nod, and walk to the counter to pay, but Luke touches my hand so that I won't pull out my wallet. And when he touches my skin, my whole body feels it. It's like nothing I've ever felt before, setting my skin, soul on fire. Peter and Michael have touched me before. The other men have touched me before, but those touches, those men, have never given me this feeling, this reaction. Luke's touch has somehow created a place for him in my heart, and this terrifies me.

Before I can pull my hand away, Luke uses the other hand and pulls out his wallet.

"Please," he begs.

With this look, I feel like Luke isn't just asking to pay for what I've put on the counter, but he's asking for something more than just sex or want.

I put my hands at my sides and stare at the woman named Valerie, as the name tag on her top says. She has bright pink lipstick and red hair. I tilt my head because, oddly, the colors seem to flow, and I want this to move my thoughts away from Luke and to the color array that stands before us.

She pops her gum. "That will be seven dollars and sixty-two cents. Cash or card?"

At the same time, Luke says, "Card," I say, "Cash."

Valerie's eyes dance between us. "What's it gonna be?" she asks.

When Luke takes his card from his wallet and smiles at his accomplishment, the woman's left eye squints.

"Hey, you look real familiar."

"I work down the road," he lies.

"Are you Ernie's brother?" she asks as I reluctantly step back so Luke can slide his card.

"Can't say that I have a brother named Ernie."

"Well, you look like him," Valerie says.

"Can we also get a spot to camp for the night?" I ask.

"I took care of it," Luke says as he slides his card back into his wallet.

We exchange good-byes with Valerie, and before we leave, I fill up our cup of noodles with hot water and push the paper lids back on. As we exit the store and walk back to Luke's car, the Texas night air meets our faces.

"I don't need you to pay for everything," I say.

"Well, I guess, on this trip, you're going to have to get used to it."

We get into the car. Luke starts the engine, and we quietly crawl to spot twenty-two.

Once we find it, Luke parks, and we both get out. He grabs the tent and the only sleeping bag we have. I balance our soup and carefully set it on our picnic table along with our waters and breakfast bars that I shoved in my jacket pocket.

Luke and I set up the two-man tent. When we're done, I walk back to the picnic table and stir our soups while Luke brings over a lit well-loved candle.

"What else do you store in your car?" I hand him his soup.

"Thank you." Luke rubs his hands together and stares at me in the candlelight across the picnic table. "Road flares. A first aid kit, a deck of cards."

"Road flares?" I say and smile. Then, I take a sip of water.

He grins. "Road flares are a good thing to have in your car, although I'm not sure how well a deck of cards will help you."

I try not to laugh. "Kill time, I guess?" I blow on my soup, smile at Luke as he chuckles, and take a bite. I allow the salty broth to settle into my taste buds. I swallow. "My mother never used to let us eat things like this, growing up." I take another bite.

"Why not?"

"She said it was cancer-causing." I shrug. "But isn't everything cancer-causing these days?"

Luke shrugs. "Everything."

It's quiet for a moment, then he finally says, "One sister?" His voice gentler.

I shake my head. "No, I'm the interviewer. I ask the questions."

"We can't have a conversation without knowing just a little bit about each other."

But the truth is, I like how, with Luke, I don't feel like the woman with the twisted family. The one who went to prison. He makes me feel like he'd meet me at the edge of water and take me for who I am, not what I've done.

"Ingrid. One year younger than me. Studied to be a nurse." I take another bite of soup instead, chew on the noodles.

Luke stares at me, swallowing another sip of water. I know what he's doing. He's tiptoeing around the wolf that's sitting in the corner.

Why doesn't he ask me what happened that night? It isn't a secret.

I want to ask him this, ask him why, but in the same breath, it's almost as if, just for a moment, I'm free of it and I'm not Catherine Clemens, that I'm just Cat and this is just a really long lunch meeting, and I like it this way.

I turn the conversation back to him. "If you died tomorrow, what are three things you'd miss the most?"

With Luke's hand on his water bottle, his eyes narrow, and he cocks his head to the right. "What?"

I wipe my mouth with the back of my hand—another thing that used to make Mother cringe. I repeat the question.

This time, his eyes are deadlocked on mine. "The ocean. The smell of fall … and you."

Please, God, let this all be a dream, and if it is a dream, let me wake up now, so I can start the healing of the wreckage Luke McCay will do to me.

I cough into my hand, attempting to act as though his words don't have any effect on me and it's the soup. "Wrong pipe," I say through the cough. "You barely know me, Luke," I whisper.

He leans on the table, crossing his arms, the candle's light reflecting in his eyes. "I know enough of you to know that, when I die, you'll have made an impact on me. That, somehow, you've wedged yourself into my forever memories, the ones I keep close to me."

I ponder this thought for a moment as my throat begins to tighten. This is a sign that I feel something that I don't want to feel. "But we haven't created any memories," I counter, trying to smile this off and take another bite of soup.

"We still have just over two thousand miles, Cat. I'm sure we'll find some."

"But you can't possibly know that I'll have made an impact on you."

"You already have." He shoves a bite of noodles in his mouth and stares hard back at me.

My phone vibrates in my back pocket, and I pull it out. Look at Luke. "I need to take this."

"By all means." Luke pushes back from the picnic table and grabs our empty soup cups. The lull of the candlelight still pulls us back to the fire, the moment we just shared that wasn't intimate, but intimate at the same time, if that makes sense. I just want a few more minutes in this moment to feel Luke.

But my sister is calling. My phone is vibrating in my hand, and Luke's already walked over to the trash can.

"Hey," I whisper into my phone.

Long pause.

"Hey."

I look back to make sure Luke can't hear me. He's in the driver's side of his car, the dome light on; he's looking down at something.

I turn back to stare at the darkness and the tent we erected together.

"Where are you?" she asks.

"Texas. How's Mother?" When I ask this question, I don't expect a change in Mother's ability to use her words. To keep house. To tend to her roses like she used to when we got older. To take care of us, but maybe a smile. Maybe.

"The same."

"Did you get the money where it needed to go?" I glance back to be sure Luke is a safe distance from me, so he can't hear the conversation.

"Yes. Still have seven more payments."

I rub my forehead with my hand, asking myself if we'll ever get out from Mother's care bills.

"We could sell the hou—" Ingrid starts to ask.

"Ingrid. We aren't selling the house. We will find a way. Look, give Mother a kiss for me. Tell her I'll be home soon."

"The house doesn't mean anything to me anymore, Cat."

"Love you, bye." I abruptly hang up because I don't want to hear what Ingrid has to say about the house.

Deep down, I know it still means something to her even if she can't enjoy it like she used to. Selling the house is not an option.

I turn around to see Luke sitting at the picnic table in the candlelight. Sliding my phone back in my pocket, I casually walk over to the picnic table and sit down.

"Everything all right?" he asks.

Everything is better than it used to be, I want to say. "Can I ask you a question?"

"Shoot." He shuffles the deck of cards.

"How do you feel about the reunion series of *LA Hills*?" I ask, feeling like a sellout, like a groupie, like someone who doesn't have anything deeper to ask, yet knowing this is part of the story Mr. Jenkins wants.

"How about this? We play War, and every time your card is the highest card, you can ask a question. But every time my card is the highest card, I get to ask you a question."

I bite my lip. Think for a minute. "Okay."

Luke hands me my cards.

We flip.

I get the win. Look at Luke across the table. "How do you feel about the reunion show?"

"I think we've all changed, and we've all been through shit." Luke runs his free hand through his hair. "Honestly, I'm not sure."

"Then, why are you doing it?"

I put a card out on the table.

Luke does, too.

I win again.

Luke drops his head, pulls it up, and smiles. "I'm not."

"But—"

"You asked how I felt about it," Luke says.

"But the media is saying otherwise."

"Hollywood thinks that there's a price to everything, and if you're willing to pay the price, well, it'll all work out."

"But not with you."

"Nah. I don't need the money. I just don't want to spend my time left on this earth tied to a show or Hollywood or anything like that. I just want to be free."

Me, too, I want to say. I feel his words in the darkest places of me, the places I store the guilt that I won't allow to the surface. The sadness I keep hidden. *I know what you mean.*

If he's read my story in the tabloids, the magazines, just like everyone else has, he knows that, of all people, I might just understand the most. My family has never talked to the media about that night.

Not Mother.

Not Ingrid.

Not me.

Not Father.

So, everything said is just speculation.

The media interviewed the cleaning service Mother had hired.

They interviewed the landscape service that manicured our lawn, trimmed our bushes into dinosaurs, swans, and Bruce Springsteen.

I could sell the story. But I never will. Some things are so private, so guarded, so secret that they become hard to let go of.

When I look up, Luke is staring at me, his card waiting for mine.

I lay down a two of spades.

He wins with a jack of hearts. "Have you ever been in love?" Luke collects our cards in the middle.

"No."

We lay two more down.

I win. "Have you ever been in love?"

"Yes."

I can't lie and say I don't feel jealous or incompetent or less than right now. Luke is on a different playing field than me. He's ten years older, maturer, more beautiful than any man I've ever met. Luke doesn't give me this vibe that I'm somehow less; it's something within me that tells me I don't measure up, that I'm not good enough.

I imagine the woman he's in love with—or fell in love with—has long, dark hair, the length that reaches her waist and lays flat against her back. Green eyes, the color between emerald and peridot. Skin so perfect that it doesn't seem real. And probably a soul so sweet that grace seems to be her motto.

We lay two cards down.

War. A seven of hearts and a seven of spades.

At the last flip of the fourth card, I win.

But it's Luke's phone that rings this time from his shirt pocket. He pulls it out, looks down at the screen, and looks up at me. "Excuse me, Catherine."

I don't say anything, but he waits expectantly for me to say something.

"Okay."

He nods, stands up, and puts his phone to his ear. He walks away into the darkness, and I hear the remnants of his whispers that move closer to my heart.

Would he whisper in my ear secrets only between two lovers?

The closeness I've never felt to a man seems present here, as if I'd known Luke my whole life. Maybe it's because he does more listening than talking. Maybe it's because he likes '70s music the way I like it. Slow, easy, full of pain, room for interpretation.

The only noise I hear is the sound of my own heart thumping against my chest. The rest of the world seems quiet, unimpressed.

I look at the night sky with the diamonds so bright. I remember when I couldn't see the stars and the moon and the sun. I remember when the sky wasn't itself at all, just four prison walls that protected the world from me.

The Texas night air is warm, and it still smells hot into the evening, like the mornings in Myers Flat when the sun rose and the scent followed, warning its patrons that today would be another warm day.

Texas heat seems somehow different from the heat in California. Maybe it's more Republican than Liberal, perhaps more hospitable than California, Texas offers a warm hug and fried chicken, whereas California might offer an opinion on recycling and vegan sushi roll.

Luke returns. "I'm sorry."

I shrug.

He doesn't offer an explanation, nor do I deserve one.

"I won. My question."

We look down at the cards.

What's her name? I want to ask. But just when my head convinces me to do the service, I remember that Luke doesn't ask about what happened. He doesn't ask about Father or Mother. He gives me that time. That space. So, as bad as I want to know about the woman who took his heart and hopefully kept it safe, I won't ask him about it.

"What's your favorite James Taylor song?"

" 'Fading Away.' "

But I'm not ready for his answer. I'm not prepared at all. I swallow the good and bad feelings that this song, its lyrics, its memories give me. The quiet voice of a desperate little girl eager to have what her parents had when this song is played and only when this song played, and yet pushing it away because when the song ends, the guessing game of how to live, how to breathe, how to survive becomes essential.

I'm writing a story, and that's what I'm being paid to do, so do it, I tell myself.

"Why that song?" My bones, my heart crush against my own words.

When I don't hear Luke's response, I look over at him. Maybe his answer is full of thoughts that he can't fill his own words with—as if the explanation won't justify the way the song moves him.

And maybe all of this is my truth and not his.

His Adam's apple bobs, and he goes to speak. But stops. Gathers his thoughts and starts again. "When all your moves, all your cards are played, who are you then? I think the song is about vulnerability. After everything is laid out on the table, what does that leave?" Luke meets my gaze as I hang on his words. The candlelight dances against his face and mine. "It leaves a man fading away, just trying to make sense of it all, trying like hell not to lose himself, and in the same breath, I think the song is also about surrender." He pauses. "I've made a lot of mistakes in my life, done a lot I'm not proud of, but what if, at the end of the day, you rectify the wrong just in time to feel some sense of right in the world?"

A single tear attempts to slide down my cheek, but I catch it before it does.

Yeah.

"I think life and death are the easy parts. I think it's all the shit in the middle that's difficult. Are you ready to go to bed?" he asks. "We have a long drive tomorrow." Luke cuts the conversation short.

He coughs into his hand and then rubs it against his jeans. I like when he does this because it makes him seem more human.

I carve out this moment right now. I take it and put it into my pocket, saving it for later, so that when I get down on myself again, I can take this moment out, savor it, and know there are people who understand, that we just need to be present to hear it.

Luke puts the cards away, and I blow out the candle.

The darkness surrounds us, and he lights the path with his phone to the tent where our bodies will lie and take in the world, a place where, hopefully, our minds will quiet and we can rest easy, knowing that we're not in this alone.

"Luke?"

He's ahead of me. He stops. Turns to me.

"I know what you mean," I try to say with clear conviction in my voice, but it comes out soft, more tender.

"Sometimes, we just need that other person to understand."

I nod because I can't speak. The knot in my throat is holding back the tears.

He takes my hand and leads me to the tent.

Luke wants me to take the sleeping bag, but I refuse. I suggest we share it by lying on top of it and using a small airplane blanket to cover us.

The Texas heat is warm, even through the night.

We both get situated. Using our sweatshirts for pillows, we stare up through the top of the tent to the starry night sky.

"Luke?" I whisper.

"Yeah?"

"Will you hold my hand again?"

"Yes."

And just like that, our hands fit together, and everything is all right in the world even if it's just for tonight.

Before
Federal Correctional Institution, Dublin

Dear Journal,

There were purple flowers on the table again when I walked downstairs.

I'd slept with headphones on and fallen asleep to mourn the loss of my virginity the night before. I loved Peter, but I wasn't in love with Peter. I'd had hopes that once we had sex, it would allow for my heart to fall in love with him. But afterward, I'd just felt rushed and contaminated and broken into small pieces. Not heartbroken, but I felt like pieces of me were scattered, and I just needed something to gather them up and rebuild myself.

"Morning, Cat," Mother said from the stove. "Pancakes and eggs."

I sat down at the other end of the table from Father. I watched as his eyes scanned the paper and wondered to myself if he was really reading the newspaper. A successful businessman, educated, surely, he was studying the stocks or reading about the economic projected growth of 1999 or the decline we'd learned about in Economics. But it didn't matter, and I never bothered to ask.

Sometimes, I wanted to hate him.

Other times, I admired him.

But all the times, I loved him.

That was the only thing that remained constant in our relationship.

"I got into Brown," I said as I took a bite of a warm pancake.

"Cat, please, get a plate," Mother said as she cleaned the kitchen.

"That's nice, Catherine," Father said and continued to read—or not read or whatever.

I took another bite.

"Catherine, a plate, please," Mother said.

"Morning," Ingrid said as she walked into the kitchen.

She saw the purple flowers, too.

I wanted to rattle off the statistics to Father about Brown—things I knew we could relate on.

They have a nine percent acceptance rate.

"Did you know John D. Rockefeller Jr. graduated from Brown, Father?" I said, knowing full well that would catch his attention because he had business ties with the Rockefellers and their political party.

"I'm aware of where John Jr. went to school, Catherine," he said.

"Did you know that Cat also got accepted to Stanford and Yale, Father?" Ingrid grabbed a pancake, just as I had, and buried her teeth into the unbleached flour.

Mother sighed, so I grabbed us both plates from the middle of the table. Handed one to Ingrid. Looked up at Mother.

"You did?" Father looked up only briefly from his reading. "That's wonderful, Catherine."

Brown was my first choice. I wanted to say this, but I didn't. Perhaps Father didn't like Brown, or maybe he thought there was a better choice. I cared deeply about his opinion even if I didn't show it.

"Did you know I was pregnant?" Ingrid whispered.

Mother said, "What?" over the running water from the sink.

Father took a sip of his black coffee.

I looked to my sister, envious and both heartbroken for her. Envious that she could speak her mind and it didn't matter to her what others thought, and heartbroken because nobody cared, except for me.

"That reminds me; come upstairs with me," I said to her.

Both Ingrid and I stood, grabbed our plates from the table, kissed Mother on the cheek, and put the plates in the dishwasher.

But when I kissed Mother, I allowed my lips to linger longer on her cheek, willing her to know that I was sorry for not using a plate, that I was sorry for turning my headphones up last night, and that I was sorry there were purple hydrangeas on the table this morning.

Father didn't look up, so Ingrid and I didn't say a word.

When we got upstairs, I told her about Peter and last night and losing my virginity.

She asked how I felt.

I told her it wasn't what I'd imagined, but what I didn't tell her was that I might have done it for the wrong reasons.

Ingrid and I had learned to lie early on. We learned that as long as everything was okay on the outside, the inside didn't matter. We learned to hold a brave face because Father hated tears—and watermelon and Sundays, maybe because we went to church and he didn't. Another thing we learned was that if you showed up for Sunday service, all the lies would be forgiven for the week, and we could start anew on Monday morning.

I'd learned to say no, even when I wanted to say yes.

I'd learned to say yes, even when I wanted to say no.

I'd learned to hold my tongue because all I wanted was for others to like me, to be okay with who you saw on the outside.

Ingrid asked if I'd do it again.

I answered, "Probably. If Peter wants to."

She paused and got really quiet. "Did it feel good?" she asked, as if she'd never experienced sex before. As if, somehow, it might be different with someone different.

I wanted to say no, but I couldn't. That sex was just sex unless love was involved. I wanted to be a better role model for her. And really, it wasn't the sex that felt good; it was what he had done afterward. Peter had lain there with me and held our naked bodies together until I stopped shivering.

Later that year, I left for Brown and left Ingrid in the wake of chaos, alone, to fend for herself until Christmas. We talked every day.

She tried to find her path, and I tried to find mine. The problem was, we were both searching for these things outwardly and not looking inwardly.

Ingrid never told me what those times were like, and I didn't ask. I didn't want to know, and for a long time, I felt guilty for that. I just wanted to escape the madness just for a while.

It wasn't until she left for Stanford the next fall that I finally felt like I could breathe more deeply again. Though Mother was still at home. At times, I felt more mad at her for staying, but it was her choice, her bed, and she just had to lie in it.

But I thought, over time, we began to build up this wall of acceptance.

That it wasn't *that* bad.

That the abuse, both physically against Mother and emotionally for us all three, and the manipulation, we learned that it was acceptable. After all, Father gave us beautiful, beautiful things. Why wouldn't we be happy?

Then, the guilt would pile in like an old, well-worn top, and I would hear Father's voice.

"I work seventy-five hours a week so that you can have private school."

"I've built an empire for you."

"I work seventy-five hours a week. I don't need to go to your dance recitals to know you dance well."

"I've run through hell and back to give you what you want."

"I work seventy-five hours a week so that you can attend your summer camps."

"You should be happy, but instead, you focus on complaining that I'm gone all the time, you ungrateful twits."

But what had started the whole litany of rapid fire was a simple comment made by Ingrid when she was seven years old: "Daddy, why don't you come to my dance recitals?"

I was eight. I should have warned her, but that never stopped Ingrid from speaking her mind, even at the young age of seven, when her heart lay there broken on the kitchen floor that day.

Something had broken in her.

Something had broken in me.

And somewhere in all of this, Mother had taken full responsibility.

After Ingrid and I were out of the house, we still called in and checked with Mother each day. I could always tell by the sound of her hello whether it had been a good day, a bad day, or a rough night the night before. They continued to throw dinner parties and act like puppets, but with Ingrid and me gone, that gave Father more opportunities to push Mother just a bit more.

I thought it was the call from the emergency room in Beverly Hills that snapped me. Mother had dropped red wine on the carpet in the living room at a dinner party one night.

Father lit into her.

Drove her to the emergency room, dropped her off, and left her to hobble inside with a broken nose and two black eyes, four busted ribs, and a fractured cheekbone.

That was when I came home, and Father left.

When we returned home the next day, I spoke to the Dean of Admissions at Brown, my professors, explained that my mother had taken a fall and she needed my care. That I'd return to the university in ten days.

Father returned home on day nine of Mother's recovery. When I left, Ingrid would come home to care for Mother. I didn't want Ingrid to see the shape Mother was in. It was my duty as the older sister to protect her from the really bad. When I had shown up at the hospital, Mother had looked awful and helpless. But that wasn't the worst of it. It was her spirit that had broken my heart.

It's a funny and peculiar thing—love. Love is the only thing that can fuck you up and tell you everything is completely normal. That it is the way things should be. That it could always be worse because when Father returned on day nine, Mother opened the door and allowed him back in while I stood and listened to him talk to her in the sunroom.

Her black eyes almost gone.

Her nose still red but bruised.

But her spirit, just as broken as the day he'd left her at the hospital.

Father cried.

Mother dried his tears.

Explained pieces of his childhood, something I'd never heard him talk about. How his father—my grandfather—

had left him on the side of the road in Florida on a family vacation. Made him walk to their next stop, which was seven miles, in the sweltering, balmy summer heat. How good Christmases were few and far between. Some years, Santa Claus had come, and many years, he hadn't. It wasn't because they didn't have the money; it was because Grandfather, Father explained, had felt it necessary to show them what it was like to go without. Food, depending on Grandfather's mood, could also be scarce.

Father cried again.

It explained why Father made sure we had all the best clothes, that Christmases were overboard, giving us both what we wanted and needed. Food was always plentiful.

I also understood Father was sick.

His explanation wasn't good enough. The way he treated Mother, there was no excuse for it. He knew it. I knew it. Ingrid knew it. And most importantly, Mother knew it.

But love, again, is the only thing that can fuck you up and feel completely normal.

And for Mother, this was the only love she knew.

A few things happened that day:

1. Ingrid didn't come home.

2. Father moved back.

3. Mother gave him another chance.

4. Father agreed to get help.

I understood. I loved Father with all my heart, and all I wanted was for him to be well. To get help, like he promised. I believe that most people have good intentions, that they don't set out to hurt people. Maybe some do. There's a big, fat line between wanting to do better and taking the steps to do better. It's called action. That willingness without action is fantasy after all.

I believe Father wanted to do better, but he never took the right steps to get there.

—Catherine

The morning sun pours in the tent, radiating the nylon, making my body come alive.

My ear is against his chest, and I panic, only at first.

What happened last night? I ask myself. *Nothing. Absolutely nothing.*

When I slept with two through nine, I'd never fallen asleep, so the guilt and shame of what I'd done did terrorize me in the morning. *This is new territory for me.*

I listen to Luke's heart.

Ba-bump.

Ba-bump.

Ba-bump.

Ba-bump.

Slow and steady, a restful heartbeat. Relaxed. I like the way it sounds. I like the feeling the rhythm, this muscle, gives.

Our hands still intertwined, I wonder if I will wake him if I move.

With only some padding from the sleeping bag between our bodies and the hard ground beneath us, my body rouses, pushing me to move.

Careful not to wake him, I move my hand from his. Even though I want to go back to the place of his heartbeat, I need to brush my teeth. When I get up, Luke rolls on his side, and

I quietly slip out of the tent, grab my overnight bag from the car, and walk to the bathroom.

I look down at my watch. It's still early, just past seven. There are two women in the shower, conversing through a wall of plastic that defines the shower wall.

As I put toothpaste on my brush, I listen.

"I heard that Louise isn't doing so well. That Paul called in hospice," Woman One says.

"Salt of the earth, that woman. Her husband, too," Woman Two says.

"When we get home, I'm going to cook them a meal. Take it over to Paul," says Woman One.

The showers run.

Woman Two breaks the silence. "Hey, what are we doing for the volunteer firefighters this year?"

"Haven't thought about it."

Again, silence.

I brush silently and wait for the small-town conversation to continue. I welcome it, pray for it.

One shower shuts off while the other one is just a few seconds behind.

Quickly, I brush my long, dark hair and throw a little mascara on. When I look at my reflection, I realize just how much I look like Mother.

When the curtain opens, I disappear out of the bathroom and go grab two coffees from the convenience store—also known as the office.

It's a new person working. Not Valerie. Oddly, I liked Valerie. Odd only because she's completely different from me—interesting, unique.

Now, the person working the front counter is completely opposite of Valerie.

"Gooooood morning." Temple, her name tag reads. "And how was your stay last night?" Her pep is too much for the morning. Like Temple escaped from summer camp that ingrained a good-morning routine. She rings up the coffees.

"Where's Valerie?" I ask.

I suppose there's a reason they have a night-shift person and a daytime person. Though I prefer Valerie.

"She's night shift. That will be one dollar and sixty-seven cents, please." Her perfect white smile lays plastically against her face.

But this is a genuine smile. I feel it because I know what genuine feels like. I pull two dollars from my wallet and hand it to her.

She hands me the change.

"Thanks," I say.

"Thank you for coming in!" Temple waves as I open the door and enter the Texas summer.

The tent has been taken down, and all that remains is Luke, sitting at the table. He smiles when he sees me, and I smile back as my cheeks turn warm.

"Black coffee," I say as I hand him his.

"Thank you." He takes the coffee and the first sip.

He didn't see us when we woke up, my head on his chest. My hand in his.

"We should get on the road," Luke says.

"Which direction are we headed today?" I ask as we both slip into the car, my clothes feeling like silk against the leather. It barely makes a sound.

"Abilene." Luke starts the car but not before giving me a longing look. Like I've somehow disrupted his life and he can't rectify what happened or when it happened, but something's shifted. His lips are the color of ripened strawberries.

You have been tasked to do a job, Catherine. Get it done. I set my coffee in the cupholder, look away, and put on my seat belt.

I still feel his eyes on me.

"Construction is what you said you did when you first got to LA. What's the most beautiful thing you've ever built with your hands?" I ask as he starts the car.

James Taylor comes over the radio again.

What I want to ask is if he feels like, somehow, we were supposed to meet. That, somehow, we were meant to cross each other's paths because in this moment right here, I feel with one hundred percent certainty that this is fate. It isn't the moment that gives me this feeling; it's the song.

"Fading Away."

My body breaks into chills.

The hum of the car as we leave.

The music.

Us.

"I wish I could have built a box around you, made of materials that could withstand heartbreak and memories and sadness. I wish I could have built you a box to climb into when the world got to be too much. I wish I could have built you a box that saved you from yourself."

"Fading Away" plays, and my heart is tender as I pick up pieces of my memories and push the tainted feelings away of the abuse.

I understand what Luke is saying.

My eyes begin to burn and fill with feeling, feelings I'd rather not feel.

Luke's face comes into my mind. The feeling of his heart against my ear. These are moments filled with hope and love and everything right.

I swallow the thump in my throat, and when I'm ready, when I know the tears won't fall, I say, "Me, too."

I focus on the broken white line that runs the course of the road in front of us. "Do you write your own songs?"

"Yeah."

"Can I hear one?"

"No."

"Why not?"

"Because I haven't sung in years."

"Why not?"

I notice Luke's hand tighten against the wheel as we get on the freeway.

He doesn't answer, and I don't ask again.

I decide I could never live in Texas as I stare out at the barren land. It's dry and hot, and the land looks needy, as if starved for attention or water or something. The land seems lonely, like it's endured its time and pain and all that's left is skin and bones.

"That's not the truth," he whispers, pensive.

"What?"

"That I haven't sung in years. Well, I guess that's part of it. I just haven't felt inspired, you know?"

"What does inspiration look like to you?" I ask, wondering if I've seen glimpses of inspiration, hoping I've somehow played a small part in the inspiration like he has for me. I can't help but feel like I'm a better person when I'm around him. This also makes me feel comfortably uncomfortable.

He smiles, and the half-smirk reaches across his face. He looks at me hard and long. "Like seeing multiple shades of one color, and every shade fits together perfectly, creating a picture in your mind of what life should really look like." He pauses. "Like a Sunday morning when love is made and there's not a single thing to do, except make more of it." Luke's eyes narrow on mine.

Chills ripple down my spine.

"When you finish a project and you know there's something special about it, real special, and you sit on it, knowing it was made by you, and all you want to do is keep it a secret." He looks back to the road. "Feels like fire in your veins. It's like … it's like falling in love. That's what inspiration on the best day looks like. To me."

His words soak into my skin, my mind, and I wonder how I ever lived a day without hearing Luke's voice. His thoughts. His hand around mine. Not in a sexual way, but in a basic-needs way. We've spent a few days in his car together, and it feels like I've known him my whole life.

You have one job, Cat. That's it. Get the job done.

But what if the job, the story, isn't in the mundane questions that I have? Maybe the story is in this trip. A story I am supposed to observe, supposed to feel, and supposed to tell but not in the interview/interviewee way.

What if, from now on, I live more on inspiration and less on what I'm told to do or get paid to do?

What if the story is us and our quest for life? I breathe in this thought, let it sink in.

"Have you made love on a Sunday with nothing else to do?" The words escape my mouth. I blush, wishing like hell I could pull them back into my mouth, eat them, swallow them, and never allow them to see the light of day again.

"Yes, but not with someone I was in love with."

Curiosity of what sex feels like with someone you're in love with unravels my mind.

I loved Michael.

I loved Peter.

But I didn't have a clear picture of what love looked like, growing up. Also, I suppose, some serve as starter loves. The relationships that teach us how to love maybe. I think they also teach us what we want and don't want. But in Mother's case, I believe she loved Father, was in love with him, even at his worst, and she kept going back because that is the sacrifice we pay for being in love.

"How about you?" Luke asks. "Have you made love on a Sunday with nothing else to do?"

The truth is, I don't know. I'm not sure which days of the week I had sex with men and paid no mind to it. But maybe that's the difference. If I had made love, I would have known what day of the week it was.

"I'm not sure."

Luke smiles. I feel his smile everywhere, and I don't like that I do. "You're not sure if it was Sunday or that you made love?"

"If it was Sunday," I simply say. "Because I don't think I've ever made love." I shake my head, wondering why the hell we are talking about this, and we've only known each other for a few days. I'm embarrassed that I started this whole thing with my mouth, my question. "I-I didn't mean to start all this."

"Don't apologize, Catherine." Luke's eyes are on the road, but I see his wheels turning with both good thoughts and bad thoughts. He bites his lip before he says, "Do you want to know what it's like to make love on a Sunday?" He drops his head in my direction.

Badly. "Yes." It isn't the act of sex I'm curious about, but I want to know what being in love feels like. "I want to know what it feels like to be in love and what sex feels like while in love. And not the kind of love I knew, growing up."

"What was that like?" Luke doesn't look away from me, still driving the car.

"Violence, manipulation, and chaos." I twist my fingers in my lap and then look back at Luke.

With a jerk of the wheel, Luke pulls off the road and turns off the car.

Without saying a word, he gently slips his hand around my neck and pulls my head to his chest, so I can hear the pounding of his heart. "This," he whispers. "This is what love feels like when someone you care about says something like that. It hurts them, too."

Tha-thump. Tha-thump. Tha-thump. Tha-thump. Tha-thump.

"For selfish reasons, Catherine, when I saw you, I wanted you on this trip with me. And not for reasons you might think," he says, but I barely hear him because I've closed my eyes, placed my hand on top of his, as if this somehow allows me to hear the beat of his heart more and better.

Tha-thump. Tha-thump. Tha-thump. Tha-thump. Tha-thump.

My heart doesn't need to try to sync with Luke's; it just does.

Before
Federal Correctional Institution, Dublin

Dear Journal,

Father went to his counseling sessions, his meetings, for the better half of a year, according to Mother.

"He's a different man," she said.

When Ingrid and I came home from college on holiday, Father seemed better, I suppose.

"Rome wasn't built in a day," Mother always said, her way of reminding us that everyone is a work in progress and we were no different.

I suppose, too, that the ground seemed lighter, or we felt lighter, and the eggshells that we walked on for years seemed few and far between.

I guess if Mother could forgive Father, then Ingrid and I should, too.

Father engaged more but with reservation.

He made more of an effort with us.

Purple flowers were never seen on the kitchen table again.

Father put down the newspaper when Ingrid and I walked in, though it seemed troubling for him. Us, too. We'd spent years experiencing Father one way that it felt like a stranger was asking us questions about school, about our studies, about life. At least, that was the way I felt. Ingrid, on the other hand, let Father know that it was awkward—said what we all felt—yet no one said anything about it, except Ingrid.

I was always proud of her for doing that.

I always envied that about my sister.

She didn't care about the repercussions. She didn't worry about keeping the peace or keeping everyone happy.

Ingrid was so mad one night, back when Father was sick in his disease, that she told Mother about the other woman she'd seen Father with.

"That's none of your business," Mother said.

Ingrid spoke up, as always, "Mother, you're not in the least bit worried that he's sleeping with another woman?"

"Ingrid Grace Clemens, hold your tongue." Mother was folding laundry. Looked up at us. Stopped. "I trust that your father will always make the right decisions for our family. Do you girls understand?"

We weren't girls anymore; we were women.

Ingrid rolled her eyes. "Mother, you're worth more than that two-bit whore I saw him with."

"Ingrid! That is enough. I will not tolerate your language or you disrespecting your father in that manner."

Ingrid went to speak again, but I touched her arm and shook my head. Both of us saw the look on Mother's face. She hadn't had any idea.

We both turned to leave, and Mother said, "One day, girls, there will be a point in your lives where you'll find that love always prevails. If it's the love you're meant to have, it always prevails. You might not understand my decision now, but you'll understand it later."

"Well, in your and Father's case, I hope it fails miserably," Ingrid said.

I thought Ingrid said that out of anger or more to protect Mother.

"Ingrid, let's go," I said.

We didn't have the internet back then or social media, and I'm glad we didn't. I don't know what Ingrid would have done, but I'm certain that it wouldn't have worked out in the other woman's favor—or our favor.

One thing about Ingrid is, she has many of Mother's attributes—she's flexible, a giver, empathetic, compassionate, loyal, and genuine—but one thing she got from Father was loyalty. Never, ever get on her bad side, and the only way anyone can do that is by stepping on the toes of her family.

One might think that Father wasn't loyal. But wasn't he? Whatever happened with the other woman, he still came home to his family every night. Whether a need was met with the other woman or a box checked, he still came home to Mother every night.

Even after Father did what he did, Ingrid still felt loyal to him, and so did I. But sometimes, late at night, deep down in my heart, I just knew things would end badly.

I've served nine years and eleven months of my thirteen years. My release date was coming.

I know what time we get up.

I know when dinnertime is.

I know what to expect each and every day—unless, of course, two women decide they need the top bunk and rip off each other's faces.

I'm terrified of being released.

I'm terrified of facing Mother.

I'm terrified of being in the house without Father.

And I can't tell Ingrid any of this.

—Catherine

I wake up to Luke coughing.

I sit up and look at him. "Are you all right?"

I open a water bottle and hand it to him. Begrudgingly, he takes it. Swallows a few gulps.

"Thank you," he says softly, handing the water back to me.

I put the lid on and set it back in the cupholder. "How long have I been sleeping?"

"Five hours."

"No, I haven't." I playfully slap his arm.

He holds out his watch. It's almost one.

"I've been sleeping for five hours."

Luke uses the back of his hand to wipe his mouth.

"I'm sorry." I shake my head. Sleeping on the job wasn't part of the deal.

"Why are you sorry?"

"I'm doing a story on you, Luke. Surely, I cannot tell a story with my eyes closed and while I'm snoring." I grab my notebook from my bag and a pencil, still groggy.

He laughs, and my heart begins to bounce around in my chest. "You do snore."

I whip my head back to him. "I do not!"

He laughs harder, and I fall for the crow's-feet that lead to his cheekbones. I try to control my heart, get it to slow down just so I can catch my breath, but I can't.

"Mouth open, head back. Here, I have a picture. Let me show you." He reaches for his phone.

My cheeks turn seven shades of red. I wince. "I don't need to see a picture."

"It's really cute," he says as he hands me his phone.

And there I am. Mouth open, leaned back. Eyes closed. "Did … did I really snore?"

"Yes."

Embarrassment doesn't cover it. Humiliating might. I hand his phone to him, and he pushes it back in his pocket.

"It was really cute, Catherine," he says.

"Trust me, every woman wants a man to call her cute." Sarcasm colors my tone.

"Look at me," Luke says in a commanding way.

I peel my eyes away from the window and look into his doe brown eyes. His long eyelashes. "Not every woman can pull that off and be completely sexy."

I try to laugh off the word *sexy* and the way it comes from his mouth, his lips. I try to push away the way he's starting to get under my skin, crawl into my heart.

"Sexy? With my mouth open and snoring—that's sexy to you? Do you also have some sort of weird fetish I need to know about?"

"See, wit, brains, snoring. All beautiful."

This time, I laugh, and he's watching me. Driving and watching me laugh.

"What?" I ask.

He shakes his head and puts his focus back on the road. "We'll be stopping in Abilene, which is about an hour from here."

"What's in Abilene?"

"Aunt Gene and Uncle Al."

"Who are they?"

"Probably the nicest folks you'll ever meet. My aunt Gene moved from Kentucky to Abilene when she was eighteen. Had seven children after she married Uncle Albert. Gives you a soda pop with a napkin. Uses mean Southern cuss words like *bless your heart* when she's real mad and *jackleg* if you're being a dumbass. She called Nathan and me jackleg quite often." The corners of Luke's mouth curve upward but fall short of a smile.

"Who's Nathan?"

"My cousin, her youngest. I'd go out for two weeks every summer, and Nathan would come home with me every summer."

I don't ask why we're paying Aunt Gene and Uncle Al a visit, and Luke doesn't offer up the information either, just like he didn't with Benny.

He said my heart could handle his story, but I'm starting to worry it can't.

We pull up to an old farmhouse somewhere in the middle of nowhere. Abilene is a city, but where we're at seems so different. Rolling hills and cows, horses, chickens, dogs, pigs, and a rooster named Marvin.

According to Luke, Marvin has outlived two cows and three dogs, and he's mean as hell.

Luke walks around the car, takes my hand and the lead, and looks back, stops, whispers, "Let's pretend, just while we're here, that you're my girlfriend."

My stomach twists and turns and drops. His touch, his voice, his eyes, his smile, the button-up shirt that he wears that shows a tuft of thin, dark hair, reaches into my body and warms my soul. I don't ask why because I don't really care.

I nod without a second thought.

We walk on the cobblestone path up to the old white farmhouse. A big oak tree sits in the front yard, off to the right, and a tire swing hangs from it, the rope reflecting time passed, age. With plush grass on either side of us, I begin to wonder how the grass is so green in September.

There are seven steps up to the front door. There's a roomy front porch with a porch swing, a chair, and two end tables, which look well used, broken in.

It's warm in September, but not scorching hot, mid-eighties, which is where our weather sits all year in Southern California.

Luke knocks.

His hand in mine, I stand behind him, close to his shoulder.

He gently squeezes my hand.

Luke knocks again.

The door opens, and the woman behind the screen door with an apron on, streaks of gray hair pulled back in a bun, puts her hands to her mouth.

"Luke!" Hurriedly, she pushes open the screen door and calls, "Al, it's Luke! Get in here!"

She pulls Luke in for a hug. Tears brim at her eyes, and I feel embarrassed about staring, but I can't seem to look away.

"Aunt Gene, it's good to see you," Luke says.

Al comes down the hallway, walking as fast as he can with a limp.

"Well, ain't this sweeter than stolen honey?" Al says as Gene releases Luke, and he pulls him in for a bear hug. "Missed you, boy. It's been a long time comin'."

Al and Gene look to me.

"Oh, my! Well, aren't you as cute as a speckled pup under a red wagon?" Gene pulls me in for a hug against her breasts. A good hug. Not a California skin-and-bone tap, but a real tight hug, and it's warm and soft.

"Aunt Gene, Uncle Al, this is my girlfriend, Catherine."

"Catherine, it's so nice to meet you." Uncle Al pulls me in for a hug, too.

"Please, please, come in." Aunt Gene hurries us in.

"Turner just installed an air-conditioning unit a few weeks ago 'cause the last one broke in June. It was hotter than a two-dollar pistol." Gene shakes her head. "Please, sit. Y'all want any sweet tea?"

"Please, Aunt Gene," Luke says.

I don't know what sweet tea tastes like, but I agree. "That would be wonderful, Gene. Thank you," I say.

Al takes his chair, and you can tell it's his chair because it's in direct line with the tube television. It's big, it's brown, and it holds all six feet of him. Uncle Al wears old Wranglers and a red-plaid button-down shirt. His hair is thin on top and thicker at the bottom. Clean-shaven, working man hands. His smile is just as bright as his eyes. It's as if he'd never met a stranger.

Gene returns with glasses of sweet tea, napkins, and a pitcher, all on a wooden tray. Sets it out on the coffee table in front of us. Gives us all napkins with our glasses of tea.

"I see that Marvin is still alive. How is that even possible?"

Al shakes his head and uses his pocketknife to clean his nails. "Tell you what. He's a real son of a bitch. Like a sheep-killin' dog, that asshole. Tried to shoot him once. Came back, and the asshole was on my chest, peckin' on my face."

We all laugh.

"Rough as a cob." Al shakes his head again, smiles. "But he takes care of the hens."

I look above the fireplace, to the right and to the left. On the walls hang pictures of children, ranging from ages six to the mid-thirties, early forties. I see a picture of Luke—longer hair, stonewashed jeans, a black sweatshirt—with a boy who looks similar in age, blond hair. That must be Nathan.

"Now, Catherine, where are you from, honey?"

"Los Angeles." I take a sip of sweet tea. Because Beverly Hills makes me sound like a complete asshole. "Born and raised." I try to switch topics. "I love your home, Gene." The pink-flower wallpaper still sits pristine against the walls.

"Well, you can't be no city girl if Luke's takin' a likin' to you," Al says.

I laugh and touch his arm as if we'd established time together. "I can wear heels when I need to and skin a skunk if I have to," comes out of my mouth, and Luke is just as surprised as I am.

"Luke was always a sucker for the nice girls. But you're the second one he's ever brought to meet us, Mr. Hollywood." Gene laughs and touches her nephew's knee. "But it sure has been a while—I'd say, fifteen years?"

Luke takes a sip of his tea.

I've decided I really like sweet tea.

Gene reaches for my glass and fills it. When God invented Aunt Gene, he made her a saint, I'm convinced.

"Thank you, Gene."

"What do you do for a livin', Catherine?" Al asks, still cleaning his thumbnail.

What I've been doing for the last year. I've been a freelance writer, but before that, I was in prison. "I'm a writer," I say, trying to keep it vague.

Luke and I didn't talk about this, and it teeters somewhere in the truth. Does he want Al and Gene to know I'm doing a story on him? Ego isn't something Luke gives off, so I'm assuming he doesn't want them to know.

"What type of writer?" Gene asks.

Thank goodness, the phone rings.

Gene stands, "Excuse me," and makes her way to the kitchen as Al asks Luke if he's still playing the guitar.

On the mantel, an urn sits, a big silver urn with grooves at the top, some sort of decorative measure. It is simple though, quiet, doesn't grab attention, and that's probably why I didn't recognize it when I looked up at the mantel before.

Gene comes back into the living room. "August is on her way. Didn't tell her Luke and Catherine were here. She'll be just tickled." Gene sits down. "Said she called the cell phone." Gene pulls out a flip phone from somewhere in her dress underneath her apron as I take another sip of tea. She opens the phone.

"Good tea?" Luke looks at me, his lips too close to mine.

I swallow the tea and swallow the nerves he gives me.

I nod, using the napkin Gene gave me to wipe my mouth and maybe create space with Luke. His breath smells like mint.

"I'm really not sure how to work this thing. August got it for us. Told her a phone wasn't necessary when we have the house phone. But"—she rolls her eyes—"August wanted Dad to have it in case he's in the pasture and something happens." She looks at Al, who's finishing up his nails, rocking in his recliner. "Al won't use it."

"If I become buzzard bait, ain't nothing gonna stop the good Lord from bringin' me home, Gene. Told August that, too. Still bought the damn thing."

"Your uncle"—she looks at Luke—"so stubborn. Anyway, talked to your mama yesterday, said you were comin'. Hoped you'd stop by, but we didn't think you'd be here so soon."

The screen door hits the doorframe, and a Southern drawl follows. "Y'all in the livin' room?" The woman's voice is soft.

Her blonde hair trails behind her. She looks just like Nathan, I notice. I assume she's August.

"Well, I'll be damned, Luke McCay. Look what the cat dragged in." August smiles.

Luke stands, and August pulls her cousin in for a hug.

"Feels real good to hug your neck, Chicken Legs. It's been a minute."

Al chuckles. "Chicken Legs. Remember that." Now, he's whittling a small piece of wood.

Luke puts his hand at the small of my back. "August, I'd like you to meet my girlfriend, Catherine. Catherine, this is my cousin August."

I extend a hand.

August slides her tongue over her teeth. Looks down at my hand and back to my face. "Nah, we don't shake hands here. This isn't a business deal. You're family. We hug." And August reaches in and gives me a hug just like her mother, Gene, did.

I try not to melt into it, but it feels really good.

"Y'all goin' to stay for supper, right?" Gene stands, brushes her hands on her apron. Looks between Luke, me, and August.

Gene looks right at Luke. "I believe fried chicken was your favorite. Don't know if that's changed since you've become the hotshot TV star." She winks. "But I tell you what. The Gatenburgs, the Austins, and us all gathered over the television at the lodge on the last episode of *LA Hills*. Girls were falling all over you here." She looks at August.

August rolls her eyes. "It was disgusting."

Luke throws his head back and laughs. Puts his hand on his cousin's shoulder. "I think that reaction right there was worth every minute of doing that show."

"Miss Libby down the road talked about you like you were a piece of meat. Made me as sick as a dog passing peach pits."

And this makes me laugh out loud.

The family stares as I try to apologize through my laughter.

Then, they start to laugh, and I can't stop giggling.

"Come along, Catherine. I think you're gonna fit into this family real well."

I nod, stand, and follow August and Gene into the kitchen. I look back at Luke. He gives me the *you okay* eyebrow raise.

Never better, I want to say.

I don't feel the eggshells in this family. I don't feel the fear of the unknown. I don't feel uncomfortable or fake or anything I'm not supposed to be.

We gather around the dinner table. Al leads the prayer. Blesses the food.

Luke takes a few bites. Stops. Puts his fork down. "Can we talk about Nathan?"

Luke looks between Al and Gene and August, and their eyes dart across the table, anywhere but at Luke.

Luke says, "I need to say a few things."

The room is still, so silent. Even the horseflies who managed a way in settle on the light that hangs over the rectangular dining room table, covered by a tablecloth with red checkers. Not the vinyl ones you find for cheaper, the ones that are easy to clean.

The room grows heavy with lack of words, and I peek over at Luke, who's staring down at his chicken, trying to find the right words.

I reach my hand underneath the table and take his because whatever he's got to say, he needs some help.

Luke doesn't look over at me; he doesn't need to. Instead, he squeezes my hand. Opens his mouth to speak but stops. Leans forward and takes out an envelope from his back pocket. Slides it over to Al, across the red-checkered tablecloth.

"What's this about?" Al curiously eyes the envelope but leaves it untouched. Then, he stares at his nephew.

Al is giving Luke a look that speaks compassion, empathy, and sadness. A shared love.

"Please, Chicken Legs, you don't need to be doin' this. Because whatever is in that envelope won't bring our Nathan back," August says in a brave voice, one that hides her heart.

I know what that feels like.

Luke looks at August. "It won't. No, but it will help with the fence and the car and the barn that needs to be fixed."

Al lets air escape from his mouth and leans back. Taps his fingers on the tablecloth.

Gene rubs her thumb with her finger, afraid to look up.

"I hope y'all plan to stay for a few days," Gene says through her watery eyes because, now, she's looking right through her nephew.

"All we want is just some time with you, son," Al says.

Luke squeezes my hand. "Yeah, I'd like that. If it's okay with Catherine." Luke looks over at me.

"As long as Gene and August teach me how to make this sweet tea and fried chicken, I'll stay for as long as you'll have us." I try to relieve some heaviness.

They laugh among the heaviness that sits in the room like a layer of smoke in a 1990s dance joint.

"You," Al says quietly, "are the only thing we got left that reminds us of Nathan. We will keep y'all for as long as y'all will stay."

This should give Luke relief, right?

It should show on his face, but it doesn't. There's no relief and no smile, only remnants of fortitude.

I'm reminded of the beauty in the process of life. Why? I don't know. I'm reminded of my sentencing to thirteen years in prison. I'm reminded of what it felt like when the honesty of what I'd done breathed life back into me. I didn't harbor secrets, and I was free. I'd paid for what I'd done, but I was free of all the secrets that kept me from the truth.

And for whatever reason, I see this trip, this travel we're doing, as Luke's reckoning of truth.

CHAPTER 17

It's late into the evening, about nine o'clock or so.

The white envelope still sits on the dining room table.

Nobody has touched it since dinner.

The front door is open, and there's a slight warm breeze that kicks up every few minutes and blows through the tiny notches in the screen.

We're in the living room, the night settling into our bones.

Gene is knitting an afghan for the Pauls, who just had a baby. They live up the road about two miles, is my understanding. Al is reading the paper, and August says it's time for her to go.

"You can sleep here, Aug," Gene says, setting down her yarn, her needle.

"Nah, Mama. I got stuff to do in the mornin'," August says as she stands.

I stand as well, and we embrace.

"You stay put for as long as Luke will let you, you hear me?" August whispers.

I nod, unsure of what to say.

Luke and August hug.

"Chicken Legs, I'll see you tomorrow."

August kisses Gene and Al and leaves out the front door.

"I have your old bedroom set up, Luke and Catherine."

Your bedroom.

Our bedroom.

One bed.

Gene thinks we're dating, that this is normal to sleep in the same bed. One couple. Sheets, a blanket. Soft pajamas.

"Left towels out in the bathroom, too, in case y'all wanna shower or anything. Come on, I'll show y'all."

Al looks up from his newspaper. In some ways, he reminds me of Father. Not in his looks or his demeanor or the way Al actually expresses emotion because that was not Father, but in the way he reads the newspaper, the look on his face as he reads, I suppose.

"Night, y'all," Al says, looking up through the top of his glasses at us.

"See you in the morning," Luke says as he reaches back for my hand.

Knots twist and turn in my belly as I put my hand in his, remembering that we're supposed to be a couple and this is supposed to be normal. And that I'm supposed to feel butterflies and knots and nerves and warmth.

We walk to the end of the hallway, and Luke opens the door to a dimly lit room. Our bags are already in here, probably something Luke did when he and Al went outside to look at the fence that needs mending.

Luke drops my hand when we walk through the door. Runs his hand through his hair, exposing his lower abdominal area.

Look away, Cat.

"I realize that this is probably awkward for you, Catherine. And I'm really sorry I asked you to do this. I didn't think about sleeping arrangements."

"Why?"

"I don't know what I was thinking. I mean, I do. It's just that Al and Gene are real private people, and to have a beautiful woman who's doing a story on me in their house … I don't know. I just didn't want them to treat you any different than you deserve. I wanted them to see you for who you are, not what you do. And I wanted you to see Al and Gene for who they are." Luke sits down on the rose-colored bedspread.

"Not why did you ask me. Why are you sorry?"

Luke smirks. "I'm not sure this is real comfortable for you. Wouldn't you agree?"

I sit down next to Luke, cross my legs, look up at the tiled ceiling. "In my life, I've done my share of things I'm not proud of, Luke. This isn't one of them." I pause and look down at my shoes and then to Luke. "But I do have one question for you."

His lips are dangerously close to mine.

"I could have been anything. Why your girlfriend?"

"I wanted to see what it felt like," he whispers to me.

My heart begins to pound. My stomach swirls. My head feels heavy and fuzzy, and I think I need some space to breathe. "And?" I will the question back into my mouth, down my throat, and away from making another awful debut.

He smiles.

And my heart wants to see more of this.

Luke thinks. "Like listening to Led Zeppelin's live guitar solo in 'Stairway to Heaven.' You feel it. You feel the words, every single one of them. You take in each note, each rift. And somehow, you come out of it more infatuated than you were before."

I need to wash him from my skin. Wash his words away. Wash the remnants of his scent, his touch. "I need to take a shower," I say as I stare back.

Luke nods.

I stand, walk to the bathroom, lock the door, and turn the water on hot.

I undress, laying my clothes on the sink.

I climb in and cleanse Luke from me.

The hot water hits my back, and I feel it in my chest.

Wash him away, Cat. Wash him away, my head says.

But my heart is asking for just another moment with him.

I've never felt anything like this. Not with Michael, not with Peter, and definitely not the nine men I was with before. But my body aches to be touched. It's been a long time since I experienced a man's touch.

I stretch my arms out and place my hands on the shower wall in front of me, allowing the hot water to run down the length of my body.

I envision Luke unlocking the door, undressing in front of the shower door, and I can make out pieces of his body, like a mosaic. I imagine him sliding open the shower door, not saying a word, and pulling my naked body to his, where I feel every inch of him, every broken piece of him, every piece well fought for, every piece put back together, built with steadiness that holds water to fire and oil to water.

It's the coughing I hear through the walls that brings me out of where I went with Luke in my head.

Is that Luke coughing?

I stand up straight and hold my ear against the fabricated shower wall.

It's Luke.

Quickly, I wash my body and my hair and turn off the water and listen quietly for more coughing. The water is only the residual leftovers that drip from my hair, from the showerhead. I grab my towel and dry off, only to realize I left my clothes and hairbrush in the bedroom we share.

Shit. Shit. Shit.

With the towel wrapped around me tightly, I quietly open the bathroom door and tiptoe to our room. I take a deep breath and step inside, shutting the door behind me.

Luke is lying on the bed, his guitar in hand when we make eye contact.

"Are you all right?" I ask, awkwardly standing in my towel. "I heard you coughing."

But he doesn't say a word. He just stares back at me. His eyes rake my body.

I stare back and allow the towel to fall only a little, exposing part of my breast.

The ache between my legs grows, and I try my best not to show this. Try not to let my eyes give off what he's doing to me, so I try to break this up by bending and grabbing my clothes from my bag, though my mind is not focused on what I'm doing.

What are you getting from your bag, Cat?

What do I look like through his eyes right now?

Brush.

Panties.

Pajamas.

"Catherine?" he says hoarsely.

"Yeah?" I say, pushing my unbrushed hair behind my ears. I stand, clothes and brush in hand, and look at him.

His eyes, his look, tell me there's more to this moment than something just physical.

Luke sets his guitar to the side, stands, walks to me. "You can change in here. I'll go."

And when he turns to go, I grab his arm and tell him it's okay, that he doesn't need to go. That I'm sure he's seen a woman's body before.

"Yeah, but not yours. I need to go, Catherine."

I've never had to convince a man to stay. I've never had to beg for anything in my life. But right now, my need for his hands on my body is outweighing any logic that tries to grab hold of my good, rational thought.

"Please, stay. It's fine." Irrational.

Luke, with a storm raging in his eyes, drops his head and then looks back up at me. Cautiously, he takes a corner of the towel and pulls it back, exposing my breast, and then the other as the towel falls to the floor.

Again, his eyes rake over my body while I see his thoughts spin uncontrollably.

Confusion.

Attraction.

Need.

He takes a big breath in as I secretly beg him to touch me with his hands.

"If I touch you, Catherine, I won't be able to stop myself," he whispers against my neck.

I know this because I feel the same way. Clarity comes, though slowly, and I realize I'm standing naked in front of a man who somehow has fallen into my heart.

Clarity. I step back and grab my panties from the stack of clothes in my hand. "Hold these, please." I hand him my clothes and slide my panties on.

I grab my pajama top and slide it over my head as I feel Luke's breath against my chest.

I do the same with my pajama bottoms, and when I go to grab for the brush, he says, "I'll do it."

Awkwardly, I nod and walk to the bed. I sit down, folding my left leg into itself.

Luke sits behind me and starts at the ends.

This tells me he's brushed a woman's hair before.

"Do you do this often?"

"I want to tell you about Nathan," Luke says.

"I'm listening."

Luke brushes. "We were best friends. We did everything together. So much so that when we were sixteen, we had Bud, the town drunk, buy us a twelve pack of beer."

He brushes. "After one, I'd had my share. Didn't like the taste. But with Nathan, something happened with him. It did something for him—not to him, but for him. It was as if he walked taller, talked larger, louder, and the beer turned a shy, well-cared for boy into a nightmare."

Luke stops brushing, and we listen to the silence between us.

"It wasn't that night. It was the days, weeks, months, and years that followed. Somehow, alcohol owned him."

Luke gently pulls at the ends of my hair. "When I came back the following summer, Nathan was gone. Gene and Al had thrown him out. And not by choice. Said he started stealing from them—money, Aunt Gene's jewelry that had been in the family for ages."

He starts to brush again, this time starting higher, but I turn and stop him. Hold my hands over his.

"I asked where he'd been seen last, and with a few hints from the family, sightings, and other friends in the community, I went to him. Found him in a bad part of town. An old, abandoned house. He'd gone from bad to worse. A needle hung from his arm when I opened the last door of the last room of that place. We were seventeen. He should have been thinking about the next home football game where he played as the quarterback—but that seems so long ago. He should have been thinking about his next deer hunt or fishing trip. But instead, he was thinking about where he'd get his next high or where to put the needle."

"You know you aren't responsible for what he did, right, Luke?"

"Yeah, I know. But I was the one who left him there in that house with the needle in his arm. Never told a soul what I'd found. Figured it was better that way for everyone. That's the guilt I harbor. If I'd just gone back in and carried his ass out of there, if I'd just said one thing, that might have made a difference."

I don't ask how he died even though I want to.

"At seventeen he went from being a college-bound star quarterback with full-ride offers from Texas A&M, The University of Alabama, and University of Notre Dame to losing it all within a year."

"Some people don't want to be found, Luke."

"I agree that's true, but I also think if Nathan had had a single moment of clarity—knowing that he'd lose his family, that his addiction would take his life, leaving his parents and brothers and sisters heartbroken—he wouldn't have taken the first drink."

"I didn't know Nathan, but if he was anything like you, you're right."

I reach over and turn off the bedside light. "Luke, lie next to me."

In the darkness of the bedroom, I hear him stand, setting the brush on the nightstand, and slide off his jeans, his T-shirt. He crawls in bed next to me, and we listen to each other breathe in the warm night air.

Two people.

Two paths.

Meant to meet.

Meant to survive.

The morning light pours in through the curtains.

I turn in bed to face Luke and realize I'm alone, and the idea of me being alone, for the first time ever, doesn't sit well with me. I sit up, pulling the covers up to my breasts. This is both uncomfortable and electrifying at the same time. I've never relied on anyone to take me places emotionally, and I've never had to. And maybe that's the thing about love. You don't get to pick when love comes along; it just does, whether you're prepared for it or not. You don't get a choice when your heart falls for the right person.

Fear starts to fester in my belly as my thoughts start to spin.

What if he leaves?

What if I lose him?

What if it doesn't work?

What if he's got this annoying habit that I can't stand?

What I have this annoying habit he can't stand?

I begin to bite my thumbnail and search the well-kept room with my eyes.

But what if it does work?

When I throw back the covers, I notice a note on the nightstand:

Went to build fence with Uncle Al.
See you soon.
Love,
Luke

I smile inwardly at his chicken scratch. It makes me think about how his autograph might look on a headshot of his. It makes me wonder how many women—and men for that matter—have a picture of Luke hanging in their bedroom. I wonder how many women fantasize about him. I suppose I've always treated Luke like a human because he is one. I've never looked at him like many people do. Maybe that's what he appreciates.

I get dressed. Take my toothbrush to the bathroom and brush. Throw a little mascara on, some lip gloss, brush my hair, and I remember Luke's strokes. They were soft, almost tender, like he was treading lightly.

I remember the story about Nathan and how heartbreaking that must have been for Al and Gene to watch their son fall from grace.

Do we all have freedom of choice?

But what if the choice no longer becomes a choice? When you have a need, a necessity, a desire so deep for that feel-good moment, that's when the choice no longer becomes a choice.

This makes me think about Father.

He made choices every day. Big choices. Huge choices. What film rights to buy. What directors to hire. Who to have over for dinner. Who to loan money to. Whether to engage with his children, Ingrid and me. Whether to browbeat his wife on a nightly basis. Whether or not to put his hands on her in the end, to hurt her so badly that she had to go to the hospital on multiple occasions.

But in the end, I'm almost certain, it was no longer a choice for Father. It became a sick need. A feeling of inferiority from his childhood. A feeling of control. A feeling of reaching a high and then coming down after the deed was done. And then the guilt in the hours that passed. I think, secretly, Mother, Ingrid, and I, knew there was no cure for Father. It was the last time he sent Mother to the hospital. We never talked about it, the three of us. Never discussed it. I think, maybe, if we did, the truth we all felt deep down, would become our reality.

One night in January, it did.

His rage turned blinding.

Something flipped inside him.

I saw it, and I also saw the fear in Mother's eyes when she pulled the trigger.

It's astounding, what a mind will do to protect itself. What mothers do to protect their children. What children do to protect their parents.

Someone knocks softly on the bathroom door, making me jump out of my own skin.

I pull it open, and it's Gene.

"Good morning, sugar." Her head falls to the right, and she pauses. "Are you all right? Why are you crying?"

Crying?

I look in the mirror and face the same person I've been facing my entire life. The one with the survivor's guilt, who I've wrestled with for years. Battled with over what is right and what is necessary.

Tears stream down my face, and I'm completely caught off guard.

I could lie, tell Gene it's eye drops.

But I could also tell her the truth.

When Gene touches my shoulder and urges me to her arms, I fold into her as if she were my own mother, just wanting to take away our own unique tragedies, just for a moment.

I bury my head into her shoulder. All the shame, the guilt, the anger toward Father rests on her shoulder. In a sense, I know what she and Al experienced. I know what loss of life feels like. One day, the person you love is there, and then they're not. And it feels so empty, so lonely, as if no one understands. How can you lose someone you began to hate and feel so sad at the same time?

"I'm so sorry about Nathan," I say to Gene.

"Oh, sugar." Gene's embrace grows tighter.

I melt into it.

I've had to hold up this facade for so long. I feel as though the walls are caving in, and there's nowhere left to turn.

"Come now. Let's have some breakfast and sweet tea, and we can talk, okay?" Gene pulls back, placing both hands on my cheeks.

I look into her deep blue eyes that remind me of the shade of blue that only comes with warm weather and white sands. They're a shade of blue that tells me kindness gets me far, and only love will get me through this.

For so many years, Mother tried to soften the blow. Tried to tell us that it wasn't that bad, and the sad part is we believed it. I knew in my heart that it didn't feel right, what Father had done to Mother, but it came acceptable because it was the only thing we knew.

Gene takes my hand and leads me to the kitchen.

I feel like I'm beginning to unravel. My undoing.

"When I was worried about Nathan, when he was alive, I'd busy myself with chores." Gene laughs quietly as she makes a plate of food.

I lean against the counter, unsure of where to stand, where to put my hands. Unsure of everything.

"I don't think this house has ever been as clean or as organized than it was the last year of Nathan's life." Her voice quiets. "I also know that people process life, grief, things a bit differently." She hands me a plate. "Go sit down in the dining room, and I'll get you some coffee, sugar."

I take Gene's direction.

She joins me and sits across the table from me.

"Thank you, Gene."

She nods and curiously eyes me. "You don't strike me as the type to cry too often."

I take a bite of bacon. Maple and salt ignite my taste buds.

"You strike me as the type who shows a brave face. And for you to be at this point, something is awfully wrong or awfully right." Gene puts her chin in her hand, taps her fingers on the red-checkered tablecloth.

The white envelope that Luke set down last night still sits, waiting to be opened.

I want to answer her. I want to talk about it. But I'm terrified if I open my mouth, years of fear, years of sadness, years of chaos will pour from my mouth.

So, instead, I take another small bite of bacon.

"Does Luke know what's on your heart, baby?"

I shake my head. Gene thinks we're dating because of the lie we told. This isn't something you tell a beautiful man you're supposed to be doing a story on. This isn't something you tell a man who you've somehow come to really enjoy being around. This isn't something you tell a man you just met. But I can't tell Gene this because we've already told her a lie.

I set down the bacon. Take a sip of coffee. Quietly cough into my hand, not because I have to, but because I need to clear the emotion from my tone. I look into the living room and see the same pictures from last night, except I notice Nathan's football pictures this time, something I didn't see last night.

"I hear Nathan was a hell of a football player."

Gene smiles as the memory touches her heart. "He was. But what's more is, he had a heart just like Luke's. Those two could have been brothers—hell, twins; they were so much alike."

"How so?"

"Since the moment those two were born, Luke and Nathan have always been givers. Nathan would give his sisters whatever they wanted, and all they had to do was start the lip quiver. Luke and his sister, well—"

"What?"

Gene stops. "Luke's sister, Ella."

I don't explain to Gene that Luke told me he was an only child or that, right now, I'm confused.

"Right," is all I say.

"Ella had Luke wrapped around her finger. He would have given her the world. Then, one summer, she just stopped comin' to our place. But I'm sure you know the story." She pauses. "Honey, whatever's causing the sadness, it's better to talk about it than to hold it all in."

I guess my problem is, I've never felt it until now. Until Luke told me the story of Nathan. "I see how happy and kind you and Al are, so open, maybe I want to get there, too."

Gene looks at me, draws her eyebrow up, reaches for my hand. "Because we love, we grieve. Whether it was a good relationship, a complicated one, or just plain ugly. It's still *the end.* And we've got to do something about all those feelings."

I laugh at my self-centeredness. "You've lost your son, and here I am, talking about me."

"I'm almost certain I brought it up, sugar. Besides, sometimes, it's easier that way—less tender, I suppose, to talk about someone else's sadness than your own, eh?"

Squeezing Gene's soft hands, I nod. "Yeah."

Gene gives my hand one last pat and gets up from the table. "Okay, you finish eatin' while I figure out what the hell we're having for lunch."

As I watch her walk back into the kitchen, I wonder why Gene was put in my path. I bet Nathan misses her. I hope her kids know what they have with Gene.

"More coffee?" She looks at me.

"No, thank you, Gene."

She nods and proceeds to clean the coffeepot.

What if God puts people in our lives to demonstrate goodness? To witness it. Feel it. What if God is disguised as Gene? What if he's not disguised as Gene, but maybe there are messages I'm supposed to listen to? What if these messages were only supposed to come from Gene?

What if I was supposed to hear the story about Nathan, so I could make the connection with Father?

I take a big gulp of black coffee, finish my bacon and eggs, and contemplate if I'll ever be able to live with a conscience as clear as Gene's and maybe be the Gene to someone in my life.

I see Luke from the field that butts up to the house. I'm shucking corn on the porch with Gene and August.

His shirt is off, and everything inside me screams. His skin is golden and covered in sweat. I try to imagine this is normal and completely fine—with Luke and his body. That the ripples from his stomach, defined, aren't making my heart beat a million times a minute. I try to collect my thoughts, and the lie we told Al, Gene, and August—that we're a couple—sits uneasy with me.

He comes closer. His shirt over his shoulder, he walks toward us.

Breathe, Catherine, just breathe. Shuck corn. Try to act casual.

"Fix the fence?" August asks, wiping her brow with the back of her hand.

The porch fan blows air, though it's warm. It creates a facade that makes our sticky bodies believe that the temperature is acceptable. That Texas in September is comfortable. It is not.

"Yeah, Al's coming up with the tractor."

Luke reaches the fence, and when he hops it, I see the muscles in his shoulders contract.

Shuck corn, Catherine.

Luke walks up the steps of the porch, waits for me to look, and when he does and he reaches me, he leans down and kisses me on the mouth.

There are times in my life when I've felt stunned, speechless, and utterly helpless, but they've never happened all at the same time.

So, when his lips touch mine, they're soft and wet, and it's nothing like I've felt before, so much so that I don't want him to pull away and I want to feel this feeling of his lips on mine for the rest of my life.

My eyes fall shut, and he pulls away.

"How's the corn coming along?" Luke asks.

I open my eyes, stare into his, the brown irises with bursts of green, and he's so close to me that I want to reach out and touch his face just to make sure this is all real. His breath is minty, and he smells like sunshine and sweat and woods. I want to wrap myself up in him.

You're dating, remember, Cat? Remember? He can kiss you.

We've never kissed before, and I can tell you, it's the best first kiss of all the last kisses I've ever had, and he's ended it for me. Ruined it. I don't think I can ever kiss another man and not think about this first kiss with Luke.

"Corn is good," I say breathlessly. I stare from his lips to his eyes and back again.

I see the conflict in his eyes now. *Has it always been there? Or did it just appear?*

My face grows warm. *Did I do something wrong?*

Luke leans in and very delicately whispers, "I want to do that again, kiss your lips, but I'm too afraid I won't be able to stop, and things here might get awkward."

The corners of my mouth turn up as my face and body ignite. Somehow, it's hard to breathe and better to breathe, all at the same time.

"Boy, Chicken Legs, you sure know how to make the ladies weak." August shakes her head, pulling at another corn husk.

Luke stands up, puts his hand on the back of my chair, and leans against it with his hip. His shirtless body is closer to me now. "How so?"

Shuck corn.

"Was down at Don's today, gettin' gas, waiting in line to pay—because you know, Rosie's don't take anything but cash. Don's too cheap to pay for a debit card machine, and I told him it'd be easier on him, cheaper in the long run because he wouldn't have to hire help. But anyway, Estelle and Carol Ann were in front of me. They didn't see me, but boy, they were rattlin' on about you bein' back in town." August laughs, looks at me, smiles. "I said, 'Y'all, he's taken now. Got him a real good girlfriend, and in fact, I think they're gettin' married. So, y'all can shut ya mouths.' Never liked Carol Ann anyway. She's got more faces than a seven-headed dragon."

Gene looks at her daughter, raises her eyebrows, continues to shuck the corn. "August, I raised you better."

"Mama, I didn't say anything but the truth."

"You said they were gettin' hitched, Aug." Gene stops.

August smiles. "I said, 'I think.' "

Gene rolls her eyes. "Well, don't hang your wash on someone else's line, is all."

I look up at Luke, and he looks down at me. The genuine smile I saw in the car earlier is back, and he wears it so beautifully, as if this is where he should be. Like Los Angeles and Hollywood and cameras and paparazzi only steal from his soul.

"I'm going to go take a shower," he says to me as if it's a secret for only me to hear. A private joke. The inside scoop.

"Okay." I smile back, and his fingers graze my shoulder as he turns to go, just as Al starts to roll up on the tractor.

He turns it off. "Where'd Chicken Legs go?"

"Shower," August says.

Al rests his forearms on the wheel. "Man, I forget that kid is a hell of a worker. He can work four grown boys under the table like nothin'."

August looks at her dad. "Get the fence fixed?"

"Shoot." Al shakes his head. "We got the fence fixed, the barn fixed, and moved some cattle to the lower pasture." He reaches up and wipes the sweat from his brow.

"Come on in and get cleaned up. Supper's almost ready," Gene says.

After dinner, when the sun begins to set and the dishes are done and the kitchen is cleaned, Luke asks for a few minutes of my time. It's a quarter past seven. It's still warm but a more comfortable warm.

"Aunt Gene, Uncle Al, I'm going to take Catherine and show her some of the property, if that's all right?"

Al has settled in his chair with the nightly newspaper, and Gene sits and grabs her knitting.

August left minutes earlier.

"Enjoy, you two," Gene says.

Luke opens the screen door for me and follows me out. I feel his presence behind me like a long-awaited day.

Luke's white button-up shirt makes his skin appear browner, his arms more defined. He smells fresh and clean, and I want to know what his skin feels like when it's wet. I want to know what he eats for lunch and what he considers to be the most pivotal point in history. Who his favorite president is. Where he stands politically—not that it matters, but his opinion is important to me. I wonder if he wears sunscreen and if he treats his mother the same way he treats his aunt. I wonder if he likes rainy days and books and movies that make you cry. And which season of the year is his favorite.

I spent many years unable to remember what the rain felt like on my face or how a hot shower felt against my body. Good books and bad books. What each season looked like to the naked eye. And yet, still, I knew what to expect every single day from prison, and I took comfort in that.

Luke walks next to me, our shoulders intermittently bumping softly as he leads me around the house to the back side of the property. He doesn't touch me. His hand doesn't slide into mine. His lips don't come near me, and I assume this is because, out here, he's not my boyfriend, and I'm not his girlfriend. We're just Luke and Catherine. He's an actor. I'm a writer. And we're working together.

I try to forget about him seeing my body last night. My face rushes with warmth. Forget about the times we've held hands because maybe this time, it is the only time it matters.

I feel this aching in my heart for Luke. A longing.

"We're going to go to the end of this knoll over here." Luke points in front of us.

After Luke showered, I did, too. A T-shirt was all I had left before I did some laundry.

"Thank you for washing clothes," he says.

"No problem."

We walk.

"I'll tell Uncle Al and Aunt Gene the truth. About us," he says.

"Why?" comes out of my mouth abruptly, selfishly.

I like to feel his lips against mine, his body close to me, to pretend I belong to a man who's genuine to his core, who looks out for others, who stands in his own truth, fesses up to things he hasn't done right. I like to be in bed next to him. I like our game of make-believe.

"It's not fair to you, Catherine. It's not fair that I asked you to do this. It's not fair to anyone."

It's quiet for a moment. My stomach grows into a fit of nerves.

Say it. Just say it already. For Christ's sake, he's seen your breasts, Cat.

"What if I told you I like how this feels?"

"Like how what feels?" His voice grows tight.

I cough slightly, only to clear my throat.

We're approaching the knoll.

"You," I say.

We stop because we reach the knoll, and I can't find my breath between the beauty of what we're looking at and what I've just disclosed to Luke.

"Can I touch you, Catherine?"

"Yeah," I whisper.

Luke comes up behind me and slides his arms around my waist, as if God built cradles so perfectly for his body to curve to mine.

I drop my head to his shoulder, feel his minty breath against my forehead.

We look out onto the city of Abilene, and it's breathtaking. City streets make the city look so perfectly put together. Green and yellow dissolve into each other. And the big blue sky goes until it meets the end of the earth.

"You like the idea of us," he whispers in my ear. "Because I treat you the way you deserve to be treated. You like the way I kiss you because it feels right, the way it should."

I feel his voice down my spine and the sting in my eyes.

"I think there are people we're supposed to meet in life, and I think our souls aren't tied to just one person. I believe they're tied to more than one. Our hearts are meant to love and to be loved. I believe that's truth to the core. It's simplistic and natural." His arms tighten around me. "I'm not going to be the last man that you love, Catherine. I refuse to accept that idea."

His words try to settle in my heart, but they won't. They create a restless feeling inside me. Not one out of anger, but sadness.

"I'm the man that you're supposed to experience right now. This trip is our time together." Luke pauses. "I didn't expect to fall in love though."

I close my eyes and feel my heart disintegrate into ashes, scattering with the wind that blows through my body, through the hole that Luke's just created. Feel my body waver and fold under his touch, under his brow. I will myself to believe that all my past relationships with men, with Father, Mother, Ingrid, they've all led me to this point, to Luke. And in a deep, existential way, I know Luke is right. That we're in the present moment, and we might not make it out together, but it's not about the end; it's about the journey.

I do the next right thing by turning around and kissing his neck, tasting of love, sweet and bitter. Tears start to form in the corners of my eyes as I feel his heart pick up pace. I don't have to say I've fallen in love because he knows.

Instead, when I reluctantly pull my lips from his neck, I say, "What now?"

We're only in Texas, and there are many hours of time alone between here and New York.

Slowly, Luke turns me around, his hands now wrapped against my lower back, holding on for life.

"We stay in the moment." He touches his forehead to mine, and then he gently and hesitantly puts his lips to mine.

I know in this single moment that I was destined to be with Luke McCay for my entire life.

His kiss deepens, and I open my mouth for him.

And I die a little more, feeling like our time is limited together.

Before
Federal Correctional Institution, Dublin

Dear Journal,

I wasn't supposed to come home. In fact, in hindsight, there were so many indicators that I should have stayed at my place. But something beckoned me, called me like the night called the moon.

I'd stayed late at work because things just kept coming up. I worked for the *Los Angeles Times*. Reporters never slept.

So, I ended up working late into the night. Something felt heavy though, and I couldn't quite put my finger on it. I ended up grabbing takeout on my way home at about midnight.

It was the night that seemed thick. Its darkness trudged through the cool, winter evening like an unwanted nightmare.

I texted Ingrid just to check in. She was still attending Stanford, but she'd come home for the weekend, mostly because she didn't trust Father. By this time, he'd become a loose cannon. He drank more and more. He had retired and stayed home more. More time on his hands.

I tried to sleep that night, and finally, after the clock read three a.m., my lids shut.

But it was the dream I had that jolted my body awake.

A sinking feeling came over me, and I knew instantly that something was wrong.

I grabbed my phone from the nightstand and called Ingrid. Nothing.

I called Mother's cell.

Father's cell.

The house phone.

Something was wrong.

I got in my car and drove the twelve minutes to Beverly Hills.

When I pulled in the estate, something felt eerie. Off. Misplaced and deathly evil.

There are places you want to visit out of curiosity of the oddities that might unfold. There are places that you steer clear from. This was one of those places.

Ingrid's car, Father's car, and Mother's car were parked in the circular driveway. The early morning fog layer lay quietly, so as not to disrupt the world and its sadness.

There are times in my life where I've felt terrified, not wanting to go, to see, but this is the only one time I dreaded to see what was just beyond the front doors of our family home. The one we spent years behind, holding on to secrets, lies, the past.

I swallowed whatever courage, self-will I had and got out of my car, slamming the door, hoping that what was happening inside, they'd hear it and stop.

The truth was, I was terrified of my own family, not for what they did, but for what they didn't do. I was terrified of what we'd become—a codependent group of hearts that couldn't seem to do anything but rely on each other.

I didn't knock. In fact, I stormed in. And I remember every inch of the scene.

Broken picture frames splattered against the tiled floor.

Holes in walls.

The smashed crystal chandelier from France that Mother had brought home from our Europe trip lying in pieces atop the dining room table.

Fear ripped through my body like a jagged knife.

The sofa cushions in the grand living room torn to shreds. Cupboards open in the kitchen as if someone had searched for something they couldn't find or someone had been trying to protect themselves.

Screams shattered through the eerie silence, ricocheting off of the walls. My body exploded, and I ran toward the screams.

My mother's screams.

I took off up the stairs, my adrenaline pushing me to the next step. And the next step. And the next step.

Ingrid's body lay against the white carpet of their bedroom. Red crimson stained the carpet in a perfect circle, too much to show signs of life.

Mother was curled up next to Ingrid in a ball, hysterical.

And I did the only thing I knew how. I curled up next to Mother, tried to quiet her screams.

But Father returned. He always did. To pay his debt, to fix his own guilt, to reconstruct the way he felt.

I remember his eyes mostly—red and swollen. Contempt and bitterness, guilt and shame flashed in his expression. He reeked of day-old liquor and new liquor and cigarettes, something Father never would have agreed to if his faculties weren't straight. His mind.

The gun was in Mother's hands.

This is the part of the story I've never told anyone.

—Catherine

The next day, Gene and Al follow us out, and when we get to the car, Gene hands me a bag of sandwiches and snacks for the road.

I pull her into a hug, wishing, somehow, I was related to this woman. That somehow, I'd get just a piece of her DNA.

"Thank you," I say in our embrace.

She squeezes me tighter. "You come back, you hear?"

"I will." I take her hand as I pull away.

Luke hugs Gene and gives Al a manly handshake, but Al pulls him in for a hug.

"Don't make it so long next time, son," Al says, pulling away.

The perplexed look returns to Luke's face. He doesn't say anything but instead gives Gene a hug.

I give Al a hug. "Thank you for everything, Al."

"Ain't nothin' to it." His scent is of Old Spice and soap. He pulls away. "Remember, always keep saddle oiled and your gun greased."

I have no idea what this means, and I try not to keep the evidence on my face, so I smile, nod. "Always."

Al laughs. "Just kiddin'. Uh, stay safe, in other words."

Luke turns to me and grabs my hand. "You ready?"

"Yeah."

The truth is, I'm sad to leave Al and Gene. From the moment we pulled up to their house, time slowed, and life got simple. I like this much better than the city life.

Wake up.

Eat breakfast at the table as a family—unless you sleep in by accident, of course.

Dishes.

Wash laundry.

Feed the calves.

Gather eggs.

Fill the wood box.

Hang the wash.

Eat lunch.

Set the table for dinner.

Eat dinner.

Dishes.

Relax on the front porch until the day turns to night.

And wouldn't you know, that envelope and its contents stayed put on the red-checkered tablecloth on the dining room table, untouched.

I wave out the window to Al and Gene until they disappear in the distance.

Luke's genuine smile is back. The one he only shows intermittently.

He slips his sunglasses on, one hand on the wheel, the other now on my thigh. I somehow wish there were less fabric to the sundress now.

The veins on his hands are large, and I trace them with my fingers. "Your hands are big. I've never noticed that before."

Luke doesn't say anything.

I lean forward and turn up the radio. "Ain't No Sunshine" comes over the airwaves.

"Headed to Oklahoma now. You all right with that?" he asks.

I don't care. As long as I'm with you. "I don't think I've ever been to Oklahoma," I say instead.

"So, I take it, you've never been to Pauls Valley."

"Nope."

"Perfect."

The music plays as Bill Withers's voice drags out, and I allow it into my soul. I wonder if he knew the song would live this long, over thirty years later. I wonder if he knew his lyrics would be so relevant and just as powerful today.

"Can I ask you a question?"

"Anything." His hand tightens on my leg. Luke looks over at me.

"It's personal."

"Off the record?" He coyly smiles.

"Off the record," I say. "How many women have you slept with?"

Luke's eyebrows rise. "Seventeen. You?"

"Thought I was doing the interviewing."

Luke gives me a look.

"Eleven," I say.

"Why does it matter?" His pinkie and ring finger are between my thighs.

I shrug. "I guess I just want to know what I'm up against." I blush, assuming it will eventually happen. Maybe a bit presumptuous.

"I've only made love to one, remember?" He shrugs. "Some were time-killers, I suppose. Some I just thought were beautiful. Others were just there in a moment of weakness."

"I slept with nine because it helped console my heart." I look out the window, too afraid to look at Luke, afraid of his reaction to my raw honesty. "I slept with nine of the eleven because it was easier to escape my emotions."

I've never told anyone this. Luke gives me the ability to speak what's on my heart, and I'm not sure how he does it.

"And the other two?"

"Boyfriends. Peter and Michael. I loved them. I did. But I don't think I was in love with them. Michael and I parted ways when I went to prison. Peter was a high school boyfriend."

"Good."

I swing my head back to look at Luke. "Good?"

Luke looks at me, protected by the black glasses that separates his eyes from mine. "It takes two-point-five seconds to fall out of bed with someone. But it takes years to fall out of love."

My heart aches at the thought of Luke making love to another woman. Of him falling so deep in love that he doesn't notice anyone else. That his world is her.

He's been in love before. Made love to a woman.

"Are you still in love with her?"

Fleetwood Mac's "Landslide" comes over the radio. I try to allow the music to deflect the fact that he hasn't said no yet. That with each second that passes, his silence breaks me a little more. I want to ask another question because the song's lyrics are pushing my heart's ache to the surface, and I'm not ready to face it right now.

"When I met Julie, I was young. I think we fell in love with the people we were at the time. Then, time moved, and we didn't."

"Are you still in love with her?"

"I'm in love with the person she was."

Can you be in love with a person who doesn't exist anymore? If so much time has passed, heart scars made, situations change who we are, is it still possible to be in love with a person who doesn't exist?

"Tell me more about Peter," Luke says.

"Not much to tell. He was my first."

Luke looks over at me. "What was that like for you?"

I laugh. "It didn't last long. It was his first time, too."

Luke quietly laughs, his left hand on the wheel, his other hand still on my leg where he gently squeezes. "I have to admit, I'm jealous."

"Why?" I say breathlessly, his hand and his words causing my body to ache in places it should and shouldn't, knowing full well I'm looking for an answer he's not ready to give and that I'm ready to hear.

"That Peter got to share that moment with you. That you trusted him enough to take something that was worth a lifetime memory. A memory you'll always hang on to."

"One thing I've learned about growing up with my family, it's not about having; it's about giving. It's about what we get from those moments that make us who we are. That we get to take those moments, tuck them into our hearts, and remember them because it helped us become better. Besides"—I pause—"I'd rather know who I am and where I'm going and not bury my head in the sand," I say into Joni Mitchell's "California" as it streams out from the speakers.

Luke gives me a hard look. Then, he says, "I'd like to kiss you, Catherine."

Slowly, I lean in and gently press my lips to his. Feel his ache in my own.

I pull away, almost involuntarily.

Luke glances at the road and back to me. "Has anyone told you that you're wise?"

"I don't know that I've ever shared that with anyone." I look back at him. "Will you help me to remember that when we get home?"

"I will. As best I can."

"Okay, so Pauls Valley," I say, trying to lighten the mood. "Who's there?"

Luke moves his hand from my leg to turn up the air-conditioning. "Walker."

I don't ask who Walker is because I know I'll find out soon enough.

"Favorite movie?" I ask.

Luke thinks on it. "*What's Eating Gilbert Grape.*"

"And why?"

"The complexity of the story. And Johnny Depp."

"Have you met Johnny Depp?"

He nods. "A few times. Nice guy."

"I thought you'd choose a movie like *The Endless Summer* or *Point Break*, I guess."

"So judgmental."

I laugh, knowing he's being sarcastic.

"What's your favorite movie?" he asks.

"*Good Will Hunting.*"

"You came up with that answer pretty quickly. So, hands down, without a doubt, your favorite movie?" he asks.

"Yes."

"And why?"

He smiles, playfully grabbing my leg again, making my body shudder underneath his touch.

"It's a story about discovery, truth, and what you choose to make of your life."

"Can I tell you a secret?" Luke asks.

"Yeah. Just don't tell me you have some weird foot fetish or something, all right?"

"Oh. Okay." He's quiet.

My eyes grow big. "You don't have a foot fetish?"

Laughing, Luke catches my eye.

I love his laugh. I could take my time with it, enjoy each tone, each note, attach myself to the way it makes me feel inside. Because it does something to me.

"I was going to say, I haven't seen *Good Will Hunting.*"

I put my head in my hands and look back up. "All right. We're stopping at the first place to rent movies." I need to confess, too. "I have a confession."

"What?"

"I haven't seen *What's Eating Gilbert Grape.*"

Luke slowly shakes his head. "It's on. Movie marathon."

It's been a long time since I watched a movie. Since I read a book. Since I enjoyed life *this* much. It's as if the guilt and regret have somehow situated themselves to take a back seat to the way Luke makes me feel. And I'm okay with that. Even if it is just for a little while. Because until I completely deal with it, it'll never go away. It will slowly pick at my conscience, wandering through the vessels of my body and attach itself to each organ and attempt to eat me alive.

"The drive today, Ms. Clemens, is roughly four hours and fifteen minutes. So, sit back and enjoy the ride," Luke says to me in a voice built for radio and a face made for all the beautiful women in the world.

We talk about sports, politics, organized religion, and Gandhi. We talk about writing and surfing and acting. We discuss the ways of the world and how times have changed since we were kids. We talk about God.

"Do you believe in him?" I ask Luke as if we were comfortable with the subject, which I'm not sure we, he, is. As if we were in a relationship and this item were on our list to discuss and we'd started the conversation like it was the second-most normal thing to the weather.

Luke's calm. He's usually always calm, but this calm is different. It's not an indifferent calm; it's an inner peace in him that I haven't seen before.

"We didn't have a choice, growing up. Went to church every Sunday at First Christian, down on the corner of Bethel and A Street. Big, old white church. Probably older than sin." He peers over at me. "I mean, we didn't have a choice whether we wanted to go to church, but I suppose my belief in God has changed over the years. But to answer your question, yes, I guess I believe even though my concept of God has changed."

I smile at his over-explanation and the way he describes his childhood church.

"How?" I ask.

"How what?"

"How do you know he's real?"

Luke shakes his head. "I've seen too much weird shit to believe he's not."

"Like what?" I ask.

"You sure you want to jump into this pile of talk right now?"

I shrug. "We have four hours and, now, eight minutes. No time like the present."

"My sister, for one. Ella is her name."

Luke
Age Eighteen

"Ella, come on. You have to do it."

"No, I can't, Luke. I just can't. Not one more round." Her eyes filled with tears. "I'm just … I'm tired, is all."

Ella sat there, weak, in bed, remnants of a full head of hair somehow slowly fading to nothing, and I couldn't remember when that had happened.

I sat down next her. Her fifteen-year-old body, all skin and bones, dark circles under her eyes, her gaunt face begging for an answer she wanted, which was, *Okay, stop fighting*, but I couldn't give it to her.

Ella had been fighting cancer for a year. Chemotherapy and radiation had left a wake of disaster, wreaked havoc on her body. And yet, still, the cancer wasn't gone.

"There's a trial in Texas we can try."

I was eighteen, an adult. Clearly, I knew better than her. Mom and Dad were sick with worry. Just sick. So, I had to be the one to convince her to do the trial.

I was supposed to protect my sister from everything. The older brother.

I touched Ella's hand. "With your cancer, they have a forty-two percent success rate. I spoke to the facility director yesterday."

"You know I don't believe in statistics, Luke."

I knew. I remembered. But this one had to be better than the current treatment she was receiving. Ella used to be athletic, tall, blonde with legs up to her ears. She wanted to be a veterinarian. Wanted to help animals.

"Ella, please, you have to do the trial."

"How long is it?" she whispered as she stared out the window of her bedroom.

"Eight weeks. We'll travel to Texas once a week for treatment."

Ella's head whipped back to me. "Mom and Dad can't afford that."

"They can't, but I can. Been saving up."

Ella slowly shook her head. Her hands touched mine. "No, I can't let you blow your life savings on me, Luke. I just can't."

I bit on my cheek. Tried to be cautious with my words. Didn't want to hurt my little sister, but things needed to be said. "You can't tell me what I can and can't do with my own money, El."

Ella smiled. Crossed her arms over her chest. "Well, guess you're going to need my consent to do anything to my body."

She was right. I watched her as she listened to the world around her.

"Do you hear that, Luke? The sparrows?"

I listened hard, straining to hear what she heard. But I never could. Ella listened and saw the world differently than anyone else I'd ever met in my life. She only saw the beauty—until now. Until her body slowly withered away right before our very eyes. Took away her dignity, her hope, and her faith.

"Promise me something, Luke?" Ella turned her attention back to me.

"Anything."

"That no matter what, you take care of Mom and Dad."

But the truth was, I wasn't sure I could. I didn't have the strength that Ella had. Fighting tooth and nail for her life these past twelve months had been difficult.

"What if I can't?"

"You'll find a way. You always do."

Not with this stuff. Not without her. Not with the way I saw this all playing out.

I shook my head because it sounded like she was giving up. "The trial in Texas. You'll try it, right? At least, just come with me and check it out."

Ella turned her attention back to the window. Watched as the world outside kept moving. "For you, Luke, and Mom and Dad, I promise I'll try it. Wouldn't hurt, checking out the facility."

"Good then." I stood and kissed the top of her bald head.

"Luke?" Ella whispered.

"Yeah?" I leaned on the doorframe.

"I know you're smoking cigarettes. You need to quit that shit, okay? Mom doesn't need to lose both of us."

How in the hell did she know I was smoking cigarettes? I thought I'd hidden them.

I shrugged. They were the only thing getting me through this. I wasn't ready to give them up. Not that I was choosing the cigarettes over my family. Hell, I was the only one I was killing. But Ella was right; Mom didn't need to lose both of us.

"For you, I'll try it." I knew I was lying. I knew it, and yet I couldn't help but feed my little sister the bullshit. I was asking her to put herself through another round of treatment, and yet I couldn't put down the cigarettes. Some brother.

I left Ella with the sparrows, and I went to find my pack of smokes.

2014

"I remember flying down to Texas with Ella. She was weak, but she could make the trip. I remember her climbing the stairs to board the plane. Midway through the climb, she had to stop, catch her breath. And it hit me right between the eyes. This fifteen-year-old girl—smart, athletic, a go-getter—and one year later, she was barely able to make it up a flight of stairs. And not from the cancer, but from the treatment of cancer." Luke takes a big breath in. Runs his hand through his hair. "Here I was, asking her to do another treatment, and here she was, showing up. I …" He pauses. "I didn't know if it was the right thing to do at the time or the wrong thing to do. All I knew was, Mom's and Dad's hearts were broken, Ella was fighting, and I just had to do something other than watch her die."

He drives.

His words consume me. His tone, the way he talks about his sister.

"Why did you say you were an only child? Why didn't you tell me you had a sister who was sick?"

"Can I answer that question later?" he asks. "I promise I didn't lie."

I nod and stare out the window at the surrounding area called Oklahoma.

"Anyway, you asked me about God and whether I believe," he says.

I listen to the faint sound of "Rocket Man" by Elton John and Luke.

"As I stood behind Ella as she caught her breath, I prayed. I wasn't the type of man who prayed, but in that moment, I called God every bad name you could think of. Cussed him out as I watched my sister struggle to breathe. In that moment, I just couldn't wrap my head around it. I told God to take me instead. To leave my sister here and let her live her days, that I'd go."

There's a long pause. "Rocket Man" comes to an end.

"Six months after we started the trial, Ella was in remission."

I look over at Luke, thinking about the miracle.

"Two months later, she was killed in a car accident."

My gut twists and turns. My body grows cold as chills take over, and my heart sinks. I can't think of anything else to do but reach over and take Luke's hand in mine, so I do. "You believe God took her cancer away?"

He shrugs. "Just uncanny with the timing of it all. I suppose the reason I told you I was an only child was because it was just easier."

Neither Luke or I say anything after that. We just let John Lennon, Bob Dylan, and Paul McCartney move us.

Two hours later, it's three o'clock when we pull into Pauls Valley. It's the prettiest place I've seen in a long time, probably the prettiest destination on this journey. My hand is still entwined with Luke's, and for the past two hours, we've let the music, the lyrics, rest in our hearts.

Pauls Valley is greener than I've seen in the past few days.

"Beautiful here," I say. "Where does Walker live?" I ask.

"Not far."

"Do you drive across America often?" I smile, look out my window at a woman walking her dog.

"Third time."

"Why wouldn't you fly?"

"Guess it gives me time to think." Luke takes a left at the stoplight.

"Where are we headed?" I ask.

"A little two-bedroom cottage I found just south of town. Under the elm trees."

He probably prebooked it, so I wouldn't cause a stink again about him paying. I roll my eyes. I'm not ungrateful. It's just hard, accepting someone else's help.

"First, let's stop by the movie place and rent a few movies," I say, pulling out my phone to find rental places.

It's not long before we pull up to a mom-and-pop shop, and it's really sweet. To rent a movie, you sign it out on a form, and they give you a return date. Everything is done by hand, except payments. They do accept all major credit cards.

"*What's Eating Gilbert Grape* and *Good Will Hunting* are due back tomorrow," I say to Luke, who tried to pay for that, too.

Our Airbnb is tucked under the elm trees on a river. It's a two-bedroom cottage, but when we drive up, I see it's much bigger and nicer than I expected. I guess I assumed that the style of Pauls Valley, Oklahoma, reflected age and time and pace, a slow pace. Not contemporary or chic.

We get out, and I try to grab my bag, but Luke grabs it instead. He drops the bags on the front porch and reaches for a rock just left of the front door, and inside the plastic rock is a key.

"Genius," I say.

We walk inside.

The kitchen has white cabinets with black handles. A wrought iron New Age chandelier hangs over the island in the kitchen.

The living room and dining room are combined, and there's a sliding barn door for each bedroom off to the right. I slide open the first barn door, and there's a desk, a closet, and a mirror, but no bed.

Luke peeks behind me. "Where's the bed?"

We walk to the next barn door and roll it open, and there in the middle of the room is a queen-size bed.

"It said two bedrooms, Catherine, I swear. I assumed two bedrooms meant two beds."

I feel the rush of warmth come over my body.

An empty house.

One bed.

And the elm trees.

"I can sleep on the couch," he says.

And I don't argue. I don't say anything, except, "Or I can."

He sets our bags down as his phone chirps, and he reaches into his pocket for it.

I walk into the living room, sit on the sofa, and pull out my phone.

No missed calls. No missed texts.

I think about texting Ingrid. Just to see if she'll respond. I know she won't though.

"I need to make a call," I say to Luke as he comes in the living room.

He nods. "Absolutely."

I dial Mother's room. I stand and walk into the bedroom without a bed and quietly slide the door shut behind me.

"Sandra Clemens's room," Pamela says, and I can hear the smile in her tone when she speaks.

"Hey, Pamela. It's Catherine."

"Oh, honey. How ya doing out there in the wild states?"

"Good, good. How's Mother?" I ask.

Nerves quietly settle in my belly when I hear Pamela. She has a way of taking the fear from me. Fear that Mother will never get better. Fear that she'll live the rest of her days in silence, unable to speak or have the will to walk again.

"Oh, she's doing great. Had a good lunch, and now, she's outside on the patio, taking in the warm Santa Ana winds." Her tone is comforting. I feel myself wanting to nestle inside it, collect the kindness and the love, and push it to my heart so that I can feel whole, just like Pamela makes me feel every time I hear her voice.

I feel it. I feel the wind and the scent of jasmine from outside Mother's room, the sun on my face.

"Give her my love?" I ask Pamela.

"Oh, honey, she knows, but I will." She pauses, and I hear her breathing. "You all right, sugar?"

"I'm fine."

I think Pamela was sent to us by an angel. She's the one who has cared for Mother since she went into the facility. At the retirement age, she still works. Still cares for patients, providing their families with love and even after their loved ones pass on.

"You sure?"

The truth is, I'm not sure. I'm not sure about anything, except Luke. The story he told me still plays in the back of my mind. The cancer with Ella and then dying in a car accident. Things like that don't just happen. It makes me think of Father, Mother, Ingrid, and me, and my mind is swarming with thoughts.

"Yes, thanks, Pamela. I'll call again soon." I try to salvage my courage.

"Okay, honey. Don't be a stranger, you hear?"

"I won't."

"Good-bye, sugar."

"Good-bye."

I think accidents happen.

My counselor when I was in Dublin said that when our emotions align with our self-will, scary things can happen.

Father spent those last final years hurting Mother, hurting us emotionally, and we endured it. We survived it, and then one day, we just stopped surviving it.

What could God say to my story? What would Luke say if he knew my story?

That it was fate that showed up that morning or that people make awful decisions because we're human and how we're brought up, raised, exposed to life and the elements of life makes us who we are? Was it fate or poor decision-making that Ella died in a car accident? Did she kill herself? I don't have the courage or the heart to ask Luke.

So, when Pamela asks if I'm all right, I'm not.

I should tell him the story. My story. Our story.

But there's something holding me back that rests on the strings of my vulnerability. As if I might open up a wound, uncover the wounds that have been closed, sealed since that night.

Lying in a courtroom full of people didn't scare me; it was living with the truth that scared me the most.

After my mother pulled the trigger, the fatal shot that killed Father, she told me to tell the truth. For the first time in my life, Mother said to tell the truth. But I knew the truth would send her to prison. So, I did what I did best and lied.

There's a fine line between the truth and a lie, and it sits somewhere in the middle. And in that is a place where the soul can rest easy, I suppose.

She begged me to tell the officers the truth that cold January morning before I called the police.

But I couldn't. My mother would not pay the price. She'd already paid for her freedom. Taking Father's words. Being his punching bag, his doormat, so Ingrid and I wouldn't have to take it. She'd paid every single night since we were little, just trying to be the strings that held the family together.

When Father had come back in that morning, Mother had reached for the gun, and I believe, because I'd come to her, that she was terrified that he'd kill me.

So, she'd fired the gun that killed Father.

And I couldn't stop it.

But she did stop the cycle, and I wasn't going to let her take the fall.

A mother's love is the strongest bond in the world. It binds love, cements it.

A mother's love is unbreakable.

But a child's love, a child's loyalty to her mother, will never break even in awful circumstances. A child protects the bond fiercely, unknowingly, because of the love that exists inside them.

Luke is there on the sofa when I come back into the living room. His tousled hair is pushed to one side. His long, lean fingers, hands, rest on his thighs. His eyes lock on me. For a long moment, we drink each other in, tell ourselves this isn't what it seems and that attraction can flip the mind into believing something it shouldn't. I don't want to fall victim to that, but also, I need Luke's hands on my body. Just to take away the pain I feel in my heart right now. Grief is fickle. It comes, and it goes, like the waves touching the shoreline. Sometimes, they're mavericks, and other times, they're just little, slow, small pushes of water. I can trust the fact that this wave hitting me now is gaining strength, momentum. I know in a few hours that it might be enormous, and the only way to rid myself of the feeling right now is to allow myself to forget the here and now.

"Luke?" a whisper falls from my lips as I watch his dark brown eyes burn into mine.

"Yeah?"

What I want to say is that I need him. That I need for him to be inside me. To show me how he makes love to a woman.

Will he caress my breasts when we make love?

Does he take control?

Does he make love like it's a need rather than a want? Does he make love to a woman while looking into her eyes?

"Please, don't make the first move, Catherine."

"Why?"

"Because I can't guarantee I will be able to control myself or what happens next."

He folds his hands into his lap, smiles, looks down at the modern wrought iron coffee table in front of him. "I've spent the last seventy-two hours trying to convince myself that what we have experienced together is just attraction. It's just a game. That someone like you doesn't really exist and that this"—he points between him and me—"is just a facade."

He shakes his head. Laughs. "But I can't deny it anymore, Catherine." He meets my eyes. "Your heart is broken; I can tell. Broken into a million different pieces. And I've spent this time trying to figure out how I can piece it back together for you. But the truth is, I can't, not when I'll be responsible for shattering it when we go our separate ways."

Luke stands from the sofa. "I can tell when you look at me, there's this small piece of your heart that beats for me. I see it in your eyes." He takes two steps toward me. "So, let's go to dinner and watch the sunset and the sunrise, and let's lose ourselves in conversation about the world, travel, and good books." He takes another step closer to me so that he's barely twelve inches away from me. "Let's get lost in the feelings of the present moment and not in love."

Pieces of me want to put my foot down, tell him no. I cross my arms. "As much as I'm sure you'd think my heart beats for you, but rest assured, it's only lust. You're a really handsome guy, Luke, but not my type," I lie and uphold the outward appearance of control, just as Mother taught me.

Don't show heartache; it's unbecoming, Catherine, Mother would say.

But it's too late.

Luke's left eye squints. He reaches for my hand. Badly, I want to keep it at my chest, tucked in safe against my breast. Safe from his touch. But if I do, it'll look like I'm irritated. I release my hand and let him take it.

But he quickly lets go, turns his mouth, and begins to cough into his fist.

Holds his finger out to signify he needs a minute. After thirty seconds, he stops and pulls his hand away, but I see the blood.

"Luke," I say. My voice changes from the brittleness of before. "You're bleeding." I take his other hand and lead him to the bathroom. Put his hand under the water I've just turned on. When he looks up, I see the tiny drip of crimson on his lip. I grab some toilet paper and wipe it. "Why are you bleeding?"

"Ulcer."

"Are you taking medication?" I ask, wiping his lip now, trying not to breathe in his scent. Take in how our bodies are extremely close right now.

Luke takes my hips in his hands and moves our bodies apart, but the look on his face betrays him.

Instantly, my chest begins to ache when he breaks eye contact. Gently, I reach up and lift his chin with my finger, and his deep brown irises with green flecks are staring back at me. I want to be in his thoughts and in his skin. I want to feel his heart as the woman who owns it, not the woman who's borrowing it. Luke's made it clear that this is just lust, but everything about that doesn't reflect what I feel from him.

"Yes."

"How long?"

"Not long." He reaches up and takes my fingers from his chin. Pushes past me to look in the mirror.

The traces of blood are gone, and so are the reminders that he might somehow look at me differently than he does other women.

"We could grab an early dinner and then come home and watch the movies?" He looks back at me from the mirror, a distant reminder that he doesn't want me to know what's going on with him.

"Let's," I say.

I quietly leave the confined space that tied us together and try to forget about the crimson, the ulcer, and Mother.

They say it takes six to twelve weeks to recover from heart surgery. That's doable. I can survive that, but I know that I won't be able to survive Luke.

At dinner, he tells a joke, although it's corny, something about a llama and school supplies, and I laugh so hard that my wine almost comes out of my mouth. When I look up, his head is tilted to the side, his eyes painted a different shade of brown. Perhaps it's the light or the room or God, but when I see his face, the look, I know Luke McCay wants more of me, and even if it is for a limited time, I'd be willing to give it. Because right now, he needs me.

"Your laugh is the most beautiful thing I've heard in a long time, Catherine." He sets down his wine.

We've drunk half a bottle between us.

Caught up by the ambiance of the beautiful restaurant and the piano playing in the background, the white linens, and the wine, I can't think of a more perfect moment I've ever had in my life, and something inside me pushes to say it.

I tell Luke something I've never told anyone, and I blame it on this moment of wine, beautiful music, and vulnerability. "I remember one particular dinner party my parents had when I was almost twelve, and Ingrid was eleven. It was the first time I had an idea that my parents were wealthy. But when Molly Ringwald waltzed through our grand entryway, I thought, *Wow*. She was beautiful, and her saffron dress followed her in."

I take another sip of wine, and so does Luke. He looks at me.

"I watched her as she sipped champagne every now and then. How she moved so gracefully around the dinner party. How her eyes lit up when someone approached. The whole evening, I just watched her. While I usually went upstairs to bed, bored from the whole thing, I just couldn't leave. I just had to watch her until the very end when she climbed into the black limousine that took her home.

"I was caught up in the moment when the door shut, when all the guests slowly trickled out like ants after that. I wasn't sure which movie stars had ever come to our home, but after that, after Molly, it didn't matter.

"When the house was quiet, when Mother and Father were in the kitchen, Ingrid came down from our bedroom and told me it was time to come to bed. I told her I'd be up later. I just needed to stay here for a few more minutes. When the yelling started from Father, I knew it was time for bed." My eyes fill with tears, and I look up at Luke to see his reaction. "I just stood up and carried myself to bed. I didn't defend my mother like I should have. I didn't tell my father to leave her alone." I shrug as I swallow the lump in my throat. "Have you ever done that, Luke? Just walked away when you shouldn't have?"

I look down and toy with the napkin in my hands. He doesn't answer. Maybe I wasn't expecting an answer; I'm not sure.

My mouth continues to move, and I'm unsure how all this will come out. "I wanted to be Molly Ringwald that night. I just knew she didn't have what I had at home. That she had come from a family where her father was nice to her mother and that they had said grace every night before dinner. And that they laughed and held hands and sang family songs." I pause. "It felt like Ingrid and I walked on cracked glass with bare feet every day of our lives, growing up. We were taught to pretend really well from a young age. We were taught to lie when opposition opposed us. We did this to survive. But one day, I knew it would all come to a head."

The waiter approaches and gives us the bill. I try to take it, unsure of what the hell I'd do with it once I got it. I didn't have but a hundred bucks on me, but I wasn't going to let Luke think I expected a free ride.

"One of these days, Catherine, I hope you'll be able to see yourself the way I see you." Luke takes the bill, staring at me as he pulls out his wallet and throws a credit card down.

I don't ask how he sees me because I'm afraid of the truth. Afraid I'll disagree. Afraid that his opinion of me will mean too much. Afraid of myself.

"Do you know what I see?" he asks.

I hold my breath, slowly shake my head.

"Well, I'm going to tell you anyway." He leans forward on his elbows against the white tablecloth. "I see a woman who has more strength than most men. I see a woman who is so beautiful that the sun is mystified of her presence. I see a woman who has fought fucking hard to be who she is today. I see a woman who brings light into a room and leaves it when she goes. I see a woman who doesn't give up, no matter the circumstances. And I see a woman who's seen tragedy, lived through it, and still gotten back up." Luke leans back. "You don't see this because you're focused on what you're not."

I stop fidgeting with the napkin. Meet his gaze.

"That's who you are, Catherine Clemens, not some drug-addicted Hollywood daughter with four rehabs and a rap sheet behind her. It seems to me that you've always accepted the responsibility for your shit and everyone else's shit."

The waiter returns, and I see the fire in Luke's eyes.

The waiter pauses. "I'm so sorry to interrupt, but are you Luke McCay?"

It's been my experience that restaurant staff always have the worst timing—or better yet, maybe it's the patrons who have the worst timing.

"Yeah." Luke signs the tag, but clearly, he's agitated. Looks up at the waiter.

"Can I have you sign this for my girlfriend?" The waiter looks over at me, a blank piece of paper in hand. "Sorry, I hope this is okay."

I casually toss my hand out in front of me. "By all means." I lean back in my chair and try to brush off Luke's words, half-wanting them to disappear from my memory and half-wanting to hang on to them, hold them close to my heart so I'll remember them and grab them when I need them.

Luke holds his finger up to the waiter. Looks me dead in the eyes. "I'll never set aside your feelings for anything, Catherine. Is this okay that I sign this?" He moves his elbows back to the table.

"Yes."

"No, it's not. Don't settle to make someone else happy. Don't settle for less than you're worth, Catherine. Not for a single fucking second."

My heart begins to pound against my chest. My hands grow sweaty as I look up at the waiter and back to Luke. "It's fine, really."

Luke smiles. Leans back. Runs his hands through his hair, frustrated. "You're lying, Catherine. Whether you mean to or not, you're lying."

My mouth falls open, and I roll my eyes. *What?*

The waiter stands there, pen and paper in hand. Looks from Luke to me and me to Luke.

"Is it okay?" Luke asks again, his eyes locked on mine.

"No," I whisper. And it's not because I want to make Luke happy, but because he's right. For years, I've been pushing my feelings aside for others. I hide how I feel to appease other people. I learned to survive uncomfortably, thinking it was all right. I learned that my idea of love was completely messed up.

Oh my God.

I cover my face with my hands. "Oh my God."

I stand, turn, and walk out of the restaurant, unable to breathe, praying my tears won't see the light of day.

When I finally reach the outside, I gasp, and the tears roll down my face, I run down to the river as dusk has settled into its rightful place.

I scream, grab the sides of my head, and yell out, "I hate you, Father! I hate you!" The ending words die off before they become a whisper.

Luke's arms are around me, and his grip is tight.

He breathes in and out with my pace, chaotic and rhythmic all at the same time.

I groan as I feel like a bandage has been ripped away from old wounds.

I scream again and try to fall forward, but Luke catches me.

"Breathe," he whispers into my ear. "Breathe and scream and do what you need to do to feel."

Quiet sobs choke my throat. I cover my mouth with my shaking hand. "How—" I start. "How did I not see this?"

"Your heart stood in the way, Catherine. I'm sure you spent years protecting your sister, dying to protect your mother, and trying to keep the shaky boat afloat. How could a little girl manage all that?" His question is rhetorical, and my body vibrates because of what his words do to me.

I'm going to be sick. "I'm going to be sick," I say as I push away from Luke, and he releases me.

I run to a nearby tree and heave up wine and filet mignon and bread. I feel Luke grab my hair to hold it up out of the way as tears and vomit fall from me.

Several minutes pass by. The world spins, and I struggle to catch my breath as my body heaves.

When I'm done, I wipe my mouth with the back of my hand, embarrassed, too scared to face Luke, though I have no choice. I stand.

With his hand still in my hair, I turn to face him, barely covering my mouth with my fingertips.

He looks at me and pulls me to him, not allowing me to turn away, and I fall against his chest and quietly allow his arms to take me anywhere but here. My eyes begin to burn again.

I come out in a sleep shirt and shorts, brushed teeth, freshly showered, feeling what's left of the weight of the world against my chest.

Luke is sitting on the sofa with popcorn and a cup of tea on the coffee table in the spot where I would sit.

"Made you some tea. No caffeine." He smiles as I sit down next to him. "How are you feeling?"

I lean back after grabbing the tea. "Like a diesel truck hit me going a hundred miles an hour, and I'm questioning how I survived." I look back at Luke. "Thank you," I whisper. My eyes start to burn again, and I fight the urge to cry, so I take a sip of tea to combat it.

Luke leans back, puts his arm around me, and hits play on *Good Will Hunting.* I lean into him, allowing his strength to give me some of my own because I'm just too tired right now. My eyes are heavy, and my insides feel quiet, less chaotic. My body feels relaxed. And this beautiful man next to me seems to hold me every time I've fallen since we met. I wonder where he draws his strength, his courage. I look up at him, take in his scent and the feel of the weightlessness of us.

I watch Luke, and he watches *Good Will Hunting.* His lean jawline and high cheekbones. His five o'clock shadow that dips below his chin and disappears. I follow the lines from his eyes that disappear, and I want to know how each of them were earned.

For the first time in my life, I want to ask for directions, for life instructions on where to go from here.

I reach forward and set my tea down, sit back and curl myself into his body, wanting to be a part of him, wanting to spend tonight, tomorrow, and the next day with Luke.

But what happens when the abuse you've lived with for so long is over, and you're supposed to somehow survive?

Luke
Age Thirty

I gently pulled the strands of her chocolate-colored hair that lay across my naked chest, and I wondered how long we could stay like this. How long we'd be able to love each other just like this. Without responsibility, without stress, without an afterthought of regret of where we'd been or who we'd been with.

We'd just finished making love. Came here to reconcile our marriage. A cottage in Santa Barbara, California, overlooking the Pacific.

How do you know when you're in love? I remembered asking myself at age twenty-two.

I wasn't sure, but I was certain that it was something like my mother and father. My mom would quietly touch my dad's back when it was time to go. When he'd give her a piggyback across the creek out on the property because Mom didn't know how to swim. I supposed it felt a little bad, a lot good, and full of moments measured by commitment, the value of love. I learned from my mom and dad that it wasn't about love notes and romantic evenings and all the good shit.

It was about seeing your love at their worst, in the throes of hell, and helping them to find their way back to you. It was about picking up the pieces after a night of fighting and giving them your best, even when you didn't want to.

When Ella had died, Mom and Dad hadn't grown apart; they had grown together, and I'd left for California, only coming back for holidays.

It was too hard to visit. Too many memories Ella had left in her room, in our home, in our town.

I just didn't want to face it all.

Julie stirred, sat up, pushed her long, dark hair behind her, and her breasts touched her stomach. I pulled her to me. Her big white smile encouraged mine.

Falling in love wasn't about making love; it was just a small piece of it.

I felt her smile against my lips right before she pulled away.

Her green eyes stared back, telling me she would always give me truth, even when it hurt. I grabbed at her naked body, just wanting two more seconds of her time. Her tan skin under my fingers looked like it should. Like my hands had been made for her body. I had written her a song, but I wasn't ready to play it for her yet. I needed to wait until I got more practice. I wanted it to be perfect, like her.

She moved up my body like silk. "I need you," she said and kissed my jaw.

My heart raced, and my body did what it did when she said things like that.

Julie and I were good together, in bed and in life.

She had been a bartender when we met. *LA Hills* had become a hit, and I had just been grateful I didn't have to work construction anymore.

And there was Julie, pouring a triple shot of Rémy Martin for a customer.

She said, "What are you having, pretty boy?"

What I liked more was, she didn't know who I was. Preferred it that way.

We talked for hours after the bar closed.

And that was that.

There was a lot to learn when you were in your twenties and felt like you were on top of the world or had the world by the balls. There were a lot of things I had done wrong, some things I had done right.

One was having sex with a woman, Candida, before Julie, who I'd met on set.

Candida said she was pregnant, and I was the father. I told Julie about it. I figured if it was real and if Julie really loved me, she'd stay.

"Well, if you're the father, we'll make it work. We have to."

I was so relieved.

After Candida reached out that first time to tell me she was pregnant, I never heard back. I tried to reach Candida by phone, but I couldn't get through. Found her place, and it was empty.

"Could have been a hoax," Julie said.

Maybe, I thought. I remembered sleeping with Candida.

"Maybe a woman trying to get money out of you," Julie said.

We let the situation go after failed attempts to reach Candida.

That winter, after Julie and I met, I tried one more time. It was Christmas after all, and Christmas was magical for kids. Maybe this time, I could get answers. By that time, if Candida was pregnant, the baby should have been born, but still, the number I had for her was out of order.

I took Julie home to Kentucky to meet Mom and Dad.

Mom and Dad fell in love with her, and so did I, just a little more.

I realized in the quiet moments of us, when she touched my back when it was time to go and I carried her across the same river my dad had carried my mom, that I was in love.

I told her about Ella and Walker and Ben and Nathan. She knew about Candida. There wasn't much left to tell her.

Some love was made to last, and other love just wasn't. Not Julie and me. No, we'd be together forever. Come hell or high water, I knew she'd be there, no matter what.

Spring of the following year, we got married. We tried to get pregnant for months. Years afterward. I thought something happened to a woman when she couldn't conceive and that was all she wanted in life. She broke before me. What she wouldn't give to hear the little pitter-patter of feet down the hallway. The belly laughs from somewhere deep inside her little body or the soft breath against her neck as the baby slept.

I wanted that badly, but I knew Julie wanted it more.

Julie took it upon herself, thought that it was her fault. And I thought everything I did reminded her of what we didn't have. She always tried to say it wasn't me, that it was her. But I knew, somehow, that I had the ability to split her in half by just a single touch. Julie had a way of pretending. A way of letting the world know that she was all right even though she was dying inside. I thought from watching that, her, something died inside me, too.

That had brought us here, to Santa Barbara, our best attempt at rekindling us. The love I'd always felt for her.

I watched her as she climbed on top of me and asked for more.

Quite honestly, I wasn't sure if it was the feeling, the love, or her attempt at another pregnancy, but I went with it to make her happy. Pushed inside her. Held her breasts to my mouth, and never once did she look me in the eyes. She used to always do that. Look me in the eyes until she shuddered underneath me, beside me, on top of me, or in front of me.

But to see the smile on her face just one more time, I'd do anything. To fuel the fire we'd felt in our early twenties. I knew though the flame would go out, and I'd be left in the dark to pick up the pieces. I was okay with that. That was what I'd signed up for.

Until death do us part.

I'd made a commitment. We'd made a commitment. I wasn't about to walk away from that.

I loved Julie too much to let us go.

We returned home to Santa Barbara this afternoon.

I heard Julie crying in the bathroom.

I wanted to knock, but I didn't. I wasn't sure why, but something inside me didn't let me. Maybe it was because I didn't want to face her. See the defeat, the heartbreak on her face again. That somehow, she'd left herself down. That she'd let me down. And that somehow, I was responsible.

So, instead of knocking, I slid down the wall next to the door and listened to her quiet sobs.

We were brought into this world pure, untainted by life, full of love, naive, and unassuming of the world. Then, somehow, we changed. We saw things. We heard things. We were told things. We felt things. And then we changed slowly, day by day.

And by the time we were taken from this life, pieces of us were so tainted, so jaded—some of it brought on by our own decisions and some of it completely out of our control—that it was hard to see the good in the world.

Julie was my decision. Her heart was broken, not by the choices she'd made or we'd made, but by things out of our control. A heartbreak was a real hard thing to watch. I wished I could take the pain away. I didn't wish it were me in her spot because I'd rather her not watch me suffer because it was probably hard to watch the heartbreak than have the broken heart and feel completely helpless.

I didn't believe we could tell our hearts who to love either. That we just fell sometimes when we were completely unaware of it.

Julie just opened the door, and she looked down at me.

"What are you doing?" she asked.

"I don't know." I looked up at her.

Her puffy red eyes stared down at me. The beautiful green eyes I had fallen in love with.

She slid down the wall next to me, wrapped her arms around my neck. "I'm sorry, Luke."

"Don't be sorry," I said with a lump in my throat. Emotion stuck where I should be gathering strength for the both of us. The pain in my chest was almost unbearable.

"I really want a baby."

We'd done all the testing. Paid for fertility drugs. We'd exhausted all avenues. There was nothing wrong with either of us. We just couldn't make it happen together.

"I know." I kissed her head. Rested my cheek against her forehead. "I love you, Julie."

"I know," she said. She got up, went into our bedroom, and shut the door behind her.

Sometimes, we had to let go, even when we didn't want to. That was what Uncle Al had said to my mother after Ella died. She'd had one of Ella's favorite T-shirts in her hand and been hanging on to it for days. Wouldn't let it go. My dad had stayed in the garage. Gone out first thing in the morning and not returned until dinnertime.

I guessed loss was universal, and grief was the same. I'd lost my sister, and I knew I'd already lost my wife. I was just waiting on her to say good-bye.

2014

I feel movement, as if someone is cradling me like a baby. Barely, I open my eyes and see that my head is resting on Luke's chest. He's carrying me in the direction of the bedroom.

I feel his shallow breaths against my ear and close my eyes again, pretending to be asleep.

He reaches the bed and draws back the covers, gently laying me between the sheets. My eyes stay closed, maybe out of fear that I'll somehow mess this up or maybe out of curiosity, as I wonder what he'll do next.

Luke pulls the covers over the top of me, and it's silent for a long moment.

But in the stillness, he kisses the side of my head and lingers there only for a second before turning off the bedside light and gently shutting the bedroom door behind him.

I should go out there, tell him to sleep in bed with me. That I won't touch him or ask him to hold my hand. That I'll be still and not move and he can sleep. That I don't snore.

Don't be stupid, I tell myself.

Listening, I try to quiet my breathing, to hear what he's doing. The darkness surrounds me, tries to swallow me before I sit up and gasp for air.

Get water, I tell myself. *Breathe, get water, and then go back to bed.*

I look up at the ceiling and trace the small grooves in the pine. Carefully, I get out of bed, walk through the room to the door, and open it.

It's dark in the house.

"Catherine?" I hear Luke say.

"Yeah?"

"Are you all right?"

"Yeah. I just need some water." I walk toward the living room, the only way to get through to the kitchen.

My eyes begin to adjust to the darkness, and I make out his silhouette on the sofa.

His shirt is off, and I notice this because I see the reflection of the light over the stove on his bare chest. He gets up and walks toward the kitchen.

I hold my breath, as if it will help me to control any temptation I feel in my body.

He doesn't say anything more when I reach the kitchen. I find a glass in the cupboard to the left of the sink and fill it with tap water.

I drink it. Chug it in fact to cool my body, praying it will take away the nerves in my stomach.

But I see him watching me in the reflection.

He's still and unmoving.

I drink my water, praying it doesn't go down the wrong pipe.

He rests his fingertips on the top of the doorframe, watching me.

When the water is gone, I panic, unsure of what to do next.

Before I turn around, I set my glass in the sink.

"Thank you for taking me to bed," I say, turning, leaning against the sink, crossing my arms.

I smile, laugh. He laughs, too, and a small dimple appears to the right of his chin, below his mouth.

"That came out wrong," I say, running my hands through my hair, my T-shirt exposing my lower stomach.

Luke's eyes narrow on mine, and I see the conflict in his eyes.

"Do you know your eyes have flecks of green in them?" I ask, reaching for anything to keep me in this room with him.

"They do not." He tilts his head to the side, looking at me. "Do they?"

"Yeah. The right one has a few more than the left one, but you can definitely see them."

He leaves the room. Turns on the light in the dining room and walks to the mirror. Stares into it. "You're right. I've never noticed that before."

Luke turns and looks at me from the dining room, walks to the light switch he just turned on, and flips it back to off, so now, it's just me and him and the darkness and the tiny stove light.

"Now what?" I whisper.

He takes a step closer to me.

The conflict in his eyes becomes clearer as he makes his way to me. There's a change in his demeanor, as if he's battling his own will and own thoughts.

"I can't pretend anymore. I can't pretend to be someone I'm not, Catherine." He takes both hands and places them on either side of the kitchen sink, so his body leans into mine, barely touching. His lips inches from mine.

"Don't pretend," I whisper, wanting him to kiss me so badly that I feel it everywhere in my body.

Again, the conflict appears, his face so close to mine. He tries to drop his face from mine, but I pick it up with my hands and crash my mouth to his.

His body, like a magnet, forms to mine as if we were melting glass.

Tonight, I tell myself as I feel his tongue against mine, quickly and then slowly, *I'll just take what I need, and that's it.*

Luke's hand slides to my backside, and then he grabs my ass as he pulls both of my legs up to his waist.

He carries me to the bedroom just like he did earlier, except this time, I force my mouth away from his, staring into his brown eyes, and say, "You're not leaving."

And he nods, meeting my mouth again with his.

He slowly lays me down on the bed, my body wired and ready for whatever he'll give me.

"You are so goddamn beautiful, Catherine," he says as he crawls on top of me. His mouth slowly moves to my neck, trailing kisses down to my chest. He looks up as if he's asking if this is okay.

I nod, pulling my T-shirt over my head, and he lets out a groan. He takes off his jeans, and I see what I'm doing to him.

Gently, he puts his mouth to my breast, and I unravel as I watch him watching me. He comes back to my lips as the ache deepens between my legs. His length falls against my folds, and through our clothes, my shorts and panties against his boxers, he slowly starts to move.

Luke moves his mouth to the other breast, giving them the full attention they need.

Slowly, he makes his way to my mouth as his hand slides down around my breasts and my stomach. With hesitation and a confident stare, he slides his hand underneath my panties, and his fingers reach their destination.

I know what he feels because I feel it, too.

My legs fall to the sides.

"Catherine, you're wet," he says as he slides his finger against my center.

I call out in need.

He uses two fingers and slips them inside me.

"Luke, please," I beg.

He spreads my legs with his own. He removes his boxers and my shorts, panties.

I feel as though this is familiar, as if this is the place I've always wanted to be.

I pull his mouth to mine as he sinks inside me.

We find rhythm and pace and oneness.

I am the moon, and Luke is Jupiter.

I am the stars, and Luke is the sky.

Lost in the abyss of feeling and love and wholeness, I find Luke, waiting, taking my hand, and guiding me.

He pushes and stretches and spreads, and I grow around him. I feel.

Opening my eyes, I find him watching me, intent, content, and everything in between.

This feeling he creates inside me, I've never been able to reach it with another person. A place where time doesn't exist.

He pulls out and turns me around and pulls me back to him where he enters me again.

He cradles me from behind and eases in and out of me.

I call out loudly this time , unprepared for my own noises.

When I reach my peak, he touches down between my legs and touches the spot between my folds in a way that is both soft and rough, all at the same time.

Luke pushes and pulls, and I stare at the exquisite beauty of the images he gives me as he divides my body into two halves. One half has fallen in love with Luke, and the other half knows my heart will get broken in some way.

But when we both come together and fall against the mattress, I feel weightless and limitless and completely satisfied.

He doesn't say another word, except, "I'm sorry," before he kisses me on the mouth and leaves me to the darkness.

As I'm still trying to catch my breath, the darkness sits on my chest like a brick, waiting for me to admit defeat, while I wonder what the hell happened as my body feels tired and completely satisfied, and my heart begins a dull ache.

"*This won't end in your favor*," the words come to my head as if they were my own. But I know it's my sister's voice, and it takes me back to that night.

I stand, tired, and walk to my bag. Grab my phone.

A missed call or something, a text, I wait for Ingrid.

It's been thirteen years, Catherine. You know the drill.

The bedroom door opens again, and it's Luke, his shirt still off, his boxers back around his hips. He hands me a glass of water, sets his on the nightstand, and crawls into bed next to me.

I thought he'd left me to sleep on the couch, and I'd accepted that as if it were all right. As if it were okay for him to use my body as a fix. *Why not, right?* I'd spent years trying to use my body to hide my feelings, to fix what was broken.

He turns on his side and looks at me. "Are you okay?" he asks and kisses my cheek. "You look surprised."

"I do?" I try to play it off, setting my phone on the nightstand. I take a sip of water.

"Yeah, you do." He reaches up and cups my breast, gently pulling me to him, allowing our eyes to meet. Luke puts his lips on mine and slowly pulls away.

"Can I be honest with you?" I ask, my skin feeling as though it will crack if I come clean from the lies I've told myself about men. Honesty doesn't always come naturally. "I thought you were going to sleep on the couch," I say, my eyes dancing between his and straight ahead.

He drops down to the pillow next to me. Picks up his head and looks back at me, a baffled expression on his face. "Why would I make love to you and then leave you?"

Make love to me?

That's what that feeling was with the moon and the sun and the stars and the sky. Dividing my body into halves. Luke. And me. And the moments of all goodness.

I say it out loud to see what it feels like against my lips, "Make love to me?"

"Yeah," he whispers, observing me.

I stare back. "I thought you said just dinner and movies. That was it between us."

He laughs. "I believed that for a second. I believed I could do it, and then when the movie was over, you were in my lap, and your face looked so peaceful. As if all that was wrong in the world was finally right."

It is. It finally is, I say to myself.

"I sat there in the moment with you and watched you. Your lips pouting as a child. Your hands curled up under your chin. I knew you were home for me."

I sigh deeply, soaking up his words and putting them into my heart. "If you see the innocent side of me, then you've seen the best in me. But for a long time, Luke, I used my body as a shield to the past. A shield to protect myself. To lose my feelings. To not feel. I slept with nine men in three weeks because I couldn't stand what was going on in my life."

He doesn't say anything but, "And what about now?"

"Now, I'm trying to do things to make myself happy. Making love to you makes this," I hold my chest, "in here happy."

He's quiet for a moment. "It's my experience in life that people are people. And they come and go. But it's what's inside us that learns to mourn, learns to hurt, and learns to love because we love. Because we love and we get to experience heartbreak."

"You should have saved that for a second date."

He laughs. "Sometimes, I'm too deep." He laughs again, and it turns into an uncontrollable cough. One where he sits up, leans forward, coughs so hard that his stomach heaves.

I jump out of bed, naked, and go to the bathroom to grab some towels.

I think of the ulcer.

The blood.

I return.

When his cough finally grows silent, I hand him his water glass. He takes a drink.

"This cough isn't an ulcer, Cat. We need to talk, and I need to tell you the truth."

Before
North Alpine Drive, Beverly Hills

Dear Journal,

I was released from prison yesterday. Ingrid was there to greet me just past the gates. Had the car there, waiting, too. Asked how I was. Quite honestly, I'd felt safer inside. Behind the steel. I guess I didn't have to deal with the wreckage, the aftermath.

Mother is fine. But I worry about her, not because she doesn't talk, but because of why she doesn't talk. Her doctor was there to meet me when I came to her room at Alder Grove Assisted Living. Ingrid warned me that Mother didn't speak. I knew, but I'd never seen it for myself. She takes medication, psych meds, to drown out that night. A buffer, I'm sure.

But I suppose growing up the way Ingrid and I did, it created a sense of mental toughness that Mother maybe knew we'd always need one day.

I think Mother knew Father would kill her one day; it was just a matter of time.

But not a day goes by that I don't recount what happened that night. Every single minute. The hours before. The day before. The days leading up to it, trying to pinpoint how everything could have been prevented. But I don't think it could have.

Father was a bubble waiting to burst. Waiting to explode and unleash his true fiery. And I know the alcohol didn't help either.

A family that looked so well put together on the outside, so lovely and loving and perfect, was slowly dying on the inside, and all it took was time and lives lived to expose it.

Home isn't home anymore. Not within the multiple walls layered with memories and the tragedy in between. A house built for gods, haunted by the past and loved by good people who weren't quite enough.

Father hadn't been enough for his father.

Mother wasn't enough for Father.

And Ingrid and I just wanted to be enough.

When I walk through the grand entryway made of white marble, to my left and to my right are staircases that curve and meet in the middle on the second story. I always took the left, and Ingrid always took the right.

I remember that night. The eerie quiet and then Mother's wails.

I try to control my thoughts.

This isn't happening right now, Cat. This is you coming home to your old traumas. Just a visit. Nothing more, nothing less.

Where is Ingrid when I need her?

Through an entryway on the left is the dining room, and in the dining room sits the same maple table imported from Italy that Mother had purchased. It's still the same table we used in the evening for dinner and for the lavish parties that Mother and Father threw. It seats twenty-four, and twenty-four open chairs that no one wants to sit in. Through the dining room is the kitchen. The white kitchen with an island as big as the sea. My voice always echoed in here as a little girl. Ingrid thought it was funny.

The drawers were as long as my arms, and into our adult years, they still seemed long. The ceiling is dome-shaped and sculpted into waves. As a little girl, I always wondered why the waves seemed so far away as a child. Now, I see it's just perspective.

The same white marble countertops swirled with the same mix as the floors in the grand entry still fill every inch of the counters, including the island.

Everything is the same, and yet everything is vastly different.

What's changed, I suppose, is me.

With thousands of square feet, a family of four had a hard time filling the space with anything but resonances of two children just trying to fill the void. And that's all it was. A big space. A space held together with nothing more than material things.

I thought about what I'd do when I was released. Would I come here? I had to after all, right? There was no choice. I knew I'd have to revisit this place.

"We need to sell the place." Ingrid moved behind me.

"It means too much to you," I said into the darkness.

"So, we're just going to hang on to it and watch it wither away? You won't live here. Mother certainly isn't coming home. All you're doing is hanging on to something that doesn't exist anymore, Cat." She walked to the other side of the kitchen island. Looked at me. "We have to let go." She rolled her eyes. "We're in a twenty-five-million-dollar home in Beverly Hills. You could be comfortable with life."

I heard her words, but I didn't feel any better about the whole situation.

"Cat," Ingrid sighed. "I'm okay with selling the house. Maybe it's you who's somehow stuck here. Maybe, somehow, it's your own grief that's keeping you tied here. You wouldn't have to worry about Mother's care anymore. It would be financially taken care of. You could buy a smaller vacation home, somewhere you want to be. What about Myers Flat? You used to love it there when we were kids."

"You did, too," I whispered.

"I loved it because you loved it."

I looked up at Ingrid.

She shrugged. "Don't get me wrong; I enjoyed it, but I needed more modern conveniences, like Nordstrom, Cold Stone, and room service at the Four Seasons."

Ingrid never came off as materialistic. She just quietly met her needs with the luxuries our life provided.

"What about you? What will you do? Where will you go?"

"I'll be fine, Cat. Stop worrying about me. Typical older sister." She playfully rolled her eyes and laughed.

I saw the same laugh from when we had been children. When we hadn't known life was slowly taking us under, that our realities would soon change, and that we'd grow more cynical and jaded to life, more aware of the real world.

"Listen," Ingrid said. "We can stay here as long as you'd like, but remember, we're only keeping the ghosts at bay. At some point, you're going to have to deal with this."

"I know. But it won't be tonight."

"Come on; let's go to bed. It's been a long day." Ingrid walks over to me and puts her arm around my shoulders, and we make our way upstairs to our old bedroom, in our old house, where no one is sleeping.

—Catherine

"What did you say?" I'm taken aback. Stunned. I've heard something that I can't quite grasp. *But you look healthy and handsome, and you have these rosy cheeks that make me want to kiss you more.*

This can't be.

My body grows shaky and sweaty.

"I'm sorry I lied to you," he says, pulling me closer to him.

This … this was supposed to be an interview. I was supposed to be working on writing a story about a reunion show, a return to television after years spent away of one of the hottest actors in the late 1990s and early 2000s.

"Cancer?" I ask, just to be sure I heard him correctly. That it wasn't my head playing tricks on me.

I'm in Luke's arms when he says this, "You need to know what falling in love feels like, so you know it when you find it, and you don't run away. You need to know what love feels like because it is the best possible solution for a broken soul like yours. You're not mine to love. You're the gift I received for the time I have left."

I sit up in my nakedness, turn to him. "There's plenty of treatment out there, Luke. Surely, we can find a way to get you the treatment you need. If what you need is money, I have it." I think about our house in Beverly Hills. Consider Ingrid's words from last year, that night when I got out of prison. It's the first time I've ever considered such a move.

Luke laughs and reaches for me, and gently, I fall back to his chest. "It's terminal, Cat."

The only outcome.

Not a place we seek to find solace or love, but good-byes and tears.

The end result.

"But have you looked at every possible treatment? I'm a researcher. I can look into this."

Luke kisses the top of my head, and we're quiet as we lie in the darkness, our naked bodies entwined. "My father used to work in the coal mines when I was a kid. I started to go with him at age thirteen. And every day that we came home from the coal mines, he used to give my mother purple hydrangeas. He said it was his token of appreciation for her. His love. The color purple means several things, but devotion, my father said, was why he did it and also to continue to love my mom and more deeply understand her." Luke pauses and then continues, "Blue hydrangeas symbolize apology. Pink hydrangeas symbolize heartfelt emotion. White hydrangeas symbolize boastful or bragging."

Luke's father did the same thing Father did but for different reasons. And maybe I was seeing purple when Father left the hydrangeas on the awful mornings, but maybe they were really blue.

Luke kisses my head once more as I feel the tears coming. One escapes my eye and falls to his chest.

"All this to say, Catherine, I've lived a really good life, and since you came into the picture, I look at life in a whole new way. And there's no one else I'd want to be on this journey with than you. Just sorry we didn't do this sooner because I feel like we missed out on a lot of love. I didn't expect all of this. You. The story. I think, too, we're meant to meet people who change our perceptions, our paths, for the better." He pauses and gently strokes my head. "But we have tonight and our trip, and that's all I can ask for. That's all you can ask for." Luke is quiet for a minute. "If you can't handle it, I understand. If you want to leave, I wouldn't blame you, Cat."

I turn my body and look up at Luke with his still-rosy cheeks. His laugh lines. The spark in his eye. "I'd rather run," I start to say and watch his face stay stoic. Then, silence follows my sentence because I'm not sure the truth will come out without tears. "I'd rather run. Allow the heartbreak to start sooner so that the ache won't last as long." I swallow. "But the truth is, my home is where you're at. And God built us to withstand the heartbreak. I know this to be true." I toy with his chest hair, feel it, run my fingers through it. "So, the question isn't if I'll stay; it's, what will we do with today?"

Tears stream down my face, as I know the inevitable. Knowing it won't be a happy ending. Knowing that, no matter what, we won't get our happily every after—Luke said as much. That treatment won't work. But it's more about living in today. Enjoying one another until we can no longer wake up together, where we can longer hold hands or kiss or ride in a car together. Maybe it's about learning to love amid adversity and forcing ourselves to live in the present moment. I don't need to ask how long we have together because I'll learn to live in the moment.

Luke gently takes my chin and pulls it up until I look at him even though all I can make out is the silhouette of his handsome face.

"Tears are a good sign, Catherine. I think we can heal and grieve at the same time."

The darkness feels light, and his heartbeat is all I want to hear for right now, so I gently kiss his lips and linger there for a moment. Then, I pull away and move my ear back to his chest. "I just want to hear your heartbeat for right now."

I feel him smile.

"Okay," he says and rests his cheek against my head.

"I love you, Luke." Something I've never said unless I knew it was forever. Three words I've saved for only Mother and Father and my sister. Three words that would have most likely died inside me if I hadn't shared them with Luke.

"I know, Catherine. I'll love you forever."

Heartbeat.

Heartbeat.

Heartbeat.

"You know one of the best qualities about you that I've learned so far?" I ask.

"What's that?"

"Your ability to trust," I say.

"How do you mean?"

"You've never asked me about that night. About what happened. Prison. And yet you allowed me to embark on this journey with you. Why? I mean, did you Google me?"

Luke doesn't answer immediately. "I Googled you, yes, but I already knew who you were."

"Oh, from all the media coverage."

He was in LA at the time.

"No, not from the media coverage. You don't remember me, do you? We met at Sam's Bar. Went to the Four Seasons?"

Oh my God. "Guy never seven." I sit up in bed and look back at him. Stare him down, praying to God the memories come back, that I'll remember him. The way his body felt, the way his hands felt. And yet nothing comes back.

"I'll take guy number seven," he says. "Come here."

I lie down with him and listen to Luke tell the story.

"It was Sam's Bar down on Sunset. This beautiful woman walked into the bar, and I swear, she turned every man's head as she walked past. She made her way up to another woman, and they exchanged hugs, words. I realized, only after I Googled you, that it was Ingrid. Saw your family picture in the newspaper." He holds me tighter as I listen.

"I watched you all night. Dance, sip on club soda after a beer. Watched you laugh. Felt a little like a creeper." He laughs. "Before I followed you out to make sure you'd make it to your car all right, I grabbed a receipt with your name on it that you'd left on the bar. If anything, at least I'd have your name to remember you by. But it was when you went to your car that you realized you'd locked your keys in your car. Ingrid had gone home by then, and cell phones weren't even a thing back then."

I remember the keys and remember being locked out.

I remember having sex with a man in a hotel room. He felt familiar and like home and comfortable, but I blamed it on the alcohol. Blamed it on my feelings at the time. I couldn't see that what I had in front of me was just what I needed all along.

But Luke felt the magic.

"You ran away that morning, Cat. Why?"

"I'm sorry," I say.

"Why'd you run?"

"I didn't run. I left."

"No, you ran. I was awake, Cat. I thought you were going to the bathroom. But instead, you grabbed your clothes, went into the bathroom, came out, and left before I could say anything."

Again, he waits for an answer I won't give.

"I got dressed as quickly as I could. Ran outside the room. The hallways at the Four Seasons are long and you were gone. You ran."

Back then, we didn't have social media. Facebook and Twitter and Instagram weren't part of our daily vocabulary.

"Luke," I whisper, "I wasn't running from you."

"Who were you running from then?"

"Me."

The wind kicks up outside. A wind chime sings, light and airy.

I take a big breath in. "I used men like a drug. I used their bodies to fix my own. I needed them to want mine. Needed an escape to busy my mind from the wreckage my father caused at home." I stop. Listen to his heart in my ear. I rise and fall with his breaths in and out. "Somehow, I thought if I could just numb or fix the hole inside me and fill it with something, I'd feel whole again. And every time, it just didn't work."

"Your father was mean to you?"

This is the first time Luke's ever asked about Father.

"The exact opposite. He wasn't. But he was to my mother. Several quiet nights after countless dinner parties, he'd berate her about what went wrong. Then, as time progressed, it turned physical. When I look back on it, I should have seen how his rage was building, but I didn't. I should have seen it coming. I think my mother always knew he'd get her in the end."

"But he didn't," Luke says.

"No, he didn't."

Luke's arms tighten around me. His heartbeats calm me. His breathing keeps me levelheaded.

I take a big breath in before I tell Luke this part. I exhale. "My mother buffered us from a lot, but after that day in January, I'd never known true sadness like I did that day and the years that followed. Prison was the easy part. Living was harder. Until I met you." I gently laugh. "I mean, until I saw you again."

Luke traces my bare back with his fingertips as my naked body lies against his.

"Luke?"

"Yeah?"

I want to tell him the whole truth about what happened that night, just so one other person knows. Just so he knows Mother was brave enough. I will take the fall for what happened that morning for the rest of my life. But I need him to know that Mother was brave enough to finally take a stand. That it wasn't me.

"I didn't fend off my dad. I didn't kill him. My mother did."

The wind chimes blow, and finally—*finally*—the hole inside me that the wind blows through begins to close a little.

I listen to his heartbeat again. Fall in line with his breathing.

I try hard to remember that night with Luke as guy number seven. I was never into movie stars or holding them on pedestals. It all didn't matter to me. I'd been around them my entire life. With the exception of Molly Ringwald. I still hold her up on a pedestal, and I probably always will.

And the only thing I can remember is the way he touched my back. It was gentle and hard, all at the same time. I don't remember his eyes because I never looked at them. I don't remember what he said because I didn't care. All I cared about was getting what I needed.

But now, I wish I did remember because that would be three more hours with Luke that I could look back on and keep with me when he's no longer here. When I can no longer hear his heartbeat, no longer measure his breaths.

"One day, you'll stop running, Cat."

"I think I already have."

Then, I realize, this trip could never be about forevers; it's about good-byes.

"Walker was my agent. My first agent. Took me under his wing, like a son. Gave me great advice. Want to know what it was?" Luke looks over at me from the driver's side as Fleetwood Mac's "Gypsy" softly plays over the radio. "Don't smoke a cigarette with the enemy; he'll learn your secrets."

I think on it. "Like, don't trust anyone?"

Luke shrugs. "That's what I gathered."

"And did it work?"

"It did. There're a lot of people in Hollywood who make promises that they know they can't keep. Walker wasn't one of them."

"Why are we going to see him?"

We pass houses that are similar in size to the one I grew up in. Filled with empty space and lies.

We pull up to a black gate, and in front of the gate is a keypad. Luke pulls out his phone and types whatever he sees on his phone.

The gate opens.

We pull through the gate, and the road ahead is lined with trees. Big pine trees. The road twists and turns, and we finally see the only big house ahead.

With a circular driveway and a fountain out front, the only thing I wonder is where they park their cars.

We always pulled in the driveway; that's just where we parked at our house. But there aren't any cars in the driveway, which tells me either they have parking somewhere else or there's no one home.

Luke pulls up front, and we get out of the car.

"Nice place," I say, shutting the car door behind me.

Luke puts his hand on the small of my back, and it reminds me of the way he put his hands on my backside as I slowly rocked on top of him last night on three separate occasions.

"Don't put your hand there," I say and push his hand away, smiling.

"Why not?" Luke looks at me.

"That's where you put your hand when we made love. Walking into a stranger's house, I don't want to be red-faced and in heat."

Luke laughs and drops his hand to my ass. "How about here?" he whispers in my ear.

I close my eyes with the memory of him taking my ass in his hands and pulling me against him as my back lay flat against the wall. "There either."

"Oh, now, you remember me."

I playfully slap his arm.

"Before, I was just guy number seven."

Luke kisses me on the cheek a little longer than he should, and I want to soak up his kiss for an eternity. Always feel his lips against me, even when he's gone. Luke just came into my life, and yet I can't imagine not having him in my life.

"Well, lucky you, now, you have a name and a face." I smile back at him as we reach the massive front doors of Walker's house.

Luke rings the doorbell, and inside, I hear the faint ring, followed by an echo.

A man comes to the door and opens it. "Mr. McCay, Miss, Walker is expecting you. Please, come in."

Luke holds his hand out so that I can go first.

Luke falls in line behind me as the man who answered the door shuts it and takes the lead.

"What's your name, man? I didn't get it," Luke asks as we follow him.

"Dean," he says. "The pleasure is all mine, Mr. McCay. Please, this way."

We follow Dean down a hallway and to the right. The home is made of rich browns. The floors, the walls. And everything is so big.

Off to the right is a sitting room with a wall of windows that looks over the valley. A swimming pool sits outside.

A tall man stands outside, watching two little ones in the pool.

"Grandpa! Grandpa! Watch this one!" a little voice says.

Dean walks out the door that leads to the outside and whispers to Walker.

Walker turns, and his whole demeanor changes. He breaks out in a big smile, turns back to the woman sitting by the pool, and yells, "Honey! Luke and his friend are here!"

"Oh! Have him come outside and meet the kids when you're done," she calls back from underneath her visor.

Walker comes inside in a Led Zeppelin T-shirt, shorts, and Toms shoes. White hair and leathery honey-colored skin tell me he wasn't raised here in Pauls Valley. That he's a transplant, most likely from a place like Arizona or Southern California.

He stops, placing his hands on his hips. His big, toothy smile is a focal point. "Luke McCay, holy shit."

Luke walks to Walker, and they embrace.

"Been a while," Luke says, pulling away. He motions to me. "Walker, I'd like you to meet Catherine. A friend of mine."

Friend.

He didn't say girlfriend. We haven't confirmed anything else, so why use a word other than friend? I'm not sure why this bothers me, but it does.

Walker pulls me in for a huge hug, too.

"Oh, thank you, Mr. … I didn't get your last name."

"Walker is my last name." The rasp in his tone makes him sound cool, experienced, a pack-of-cigarettes-a-day smoker at one point in his life. It's inviting and intimidating at the same time. The words roll off his tongue so casually and so rhythmically, like written song lyrics that have existed for years.

"Luke still calls me Walker. You can call me whatever you want, but the name is Sam Walker, and that out there, that's my wife, Gail Walker. And our two grandsons, Steven and Sam Jr. Twins. Who knew?"

Luke eyes the boys. "Are they Tammy's boys or Rick's boys?"

"Rick's. He's on a getaway with Letty."

The boys look to be about six or seven. Towheads.

"It's been a while, Luke, and it's sure good to see you. In fact, when Gail sees you, you'd better plan to stay awhile. Of all the clients I represented in Hollywood, you're the only one she loved like a son, and you're the only one she still asks about."

"Well, we're passing through on our way to New York, and I wanted to give you this." Luke hands Walker a white envelope from his back pocket.

Walker's big grin appears again and quickly fades. He stares at the envelope, takes it, and looks back at Luke. "What's this?"

Luke shrugs. "What I owe you."

Walker's shoulders drop. "You don't owe me a dime, Luke."

Walker looks at me with questioning eyes as if I had something to do with this.

"I'm just an innocent bystander," I say.

He tosses the white envelope onto the counter where we're standing, clasps Luke's shoulders in his big hands, and says, "Missed you, kid."

We're at the dinner table, and it's the four of us. The twin boys are off playing a video game they were promised if they behaved at the dinner table.

I feel like an intruder. Walker, Gail, and Luke have lived a life together that I wasn't a part of and I'm looking through a window, listening, watching.

Out of the blue, Luke begins to cough, and I know what to do. I grab a napkin and shove it in his hand to catch the blood that might come out. I try not to make a big deal about this, try to make it seem like it's just a cough.

I smile at Gail and Walker and ask, "So, how long have you guys been in Pauls Valley, and how on earth did you end up here from Los Angeles?"

I take a bite of my steak even though I want to throw it all up. The sound of Luke's cough has changed, and it worries me even though I try to play it cool. I chew the piece of meat and Luke coughs and Walker and Gail look at me, waiting for an answer I can't give. I put my hand on his back.

"Well—well," Gail begins as Luke's coughing fit begins to subside.

I want to throw up, and yet I keep chewing and keep pretending everything is okay.

Luke looks at me, his eyes straining. "I'm going to use the bathroom."

I nod as he stands, my hand falls from his back.

"Are you all right, honey?" Gail asks.

Luke says, "Yeah, just a tickle in my throat."

But I saw the blood in the napkin.

"So," Gail begins again—she, too, catching on to the *act normal* façade—"I grew up here, and when Walker retired, we came here to be closer to my parents."

"It's a beautiful place," I say, trying to focus on the conversation at hand and not Luke.

"What do you do for a living, Catherine?" Walker asks in his smooth way.

"I'm a writer actually." *And I went to prison for murder.*

I'm sure Walker knows exactly who I am if he saw my full name in the headlines of my daily newspapers thirteen years ago. I'm sure what happened was a part of his world, too.

"What do you write?" Gail asks, taking a bite of salad.

"I've written for a few publications. *US Monthly* magazine is who I currently write for."

"Ah, does David Jenkins still serve as acting chief editor?"

I swallow hard. Put my water glass down. *Shit.* "Yes, he sure does," I say as if I know the guy. As if I'd spent Christmases with his family. Babysat his kids or something.

Luke returns to the table, thank goodness. Sits down. Looks at me, and I give him the *you all right* look.

Luke smiles. Plays it off.

"Everything okay, Luke?" Gail asks.

"Just a tickle I couldn't get rid of."

In this moment, I believe Luke. I want so badly for it to have been just a tickle. A small tickle, and that's it. Not a deadly disease festering in his body. I also realize how well Luke plays the part. How well he brushes it off. How well he pretends. He's an actor, I know. I look at Walker and wonder if he knows the truth. If he knows Luke as well as he seems to. Does he see through the bullshit?

This time, Gail stands. Takes her plate and Walker's plate and reaches for mine.

"Oh, no. You cooked. I have dishes."

Gail smiles at me from across the table, plates in hand. In this moment, I can see why Walker fell in love with her. Her smile is sincere and genuine and full of love. I can see why Luke came back.

Are the white envelopes an explanation to people?

Is each one full of money?

A letter?

An apology?

A map to treasure?

I reach my hand across the table to take the plates from Gail. She's hesitant, but she gives them over.

"Thank you," she says.

"Thank you for dinner."

I take Luke's plate, and he thanks me with the soft touch on my lower back.

"I'll help you," he says.

"No. Visit." I eye him.

Luke smiles, and the fear in the pit of my stomach disappears.

I walk into the kitchen, and Gail follows me. We start the dishes.

"You know," she says, "I've never seen Luke look at a woman the way he looks at you. Not even Julie."

Julie?

Sometimes, it's better to listen than to ask questions.

"That young man in there is absolutely in love with you, Catherine." Gail smiles and leans against the counter as I submerge my hands in the water.

Breathe, Catherine.

"But I'm sure you already know that." She laughs.

I grab a pot and begin to wash it, allow the warm, soapy water to ease the tension in my body.

"We met a week ago," I say, willing myself to be honest.

Gail shakes her head, smirks. "Well, if you heard my and Walker's story, you'd know that I believe your story to my core."

"How'd you guys meet?"

Gail is petite with short brown hair and a beautiful face. Cheekbones and a narrow jawline.

"My mama said I wasn't tall enough to be a model, so I left Pauls Valley for the big city of Los Angeles to prove her wrong. It wasn't more than three weeks when I got there that I met Walker. At the time, he was just building his business. It was 1973. I was just eighteen years old, and Walker was twenty-two. That man has always been a go-getter. But what I fell in love with was his passion and understanding of people. Since the day we met, I've always told him he was in the wrong line of work and that he should be working for the Red Cross or some disaster relief outfit. And do you know what that man said to me?"

I hand the pot to Gail to dry.

"He said, 'Marry me.' " She giggles.

Her giggle reminds me of Dolly Parton's. It's high-pitched, and it ends on a kick.

"So I did. We were just so young and so naive." She shakes her head. "That was forty-one years ago." She smiles. "My mama said it wouldn't work. Said we were too young." Gail bites her lip when she sets the pot down.

"My mama was a strong lady, but she was wrong about two things. One, the right person falls in our lap when we need them most. We're still married. And two, petite women can become models."

We both laugh.

I bury her words in my heart for a time when I'll need them, especially the first thing about the right person falling right into our lap when we need them most.

"Oh, my mama. God rest her soul. She was a tough, old bird, but boy, she raised us right."

Luke and Walker come from the dining room, bringing the leftovers from the table just as we finish up the dishes.

Luke leans into me from behind, whispers in my ear, "Are you ready?"

I feel the warmth his breath provides against my ear, my cheek. He gently kisses my cheek, and my heart picks up pace.

Live in the present moment, Cat, I remind myself.

So, instead of falling to fear of the future, I breathe him in, just as if he were gone. I breathe in his scent, his words against my cheek. I picture his smile and the lines that run from the corners of his eyes. His dimple and the two creases in his forehead that you'll see if he laughs hard enough.

I'll remember. "Yeah," I say, "I'm ready."

CHAPTER 30

The drive back to our Airbnb is quiet, not in a bad way, but in a good way. It's peaceful. I realize our days together are numbered, but I'll give Luke what he wants, what he needs until he can't tell me anymore.

He hasn't brought up the cancer, and neither have I. In fact, I wish it didn't linger in the back of my mind, but it does. It's always there.

The night feels good against my face, the September air of Pauls Valley, the mood of the evening. I look over at Luke, who's got one hand on the wheel and the other hand between my legs.

Live in the moment, Cat.

I've said before that I felt safer behind the metal doors, in prison, but now, after a year of adjustment, I can't imagine going back.

Luke could choose to look at his diagnosis like a prison sentence. I could choose to view Luke, our trip, as a prison sentence with an unhappy ending, but I can't. I don't think he can either. We get time together.

I take my fingers, and slide them through his hair, and he gazes over at me.

"What are you thinking about?" I ask.

"You."

"What about me?"

"I realize I've fallen in love with a woman, and I don't even know her favorite color or what high school she went to."

"Blue and Harvard-Westlake." I pull my fingertips through his hair. "What about you?" I ask, lingering on the words *in love.*

"Blue and Bardstown High School," Luke says, pulling into the driveway.

The gravel crunches underneath us as we come to a slow stop.

The moon shines its brilliance, the river behind the cabin making a consistent *shh* sound, and all I can think about is the contentment I feel, being with Luke. Like, no matter what happens with life, in this moment is where I'm meant to be. I want to be the keeper of his heart. I want to take all his sadness, his fear, and put it in a box and tuck it away, so he can live whatever time he has left in peace, just as I feel it.

I know that isn't a reality, so I say, "What happens now?"

Luke turns off the engine. Pulls me from my seat in a commanding way and says, "We make love."

Luke's head falls to the headrest, and he looks at me as if I am the most beautiful flower, the most boldly colored flower he's ever seen. His eyes, in the darkness, make him look mysterious, but I know who they come from. I know that this man in front of me is worth every ounce of grief I'll eventually feel, every minute of stolen moments from my future, every ounce of love I have in my body.

I was taught to love with consequence—this I'm very familiar with. I was taught to love with strings attached. I was also taught to love with lies. While I can lie to myself and tell myself that I can withstand the hurt when he goes, what I cannot do is sit here and tell myself that I won't fall in love because I already have.

Luke picks up my body, lifts me over the console, and sets me down on top of him. I take my hands, put them on his cheeks, and hold his face in my hands. Allow my skin to feel his, allow my mind to collect these memories, ones I'll miss so intently that my heart will cry out, I know.

Because when my family was a family, I wish I had collected the good memories and not the memories of Mother and Father fighting so loudly that we could feel it in our hearts and in the walls of the beautifully broken home on North Alpine Drive.

"I wish I could have more time with you, Luke. I wish I could collect your thoughts, your feelings, and stow it away for when you're no longer here to tell me them. I wish I could always feel your heartbeat."

Before he can answer, I gently press my lips to his and feel his sadness, a kiss littered with push and pull and conflict, of the unknown. My legs settle down comfortably on either side of his thighs, and I feel him harden underneath me. The only thing between us is his shorts and my panties because of the sundress that's up over my waist.

Luke grabs the back of my neck and nudges my chin up with his head, so he can get better access to my chest but not before fiercely staring at me in the eyes. Though his look is intense, his touch is found somewhere between soft and hard. Needful.

He trails kisses down my neck and against my bra.

Somehow, I get his zipper on his shorts down, and I put myself against him. He pulls my panties to the side, so I can feel all of him.

I tilt myself up so that my opening is on top of his sex, hard and waiting. Knowing my body, I ease myself down, and he's inside me.

Slowly, I rock.

He closes his eyes, and his head falls to my chest, but I can't help but move my body.

"Look me in the eyes." I rock against him.

He pulls his head up. Need bleeds through his dark brown eyes. He bites his lower lip, and he intently stares back at me.

Badly, I want to go faster, to feel him fill me up, take all of what he has to offer. But I keep the pace slow, even, and he grabs my ass and holds me tight to him.

He takes my mouth in his and kisses me like tomorrow won't be here, like we won't have each other, as if we'll wake up and this will all have been a dream.

Luke pulls away, opens the driver's door while inside me, gets up by lifting us both, shuts the car door with his foot, and walks to the front door while he peppers me with kisses along the way in.

It's a feeling to be outside, in the moon's light, committing an act that should only be done behind closed doors. A rush of euphoria shoots through my body when he rests my back against the front door and pumps inside me. My legs feel like jelly, and this feeling he gives me between my legs makes me want to whisper, *Faster*, because it feels too good. But I don't. I want to savor Luke for as long as I can.

Luke gets a full grip on me before he opens the door to our cabin and carries me in.

I don't care where he puts me or where we make love. I just need him—and this thought both terrifies me and makes me feel whole.

He walks to the couch and sits down. He takes off his shirt while I watch. I reach out and run my fingers down his chest and all the way to the base of us, where we're connected.

I push my lips to his as he takes me in, pulling my hair back from my face and then grabbing my jaw and kissing me hard. He pulls away and stares at me.

"You are why I was made," he says. "You are why I am here. I believe my sole purpose in life is for you to feel loved by me, Catherine." He pauses. "And I think your sole purpose is to learn to love completely, without strings attached and without lies, only all things innocent and pure. To know what true love is like, so you can take it with you as you live. I think I'm the one who's supposed to teach you that."

Tears well in my eyes, and they start to fall. Luke takes my hand when I try to wipe them, shakes his head, and watches them fall.

"It's really hard to live in the moment, Luke." I push my thumb across his lips.

"I know," he says.

I know that my life up until now matters. I also know that we must walk through the fire to get to the ground of knowing. All of this is worth it, and I know this with every burning ember inside me.

I fall to his mouth and rock against him as he holds me in his arms and allows me this time to just be.

We come together quickly after that. I fall to the side, and we lie here, tangled in each other, panting for a few seconds.

Luke watches me as I stare at the ceiling.

"What are you thinking about?" he asks, rubbing my thigh.

"I'm wondering if the cabin is old."

The roof has a glittered ceiling that was popular in the eighties.

Luke looks up. Smiles. "I have a hunch."

I wince when he says this. His tone and the grittiness, I'll miss them with all my heart.

And when he sees this, Luke scoots to the edge of the sofa, lets his shorts fall down with the zipper still unzipped, and picks me up, carrying me to the bedroom. "Let's go to bed, Catherine."

Luke walks into the bedroom and lays me down but not without taking off my sundress, my bra, my panties. Then, he tucks me into bed. He takes off his boxers and crawls in bed next to me, pulling me to him so my head is against his chest and I can hear his heartbeat. I will myself to remember its beat, and I close my eyes.

"I love you, Luke."

"I'll always love you more, Catherine Clemens. Always more."

"No." I smile. "I love you more than all the pepper flakes in the world."

A slow, throaty laugh sounds from inside him. "I love you more than all the grains of sand in the world."

"I love you more than the stars in every galaxy."

"I love you more than all the book pages from the beginning of time to present."

I'm silent. I look up at him. "That's a lot of love."

"I know."

I rest my head on his chest again and find his heartbeat. "I'll love you even when your body is no longer."

"I'll love you from death."

I smile against his chest, kiss his stomach, and say, "Okay."

If this is what living in the moment means, then maybe I can survive it. I just hope Luke can, too. Not that his body can because I know that would be false hope, but I hope he can remember us, the feeling that us together gives him, so when the pain gets too unbearable, he can let go of us, knowing that I'll survive. I'll be all right without him … eventually.

Luke
2001

I took another sip of the whiskey from the glass that sat in front of me. I didn't drink much, but this day warranted as many drinks as my body would allow. Lou, the bartender, was half-Korean and half-black, and he stared at me from across the counter.

"Boss, you okay?"

I took another sip of the whiskey, winced as it slid all the way down my throat, burned and then ignited in my stomach. It made my head feel a little lighter, and the weight of the world just seemed to ease only a little.

The bar was just down the street from mine and Julie's place in Carpinteria.

LA Hills had finished filming, and our last episode aired on May 17, 2000. I thought I'd lost some of my purpose after giving up the character Dylan Klein. My marriage was in turmoil. Julie still wasn't pregnant, and I felt so helpless every day I came home to her. Cold, silent, bitter. Even though she tried to pretend she was all right, I knew. I noticed when she winced every time I went to kiss her on the mouth. I noticed every time my hand brushed against her hair, she'd move away. I noticed she didn't sleep. I noticed her smile had changed. I noticed everything. And yet, I couldn't fix a fucking thing.

So, Lou's is the only place I'd thought to come when I got home and saw Julie's note. The note that sat on the bar in front of me.

I couldn't answer Lou because I wasn't sure I was okay. I wasn't sure of fucking anything anymore. I wasn't sure if I wanted to stay an actor. I wasn't sure if I wanted to go back home to Kentucky.

I took another sip of whiskey, that sip bigger than the last two.

In my jacket pocket, my BlackBerry buzzed. I didn't give a fuck who was on the other end. I just wanted it to stop buzzing, so I pulled it out of my pocket and stared at an unfamiliar number.

"Hello?" I said when I answered.

Silence.

"Hello?" I said, more agitated.

Still, silence.

I went to hang up but I heard, "Wait, don't hang up."

"Who is this?"

"Candida. Candida Briggs. I-I'm not sure you remember—"

My throat grew extremely dry. "I remember you, Candida."

"I shouldn't have called," she sighed into the phone.

I didn't move. I couldn't. My stomach twisted and turned, and I couldn't quite understand why she was calling after all this time—except for only one reason. I remained silent and waited.

"Luke, I'm sorry. You have a daughter, and her name is Fiona. She's seven years old. And I'm sorry I didn't call you sooner."

There had been times in my life where I'd felt like I couldn't breathe. Times in my life where I'd felt shocked, like when Ella died and Nathan died. But this was different. I couldn't seem to find the right words. They didn't come to me.

"Look, I know what this seems like. I don't want anything from you. Not a damn dime. But Fiona's been asking about her father since the father-daughter dance at school."

Father-daughter dance?

I felt like I'd just gotten punched in the gut.

My biological father was no father at all. He'd left my mom when I was born. Said he was going to work and never came home. My mom met James three years later. Three years it had taken my mom to find the ability to breathe again, to live.

Tears filled my eyes. I blamed it on the booze, and I brushed them away as they began to fall. "I called you. I tried to find you—" My words were broken.

"I know," Candida whispered into the phone. "And I'm sorry about that."

I'd missed Fiona's birth. I'd missed seven birthdays because I didn't know when her birthday is.

I don't know when my damn daughter's birthday is, I thought to myself.

"When's her birthday?" Disbelief colored my tone.

"July 15."

The math worked out. Julie and I had gotten together in 1995. Candida and I'd slept together in 1993 or so.

"I-I'm sorry I didn't call sooner." Candida said that like it was on a checklist. *Call the father of my child and let him know he has a child.*

Anger set in.

"It's a little fucking late, Candida," I said and hung up on her.

"Lou, can you bring me another whiskey, please?"

Lou nodded. "Can do, boss." He poured it and slid it down my way. Lou put the whiskey bottle back in its place and walked over to me. Threw his towel over his shoulder. Stared at me again. "You're sure you're okay, boss?"

I smiled a sarcastic smile before I put my glass to my lips. "No. No, I'm not, Lou."

Lou didn't say anything.

The note from Julie stared back.

Her wedding ring taped to the inside.

After I downed the whiskey in full, I picked up the note again. Read it again.

Dear Luke,

It wasn't supposed to be like this. And I'm not sure where we went wrong, but I know where I went wrong. I can't be the woman you should want. The woman you deserve. I'm not the woman you met in 1995. I'm different. You are, too. Things change, and we change. Nothing ever goes as planned. With time, people grow together, I suppose. And, also with time, people grow apart.

I'm not sure when we started our descent to this place we've been, but, Luke, most of it is me. I really want a baby. I know you do, too. But I found out, with testing I had done on my own, that it's me. I can't have your baby, our baby. I'm not quite sure how to process all this. I'm not quite sure how to live life without you, but I need to.

Our marriage felt stifling, thick, as if the air I breathed every single minute was just us and the weight we carried. Every time you came home, you checked on me. Asked if I needed anything. Sat outside the door and listened to me cry. Watched me as I pretended to sleep. Asked if I was okay every minute of every day. It made me sick in my heart that you worried so much about me.

The truth is, I'm not okay. But you and me apart is okay. I'm so sorry. There's no other way to describe it. I feel like I need to be alone.

Please know that I love you, and you will always have pieces of my heart, but in order to love others, I have to learn to love myself, and I just can't seem to do that right now.

Love,

Jules

I called her Jules. My Jules. That was my nickname for her.

I shoved the note with the ring attached in my pocket, felt the whiskey on my breath.

What had once been, I'd thought, a love story for the books somehow became a sad, misunderstood relationship that didn't survive.

And a daughter.

I wanted to throw up.

I'd never been a father. But I figured I could be, not by my biological father's standards, but James's. He'd taught me how to be a good father. To love unconditionally. To be there through all the shit and all the death—*you never leave your family.*

I have a fucking daughter.

I felt the anger build. I wanted it to go away, but it wouldn't.

"Lou." I took out my wallet, threw down a hundred-dollar bill.

"You walking home, boss?"

"Yeah, yeah." I blew him off and left the dark bar into the sunlight.

I slid my sunglasses on, pulled down my hat. I didn't want fans. I didn't want sunshine. I didn't want any of it.

Made my way home, and the world felt a little lighter. The booze I knew.

When I returned to our place again, Julie wouldn't be there. Her things would be gone, her scent still there, I was sure. The memories stored inside me forever. The place with four walls that held our love, our happiness for a long time now only held pictures and evidence of two people who'd once thought that love would win.

I should call Candida back. I'd hung up on her after all.

I should call her back and demand to see my daughter.

Does Fiona have my eyes?

My nose?

Does she look like me?

Does she like me?

Does she think I abandoned her?

What has her mother told her?

The weight of the world was too heavy.

The sunroom was the place Julie and I had liked to make love in during the early morning hours. Make love until the sun rose. Held each other until we felt satisfied.

There wasn't much gone from our place.

Her clothes. Her jewelry box. The things on her nightstand. The picture of us at the bar she'd worked at the night we first met.

Everything was the same, and yet everything was different. How could one place that had brought us so much happiness now feel like an ache in my body and create this feeling in my heart that I just wanted to go away?

I pulled my fist back and crashed it into the wall, making myself bleed.

I slid down to the floor, to a puddle, and just lay there until the darkness ate me alive.

I woke up in an awkward position on the floor. It was dark outside. My head ached, and my body needed water or booze. Water would sober me up; booze wouldn't cure anything, except the way I felt and that wouldn't last forever. I peeled myself from the floor and staggered into the kitchen. Grabbed a glass from the cupboard—glasses we'd gotten from our wedding. I filled it with tap water. I drank it down. Filled it up again. Drank it down.

Groggy and tired, I didn't want to go into our bedroom, the master suite, so instead, I stripped down to my boxers, grabbed a blanket from the linen closet—the blanket Julie had made when we moved in—and went back to sleep on the couch in the living room.

Julie had designed and decorated our home. She was good at it. After we'd started dating and things were serious, I'd told her she didn't have to work anymore if she didn't want to. But Julie wasn't the type to not have a job and not be able to take care of herself. So, it wasn't until after we got married that she stopped bartending. She opened up her own home-designing company with money she'd saved. She said she didn't want a dime of mine. I saved a lot of money over the years. I, we, just didn't need much. I donated a lot. We donated a lot. Still, the show had made a killing, and I'd continued to collect.

Money couldn't buy happiness.

I lay on my back on the couch.

I could invest in Fiona's college. I could buy her a car. I could buy her whatever she wanted. Whatever her little heart desired. But it wouldn't give us the seven years we'd lost together. Unmade memories. The first time she had ridden her bike. Learned to tie her shoes. The first day of kindergarten.

Fuck.

The anger built again.

I wanted to yell at Candida. Scream at her for not allowing me to be part of Fiona's life.

My dad always said, "Everything happens when it's supposed to happen, Luke. You're right where you need to be."

I pulled my BlackBerry from my pocket. I should call Candida back, but instead, I called my dad.

"Hey, son. How are you?"

"Not … not so good, Dad. Can we talk?"

"Always."

I wanted to be my father. I wanted to be the man he was to his wife, his daughter, and me.

CHAPTER 32

2014

We cross over the state line from Oklahoma into Louisiana. Luke's got one hand on the wheel, and his other hand in a fist where he's casually resting his head as his arm sits on the windowsill. He looks over at me.

"What?" I ask.

He has something to say, but I can tell he's perplexed about it.

"I need to tell you something, and I'm just not sure how to tell you. I should have said something sooner. Things just happened so fast between us that I didn't know when and how to tell you."

Don McLean's "American Pie" plays over the radio.

"Luke, I'm not sure there's anything you can tell me that would make me run for my life. Except bodies in the trunk. That might be a game changer." I smile at him.

Luke laughs. "Wouldn't that be a media shitstorm?"

McLean hits the part in the song where it starts to slow. The calm before the storm.

"I have a daughter named Fiona."

Except for Don and the light AC that blows in my face, making my throat extremely dry, nothing sounds.

"She just turned twenty. I, uh, got a call from her mother when she was seven. Said I had a daughter. I hung up on her, too ashamed, and not in a good place to face news like this so I sat on the news for months.

"What had kept coming to my head was, *Be the father you had.* I called my dad and asked for his advice. I wondered if Fiona looked like me. If she had any of my characteristics. My dad said it was in me to be a good dad; I didn't believe it at the time. All he said was, 'Make the call.' " Luke pauses and adjusts his hand on the steering wheel. "So, I did."

"And?" I look at Luke as I see the spark coming from his eyes, the love for his daughter.

"I made the trip out to Louisiana." Luke is quiet for a moment and then says, "You asked if I believed in God, and I wasn't sure how to tell you this, but when I looked into my daughter's eyes on that first trip out to Louisiana, her big, beautiful seven-year-old brown eyes, I knew I'd seen the eyes of God. She not only had my eyes, but also my mouth, my forehead. She had everything in me that I'd ever wanted to give a child."

As I watch Luke talk about a love that is so pure and so untainted by the world and pieced together by fate, I think that maybe my heart is capable of the same.

"So, I need to tell Fiona about the cancer, and I'm not sure how to do it."

Mother lied to us about things to keep our hearts protected. I think she told us to lie to Father to keep our bodies protected. Her motives were pure in nature, but she made the softer choices, the easier ones.

"You tell her the truth," I whisper to Luke for Fiona. "You tell her the hard stuff, so she'll know how strong you are. You tell her what's going on because she'll love you for it later."

"American Pie" comes to an end.

Luke's head falls in my direction, but he doesn't say anything. Looks back to the road. "I remember when Fiona was eight, and wanted to learn how to roller skate. I got to teach her how to do that. She'd fallen and scraped up her knee, so I took her inside of the house I'd been renting for the week, got her fixed up. Some milk, cookies, and she was all better.

"When she was thirteen, Cannon Davis broke her heart, so I took her to my parents' house in Kentucky, and I told her that Cannon Davis wasn't worth her brains or her beauty, that one day she'd look back on this situation and laugh about it." He pauses. "We did."

Luke shakes his head. "I can't fix this one, Cat. It's going to break her heart, and I can't do anything about it. And I might not live long enough to pick up the pieces."

The sun is setting, and I watch as it creeps below the horizon. "Grief is inevitable. Losing a father isn't." I slide my hand over and cup the back of his neck, feel his skin beneath my hand. "But you can tell her about all the qualities that make her strong. That it's okay to be sad. And it's okay to cry." I pause. "Let her see you laugh. She'll hang on to that memory, Luke, for a lifetime."

I make sure my voice is level before I say this because I feel the heartache building. "After you go, Luke, if she'll have me, I'll be there for her," I offer, unsure of how I can be that person but I feel as though it's what I need to do—not for me, but for Fiona and Luke. Maybe to help keep Luke alive in memory. "There aren't any promises that life is easy, but I know it's just worth it. All the good, all the heartache, all of it."

Luke smiles. "You went to prison for the better half of your twenties, for something you didn't do, to protect your mother. And you sit here and tell me that all of it is worth it."

He gently brushes his hand against my cheek, and I fall into it.

"You taught me that."

Luke gives me a sideways glance that just about makes me come unglued. "You amaze me, Catherine Clemens."

"I could say the same for you, Luke McCay."

We drive, and let "How Deep Is Your Love" by the Bee Gees take us down the highway and let try to leave behind what stands in our way of growing into better people.

Luke knocks on the door of a two-story French-style home in Bastrop, Louisiana. Luke called Candida and told her we were on our way.

I'm staying in the car for several reasons. One, it's not my story. Two, it's not my place. And three, a daughter needs time with her father.

So much for the story I'm writing. I smile and think about Mr. Jenkins. I'll reimburse him for the money he paid me.

I'm going to sell the house in Beverly Hills that I don't need. That Ingrid doesn't need. That Mother doesn't need.

Fiona comes to the door, and she's just as beautiful as Luke. Milk-chocolate brown skin, same exact eyes as his when she smiles, the same forehead. Dark brown hair with tight curls that go on for days. My heart swells, and my eyes grow full of tears when I see Fiona's reaction to her father. I can't hear what they're saying, but when she throws her arms around her father, I can read that language.

She looks surprised that he's here and excited.

Luke holds out his hand, and Fiona takes his. They slowly walk down the walkway, laughing, their smiles big and bright, mirroring each other like a looking glass. And I continue to watch until they disappear.

I think healing starts when truth is given. As much as I loved Father, I knew I couldn't help him unless he was willing to help himself. And when he died, I cried.

I cried for us. I cried for our family. I cried for myself. I cried tears of gratitude that Mother wouldn't have to feel afraid anymore. I cried.

But on this day, as I see Luke and Fiona make their way down Spruce Street, I know the healing will begin the same time the sadness begins.

And when Luke is gone and all that remains are the memories, we'll remember them, feel through them, and tuck them into our hearts for another day.

I pull out my phone and try to collect the reality around me. I call Eddie McGavin, my old attorney.

"Catherine?"

"Hi, Eddie."

"Well, I'll be! How are you doing? How's your mom doing?"

"We're all okay. But I want to talk about the house. I want to sell it."

This is met with complete silence.

"Are-are you sure about this, Cat?"

"Yes."

"All right then. I'll take care of all of it. Get in touch with a good friend in real estate."

He knows that when I make a decision, I stick to it, and seeing as though I'm the only one who can communicate that, I'll be the one to make the decision. It will help pay for Mother's care. It will help me let go of the memories I'd rather not remember. Besides, Ingrid said it was time to let go. Why it's taken me so long to come to terms with this, I'm not sure.

I come back to the phone conversation, and Eddie is rattling on about the real estate guy and stops with a sigh. "Don't worry, Cat; I'll take care of it. I'll call you when I need to."

"Thank you, Eddie," I say.

Eddie has been around since Ingrid and I were little. My father met him on the golf course. One thing Father did well was pick good friends.

"Take care of yourself, Catherine."

"You, too, Eddie."

"I'll be in touch."

We hang up just as Luke and Fiona are slowly making their way back.

Fiona isn't crying.

But I see her holding her father's hand, walking in step with him, and I wonder how many times they've taken this walk together. How many times he's helped fix her heart, but more importantly, how many times she's helped him fix his.

Luke looks in the car and motions to me.

My heart starts to pound. I have to get out and meet her, but my body doesn't move. It stays still, and I will my legs to move, but they won't.

I hear Ingrid's voice. *Go be the person we needed as kids.*

She's twenty, I try to argue.

And look what you still needed at twenty.

Without another thought, I open the car door, get out, and walk to Fiona and Luke.

Fiona is even more beautiful up close.

Luke reaches for my hand. "Honey, this is Catherine, my girlfriend."

Fiona's head tilts to the right, and her eyes narrow. She looks back to her father and then back to me.

"Daddy's never introduced me to a girlfriend before," Fiona says as she reaches for my hand.

I take hers in both of mine, feel the warmth of it. "It's so nice to meet you, Fiona."

"You as well."

Our hands linger for a moment as Fiona looks back at her father.

"Fiona is going to meet us in New York when we get there."

"Wonderful," I say.

"Told her we were on a road trip, and Bastrop had to be a stop along the way to see my girl," Luke says, pulling his daughter in and kissing her on the forehead.

"Call me when you get there, Daddy."

Fiona starts to walk back toward the house, and she gently touches my shoulder. "It was really nice to meet you, Catherine." Her words are like a fine wine as they flow in and out of her mouth so smoothly.

Fiona walks to the door, and we stand here and watch her. Luke puts his arm around me and pulls me in as we turn and walk back toward the car.

"How'd it go?" I ask.

"I didn't tell her." His voice breaks. "I couldn't."

I've never put Luke up on a pedestal. It isn't right for anyone to be there, with the exception, maybe, of Molly Ringwald. Because, inevitably, they will fall from grace. Eventually. Something happens. Something is done, or something is said. Luke is no different.

We're somewhere between Arkansas and Mississippi when I ask him why. It's the question that has been lingering in the back of my mind.

"Ain't No Mountain High Enough" plays. Not loud but loud enough to hear the angst when Diana Ross throws it. Plus, you just feel it.

Music is healing. It allows me to think. For my mind to wander against the lyrics, sit in them, let them sink into my skin until I can understand what the songwriter was feeling when they wrote the lyrics.

"Why didn't you tell her?"

Again, a long silence.

"She started talking about college, Dartmouth. She was accepted for spring. It's the college she's dreamed about since she was a little girl. Her eyes were so bright, Cat. I couldn't bring myself to ruin that moment for her. I just want my little girl to have these pockets of happiness. That is what I live for."

I understand where Luke is coming from.

Every time Father apologized to Mother, I'd see the hope in her eyes, that it would somehow get better. Somehow, a magical potion or elixir or a miracle drug would fix Father, and the hope in Mother's eyes would give Ingrid and me hope. Somehow, I would trick myself into believing that everything would be okay. Ingrid would ask me if things were going to be all right, and I would say, "Yes, probably." Every single time. And every single time, we both bought it—until we couldn't anymore.

So, I understand why Luke couldn't tell Fiona because it is the same reason we couldn't tell Mother that Father wouldn't get better. It's a devastating truth to know our mind can be stronger than our heart.

"What's your plan?" I ask.

"I don't know."

"Brass In Pocket" by The Pretenders starts to play.

Luke begins to cough.

"Pull over," I tell him. Rub his back, grab a few paper towels from the roll we stashed underneath the seat.

Luke pulls over.

I hand them to him. I take in our surroundings, and it's just past four in the afternoon.

I reach down and get the trash bag ready. Gently, I take the bloodied paper towels and hand him two fresh ones as the rasp in his cough gets worse.

It looks like it feels awful now.

I feel the strain in his face and his body every time he heaves forward.

Sometimes, he gags, and I want to take it all away for him.

If I could take his spot, I would. He's got a daughter who will need him one day when she walks down the aisle. She'll need him to fix the leak in the sink when her partner is out of town or when she needs help with the baby. Fiona will need her father. And all that will be left is his memory.

I exchange the paper towels once more, and the coughing fit slowly ceases.

I hand him a bottle of water and tell him I'm driving.

Luke doesn't argue, doesn't counter with a rebuttal. He simply gets out of the driver's seat. He knows as well as I do that he can't drive.

While Luke gets into the passenger seat, I get in the driver's seat.

He's tired. I see it in his eyes. Looks like he's lost weight.

"Are you ready?" My best attempt to live in the present.

"Ready when you are." He wipes his mouth one last time. Takes in a few deep breaths. "We'll pull over in a few hours and stay in New Albany."

I hit the blinker and ease on the gas pedal as we get back on the highway.

"You look familiar," Clara, the front desk person at Miss Sarah's Inn, drawls. She looks to be about my age, maybe a little younger.

I wonder if Luke ever gets tired of this whole song and dance. Never once does he roll his eyes or lose his patience. He gives the smile that tips up to the right, the one I love, shrugs, and tries to play it off. But ninety percent of the time, the other person catches on.

"Oh, my good word." Clara covers her mouth when she sees the name on the card. "Are you really him?" Clara hands Luke's card back.

I whisper into Luke's ear, "I'm going to go clean out the car while she fangirls. Remember, I'm the one who gets to make love to you tonight. Don't let this shit go to your head."

Luke looks breathless at me. Then, he says, "That's hot."

I briefly kiss him on the cheek and walk back outside to the car.

I'm finishing up when Luke walks out. I notice in the sunlight that his eyes look tired. I see the dark circles beginning to form under his eyes.

I'll do the driving from now on, I say to myself.

We get into the car, drive to room four, and park the car.

"Cute place," I say.

"Yeah," Luke agrees as we get out of the car and grab our bags.

The room is cute with a sitting room and a king-size bed. All the amenities.

But before I can set down my bag, Luke comes to me, slides his hands around my waist, kisses me gently at first and then with need.

Immediately, my body responds.

"Shower with me," he commands as he pulls away and gazes into my eyes.

Without another thought, I slip off my sundress and stand in front of him in my bra and panties.

He doesn't break eye contact as he reaches behind me and unhooks my bra, allowing it to fall to the floor. Luke looks down at my body and drinks me in, gently running his hands over my breasts, watching me as he does it.

And I can't help what my body does every time he touches me.

The ache between my legs starts.

My body breaks into the chills.

And my breathing becomes labored.

He slides his finger in through the side of my panties and checks to see if I'm wet.

I pull him to me tightly as he pushes against my middle, and I almost scream it feels so good.

I feel him harden against my stomach, and then he pulls his finger from my panties, pulls away only for a moment, and slides off his shorts and T-shirt.

"Shower, Ms. Clemens," he whispers as he pulls me near again, and we saunter to the bathroom, his hard body against my backside.

We make our way to the shower, his lips trailing up and down my neck. His hands full with my breasts.

Somehow, Luke turns on the shower, and we get in.

He's holding me from the front now, and I am staring at his brown eyes with the flecks of green. I wonder how long I'll get this beautiful sight. I take my fingertips and guide them down his face. The hot water hitting his back.

I trace the wake of his smile, starting at his forehead—the three lines that are permanently there—dropping my finger down his nose and then back out to his eye, the crow's-feet that stay, and falling down to his lips.

The lips I've kissed.

The lips that have kissed me places that make me blush.

I kiss them sensually and pull back. "I wish we could stay like this forever, Luke."

"Promise me something."

I smile, still looking at his eyes. He knows I'll make the promise, no matter what it is.

"When you look back on this moment after I'm gone, you'll remember this and not what it will be like in the end."

"How? I won't be here for the end. You're on your own at that point," I whisper.

But he knows I'm kidding. I feel the tears start to fill my eyes.

I brush my lips against his. "I want to remember everything," I say. "I want to remember your beauty, your sadness, the highs and the lows because I refuse to waste any memories."

He takes himself in his hand and puts it to my opening. He pushes inside me, and I take all of him in.

My arms tighten around him, and he squeezes his grip on my waist.

With each of his thrusts, I watch him just as he watches me, and I wonder if two people can feel the exact same thing at the exact same moment without an exchange of breath or words or kisses.

We take each other in and make unspoken promises. I feel them in my heart.

Until death do us part.

We push against each other.

This love will never end.

We pull against each other.

No matter how much time has passed, I want to remember Luke in this way. Giving me love and showing it through his eyes.

I tighten around him.

His eyes close as he pushes inside me again.

"Again," I say with need, the water falling all around us now because we've somehow moved.

I begin to feel light-headed and know that I'm close to letting it all go. "Luke, I'm not sure I can hang on much longer."

"Oh, God, why do you do this to me?" He nips at my neck and says, "Go first. I need to watch you."

He takes a few steps toward the back of the shower and lets my backside rest against the shower wall. Then, he pumps into me. I watch what his body does to mine. I see how we fit together so seamlessly, so effortlessly, and that's how I know this is forever.

My body feels it coming on as I grow weak, and I begin to peak.

Luke watches me intently.

And the feeling gets to be too much. I unhinge just as Luke does.

It takes us a minute to come down. His body is against mine, and he's shaking.

"Are you okay?" I ask, trying to find my breath.

"Yes. Are you?" he asks.

"Yeah."

He pulls out of me and begins to wash my body with just a bar of soap. Over my neck, shoulders, chest, breasts, stomach, my back, between my thighs, and I'm free. He washes my hair with ease and a sense of tenderness I've never found in another man before.

I return the favor, but when I get to his stomach, his abdomen, I lean down and kiss both sides where his lungs are. I wish I could will them to be better. Instead, I silently pray that he'll be okay. And that it will be a miracle. That he'll be cured. And then we'll be able to live out our lives somewhere, as long as we're together. And that Fiona will still have her father, and he'll be able to walk her down the aisle when she finds the love of her life.

When I stand and look back at Luke, with his thumb, he wipes my cheeks and frees them from their sadness.

"I know you want a different outcome, Catherine. I do, too. But the sooner we can accept this, the sooner we can live. The easy part is on my end, I know. Because the thought of losing you—" Luke stops. Looks down at my lips and back to my eyes. "I'm not so sure I'd be able to make it through."

"Yes, you would," I say and kiss his lips.

We all have that one fear in our lives that we keep in the back of our minds. All of us. Every single one of us. Whether we talk about it or not, it's there, waiting to be acknowledged. I didn't know my biggest loss until I met Luke. And now, here I am, walking through it with him.

But I ask myself the more important question: *Will he be able to let go when it is time?*

Tennessee really is a beautiful state. It reminds me a lot of Myers Flat in Northern California. The leaves are beginning to turn with their burnt-orange vibrancy and their reds.

Fall is my favorite time of year.

Mountains, streams, lakes, and sunsets seem to be the focal point here. I could live here. The nip in the air isn't quite here yet, but the feeling of fall has arrived.

"Let It Be" by The Beatles is playing through the car speakers. Maybe it's the trees and the air and the color of the leaves and Luke, but a feeling of complete contentment comes over me. I can breathe deeper, my mind is clearer, and all I want to do is live this one life I've been given right now. In the moment.

I look over at Luke in the passenger side. I've been driving since Mississippi. He's asleep, and he looks just like a little boy who's dreaming sweet dreams, whose biggest worry is whether or not to play with the boat or the truck today. Whose excitement isn't money or the right address or the best car or the right image; it's whether or not he gets another day of living.

I try to pretend Luke isn't sleeping, that his heart no longer beats, that he no longer needs air, that his soul has left his body. I do this maybe to soften the blow when his time, our time, has run out. Maybe to help ease my heart. But my throat tightens and my chest begins to ache and my head doesn't allow for my heart to feel. He looks too peaceful, okay with the world and his life and what's happened.

When we're ready to be called home, it won't matter how much money we had, what house we lived in, what car we drove, what image we had. It will come down to one question: did we right our wrongs? When it comes down to the end, were we good people?

It hits me like bricks.

Is that what Luke's doing? Righting his wrongs? The white envelopes. The stops to family and friends. Maybe he isn't telling them he's dying but making sure he's righted things he did in the past.

Luke stirs. Slowly, his eyes flutter open, and I'm grateful I'll get to tuck this memory under my hat and remember it when his eyes no longer open. I watch as his body and brain come alive.

He looks over at me and smiles. "Must have dozed off," he says, his voice raspy—maybe from sleep, but maybe from the cancer and I'm too afraid to ask which.

"A state ago. We're in Tennessee now," I say and smile, my hands on the wheel.

I want Luke to take good memories with him when he goes. Though I'm not sure he'll need them where he's going, I want to give them to him anyway, just in case.

"Where exactly are we?" He looks out the window.

"You said Nashville, right? We need to go to Nashville?"

"Yeah, yeah, that's right." Luke sits up, adjusts himself in the seat.

"We're in Dickson. And according to my iPhone, we have about forty-eight more minutes."

"Holy shit, I did sleep a long time."

"You need the sleep, Luke."

A song I'm unfamiliar with comes over the radio.

"Where do you think you would be if the show hadn't happened?"

Luke laughs, shrugs. "I guess I'd be in the same spot." Luke looks out the window and takes in the scenery. "If you take away all the money, the notoriety, the fame, all that shit, I'd still have terminal cancer. I guess, what's the hardest in all this is leaving Fiona. You always need your dad. Right?" His head shoots back to me. "I didn't mean it like that."

I smile. "Yes, you did, and it's all right. I think you're right in most cases. I need pieces of my father. The good pieces. The two percent of who he was. I could do without the remaining ninety-eight percent."

I see the worry in Luke.

"She's going to be all right, Luke. She will be okay eventually."

"And then there's you," he whispers. "I never expected to fall in love with you, Cat. This … this wasn't on the agenda or my timeline." He laughs. "But sometimes, the unexpected happens at the moment we need it most." He looks at me.

"What are we doing on this trip, Luke? What's the point of it all?"

"Trying to clear away some wreckage of my past." He's quiet for a moment. "Sometimes, we get second chances, but I can't miss this. When my sister died, I didn't get to tell her things that I wanted to. I think she felt the same way." He bites his lower lip. "Life can get cut short, and we might never be able to tell the ones we love most how we feel, you know?"

Yeah, I do know.

"What do you wish you had said to your dad, Cat?"

I take in a deep breath and let it out. "I …" I start but stop. Think on it. "I wish I had told him that I was terrified of him. That he scared me. And that I was tired of him hurting our mother. That my heart was broken for him and for my mother and for Ingrid and me. I wish we could have been the family that my mother and father had painted us to be, but we just couldn't."

A long minute passes, and we don't say anything. My mind wanders to private moments with my family where things could have worked out so differently. When Mother didn't have to ask us to lie and Father could just be present and in the moment without a reason to bring the hydrangeas. And all the times Father could have held his tongue instead of berating Mother.

"What would you have said to your sister?" I ask.

"I would have told her that I should have said yes when she wanted me to play school or Barbies. I wish I could have protected her when kids teased her for being bald. Kids are assholes," he sighs. "I wish my sister hadn't seen Benny and me beat one of her ex-boyfriends to a bloody pulp when he told everyone he'd gotten her pregnant and bragged about it. He'd never gotten her pregnant and Ella swore they never had sex."

I can't picture Luke or Benny doing this. But people make decisions, unimaginable decisions, based on emotion, a reaction, and without thinking. I wonder if the driver in the car that hit Benny that night had made a conscience decision to drink and drive. I wonder if Father attempted to make right what he'd done wrong the night before, only to end up in the same spot he'd been previous nights.

If the goodness in this world were done with bigger intentions, I wonder how much better the world would be.

Luke doesn't want to talk about this anymore because I see him pull out his phone and tell me to take the next exit off the freeway into downtown Nashville.

"Who are we going to see in Nashville?"

"Kane."

"Kane who?"

"Kane Voss."

I slowly turn my head in Luke's direction. Look back to the road and then back again to Luke. "As in Kane Voss and the Strikers?" I focus on the road.

"That's the guy."

They're one of the biggest bands in country music right now and cleaned house at the CMA Awards last year.

"We'll check in to our hotel and get showered and then meet him at dinner, if that works for you?" he asks.

"I'll check my schedule," I say, smile, side-eye him.

I decide I will miss Luke's lips the most. So, I capture this moment, memorize it, and tuck it into my heart and hold it there.

I was used to posh places, growing up. It wasn't like I took advantage; I noticed everything. I noticed the crystal wineglasses in our hotel rooms as children. The large, grandiose beds that we laid our heads on at night when we traveled. The music that played in the lobby just sounded more expensive, more educated, more sophisticated. The places we stayed when we went overseas, how we were treated like royalty, making me feel uncomfortable in my own skin. When people asked to take our bags or fetch us breakfast or lunch and served us dinner, I wanted to help, not be at the receiving end.

And prison felt better. Prison felt better because I didn't have to walk on eggshells anymore. I knew where I stood in life, and my responsibility to my family and the world was serving my sentence. Somehow, I just felt safer in prison than I had throughout my childhood—maybe because I hadn't been free at all. I had been tied to a family whose secrets kept us bonded to ourselves. Chained.

But in prison, I no longer had to live the lies. I no longer had to live without knowing what to expect from day to day, night to night. I knew where I stood and learned the expectations, and if I followed the expectations, I'd be all right.

This place that Luke has booked for us reminds me of those places I stayed at as a child—the marble floors, the elegant mahogany four-poster bed, the crystal water pitcher and wineglasses, and the most amazing view I've seen since Al and Gene's overlook in Abilene.

A wall of windows overlooks the night skyline of Nashville. The different shades of white, orange, yellow. The colorful reflection on the Cumberland River.

This place is magnificent not because of what surrounds me, but because I am finally free. I am free from my childhood and its uncertainties. I am free from the walls that kept me confined—albeit safe, but confined—and for the first time in my life, even with Luke's cancer, I am able to be free in this moment.

I feel his hands gently slide around my waist.

Luke had arranged for several dresses to be sent up to our room for me to try on. Until I was blue in the face, I told him that I'd like to reimburse him for the lacy yet somewhat conservative black dress I'd chosen.

He laughed.

We showered together.

Made love twice.

I listened to his heartbeat just because I could, and we got ready for dinner with Kane.

"What are you thinking about?" Luke asks.

"How free I feel in this moment."

I feel his lips smile against my neck. He kisses me lightly, sending chills up my spine.

"Do that again, Mr. McCay. I'm not sure we'll make it to dinner."

There will come a day where Luke and I won't be able to make love anymore. Where his body will be too weak, where his organs will slowly shut down and stop working. Where his breathing will become labored and slower. And then his heart will eventually stop beating.

But not tonight, I tell myself as I push the sadness that constricts my throat. *We have tonight. Tomorrow isn't a promise.*

"Marry me, Cat."

My mouth falls open, and I slowly turn to face him. "What?" My voice is broken, my tone wavering on disbelief, and love and sadness—because I know in my heart all we have is today even though I want so badly to live out the rest of our tomorrows until we're old and gray.

"Marry me." His voice is strong as if sickness weren't there.

He towers over me and lightly cups my jaw in his hand. I lean into it and close my eyes.

Luke continues, "It's the way you chew on your lip when you're in thought. It's the way your head moves when James Taylor comes on the radio. It's when it's quiet around us, and you look at me in wonder. It's the way you took Fiona in your hands. The look on your face when you saw her was like witnessing active beauty, not because of your admiration of the way she looked, but because you could see her heart, because you know mine, because you own mine." Luke puts his other hand on my other cheek. "I've longed for you, even when I didn't know you were the person I needed in this life. But now, having met you, having felt you, my only regret is not having more time with you."

"We're given what we need when we need it," I whisper because I believe this in my bones. I need Luke to teach me how real love works and how to deal with grief when it comes.

Luke smiles and kisses the tip of my nose. "You still haven't answered my question. Will you marry me, Catherine Clemens?"

"Yes." My answer is rushed and hurried, and it doesn't sound like I want it to, so I say, "I would love to be your wife, Luke."

"I'm really glad you said that because"—he reaches into his pocket and pulls out a bright blue box and he gets down on one knee—"I will spend the rest of my life loving you the way you deserve to be loved. Give you everything I have in my heart. Keep you safe. Battle whatever comes our way, and

I will continue to fight until I can't anymore. Will you make me the happiest man alive and marry me, Catherine Clemens?"

Luke pulls open the box, and all I see is light. Light and rainbows from all different directions.

"I will."

Luke stands, takes the ring from the box, and places it on my left ring finger. I don't look down at the ring. I just pull his mouth to mine and kiss him as if it were our last kiss. I will him to feel the overwhelming sensation I have in my body right now. One of his hands slides around my waist, and the other goes underneath my long hair where he holds my head.

We break for a moment and stare at each other.

Smile.

Laugh.

Kiss again.

"I love you, guy number seven," I say to Luke as my hand slides down to his, and we make our way to the door to go to dinner with a guitar player who's magical on strings. "You know I'm only marrying you because of who you know, right?"

Luke laughs. "If that were the case, I would have asked you to marry me when you came to my house in Carpinteria or the night we'd slept together all those years ago."

"I wish you had," I say as Luke holds our hotel door open for me.

"Catherine, it's nice to meet you," Kane says, holding his tie close to his body as he sits down in his chair.

"Kane, you're killing me. I'm really trying to hang on to this woman"—Luke gazes at me—"and your Southern drawl isn't helping me any."

Luke and Kane laugh.

"Did Luke tell you how we met, Catherine?" he asks.

"I'm afraid to say, Kane, that he just told me today that we'd be going to dinner with you."

"Ah, well, we met in LA—at the beach, of all places. I was strumming on my old Gibson. Who would have thought this guy could kill it on the guitar? He told me I was playing the note wrong. I told him to eat shit and die."

We laugh.

"He offered guitar lessons if I could show him how to surf. Played a lot. Did some gigs together. God, we were young. And dumb." Kane shakes his head.

Luke stares at his friend across the table.

"Then, he takes on this big-ass role as Dylan Klein. All shit breaks loose, and he disappears for years. Then—get this—one day, while I was still struggling to make it in the music industry, I get this Gibson Hummingbird fucking delivered to Tommy Page's, a guy whose couch I was sleeping on at the time. The delivery guy walks up to the door, and I answer it because I'm the only one home. Because I play gigs at night, right? My hair is a mess. I'm tired. Probably a little hungover. The guy says, 'You Kane Voss?' I'm like, 'Yeah,' thinkin', *What the hell does this guy want?* He hands me a long package with a note that says, *From Chicken Legs*."

Kane beams at Luke, and Luke sets down his water glass.

"That's what made my career."

Luke shakes his head. "You made your career, not the guitar."

"No, I mean, out of all the shit this career has given me—the awards, the people I've met—nothing tops that day, man. Nothing. I'd felt invisible. And that somebody was willing to spend that kind of money on me, it meant they believed in me."

The waiter approaches our table, and you can tell he's a bit out of his element—nervous and excited, all at the same time.

"Miss, may I get you something to drink?"

"Water, please. Thank you."

"Mr. Voss, and, Mr. McCay?"

"Just water," they both say in unison.

The waiter scribbles it down on his handheld electronic device—a way to take orders, I suppose. "I'll be back with your waters."

By the end of dinner, I've laughed so hard that my cheeks hurt. Kane is an amazing storyteller and hysterical. And he and Luke together are just as magical. I can see why they gravitated toward each other. How, in Los Angeles, out of the four million people who live there, Kane and Luke found each other.

Luke bites on his lip and grabs the white envelope out of his back pocket.

"What's this?" Kane asks, setting his water glass down on the table.

Luke shrugs. "A parting gift."

Kane puts his elbows down on the table. "You mean to tell me, you came all this way to break up with me?" A smirk begins to form on Kane's face.

Luke rolls his eyes and sits back in his chair, crossing his arms. "I traveled all this way for a lot of people. Don't feel that important."

We all laugh, and then it's quiet.

"What's in the envelope, Luke?" he asks. Kane picks it up. Smells it to be funny. Runs his fingers along the sides. Sets it back down on the table.

Kane's cell phone starts to sound from his back pocket. He pulls it out to look at the screen. "Sorry, I need to take this real quick."

He answers, and all he says is, "Mikey." He listens. Rolls his eyes. "Again? Yeah. Yeah. Leaving here now."

Kane hangs up. "Skipper, our drummer, is going through a breakup. Apparently, he took a bottle of Crown from a liquor store, and no one can find him." Drops his head. "The media is going to have a field day with this one. Anyhow, I'm real sorry, but I have to cut this short to go find the little fucker." Kane stands and shoves the white envelope in the back pocket of his jeans.

We stand.

Kane comes over, and we hug. Quietly, he says, "Take care of this guy. He's a keeper, okay?"

"Yeah, I will."

I wish I could take care of him forever. My stomach turns into knots. We've joked and laughed and exchanged stories as if Luke were no different than a healthy man walking down the street. As though he didn't cough up blood on a daily basis and he hadn't been told that the cancer would take his life.

Kane walks to Luke, and I see Luke's genuine, big white smile again. They both laugh about something and embrace.

I wonder if Kane knows this will probably be the last time he embraces Luke. I wonder if that white envelope that Kane has in his back pocket will tell him what he needs to hear after he's gone. I wonder if Kane will look back on this moment and wish he had hugged longer, stayed longer, and forgotten about Skipper the drummer.

Luke feels good enough to drive back to our hotel. On our way up to our room, Luke starts to cough. There's more blood this time. I take off my light sweater that Luke bought with the dress and put it over his mouth to catch the fallout.

His hands have blood.

He takes a sharp right into the bathroom and shuts the door behind him.

He coughs so hard that I hear him throw up.

Again.

And again.

And again.

And again.

I know he wants his privacy. I know this is hard for him.

My stomach turns, and I, too, want to throw up. But I also want to be in there with him.

"Luke," I whisper. "Please let me in." I slide down the wall on the other side of the door. "Let me help."

The bathroom is silent. I hear the toilet flush.

"Luke," I say again, louder. "I need to be in there with you. Please, let me in."

A click sounds on the other side of the door, and I scramble to my feet and walk into the bathroom. Luke has his head between his knees, his hair wet from sweat.

I get down on the floor next to him. Pull his head to my chest and hold him. My sweater is balled up on his face. His body feels tired and heavy.

I stroke his hair and collect memories. Even the bad ones will do. What his head feels like against my chest. What he smells like. His breath against my skin.

We don't say a word.

I hold him, and he holds me up.

"Would you like to get in bed, Luke?"

He says something, but I can't understand it. It's muffled and soft. But he gets to his feet and reaches down to help me.

Darks circles have already formed underneath his eyes, and he looks exhausted. It's the first time I think a hospital might be a better idea. I take his hand and lead him to our bed. I take off his clothes and put him to bed.

"You feel warm, Luke. Should we go to the hospital?"

"No hospitals, Cat. I won't go. Not yet. We still have six states left. When we get to New York, then I'll go if you think we need to." His voice is weak, tired.

I nod and kiss the side of his head.

I go to retrieve water to put by his bedside. I fill the glass in the bathroom and stare back at the woman in the mirror.

This woman isn't the same woman I've known for the past thirty-four years. She's different. She's more. She's more whole than she was two years ago. Love is stained in her cheeks, in her heart. Her eyes are somehow brighter, more alive, and more forgiving. She carries the weight of her world on her shoulders armor, taking the jabs, the swing of life. And the grief that sits behind her eyes is only visible when she allows it to be. But tonight, she's not hiding anything. She takes down her hair, steps out of her dress, and stares at herself, the woman she's proud of becoming.

A new skin.

She realizes her greatest heartaches, her greatest failures have become her greatest assets.

She no longer has to live bound to herself.

She can be vulnerable.

She can be who she is, and she is okay with that.

She has the strength to withstand anything.

She can feel through it all and come out on the other side even if her heart still aches.

She is me.

I begin to cry, leaning over the counter, covering my mouth to hide the sobs. Heartache is the price we pay for love. Real love. The kind of love that's beautiful and broken and stained with memories that give two things: clarity and grace. Clarity, because it allows me to see things for what they are, even when they're hard. And grace, falling on the toes of clarity, we're reminded that we are imperfect and so are others.

I peek in the other room, and Luke is sleeping.

I cry quietly, tears spilling uncontrollably from my eyes.

In this moment, I'm able to forgive myself for not being there with my family that night. Forgive Father, who didn't deserve grace, but love allows me to give it. People put in our lives for a variety of reasons. I believe I was meant to fall in love with Luke, and it was his journey to leave.

I cover my mouth tightly, so the sobs don't escape. I swallow, pushing them into my throat.

I look back in the mirror to a woman who's crossed over to a new skin, a new strength, and a renewed sense of self. I know it will take my heart time to heal with past traumas, past hurts, and it might not ever heal completely, but I have faith that I'm right where I'm supposed to be—finally.

Dabbing my eyes with tissue, I look back at the woman, and in the mirror, I tell her, "We're going to be okay."

I walk back into the room where Luke is sleeping, set down the glass of water by his bedside, kiss his forehead, and walk to the other side of the bed.

And in my new skin, I crawl in bed next to the man who will always have my heart, no matter how far apart we are.

The farmhouse sits just off town in Bardstown, Kentucky, and I assume it's Beth and James on the porch when we drive up. It's a modest ranch-style home with a wraparound deck and land behind them that you can see for miles.

Luke parks. "Are you ready to meet my mom and dad?"

"Been ready."

Luke nods, and we both get out of the car.

He wanted to drive today, felt strong enough. I've learned with Luke and his cancer that some days are really good days, and it seems like the cancer is gone. He has energy and seems normal.

When James and Beth approach, James throws his arms around his son. The son he didn't create, but the son who chose his dad.

I see the whites of James's fingertips as he squeezes Luke.

"It is so nice to meet you, Catherine," Beth says as she pulls me in for a hug.

I've decided that Midwesterners are far nicer than Californians.

She smells like roses, and I've decided that's the smell of heaven.

"Let's see that ring," Beth says and takes my left hand to admire it. Beth examines the ring. "You've done well, son."

James reaches in to hug me as Beth embraces Luke.

"It's so nice to meet you, Catherine. We've heard a lot about you," James says.

When? I think to myself. *Between Arizona and New Mexico? Texas?*

"I've heard a lot about you, too. I'm glad we could meet."

Beth takes Luke's hand. "Come on; let's go inside. Supper is on the table."

James takes a sip of his lemonade. "Luke tells us you're an ex-con?" James smiles.

Beth looks at James.

James looks at Luke.

They all burst out laughing.

I start to laugh.

James reaches for my hand. "Excuse my sense of humor, Catherine. I think, when we laugh, we begin to heal. Humor is what helped us with Ella, and so I assume everyone needs to laugh." He gives my hand a squeeze and lets go. "You're safe here. And we really enjoy your company."

"Thank you, James."

"Honey, you're about as perfect as a peach." Beth winks. "I can tell by the way you carry yourself."

Luke takes my hand and kisses the top of it. "She sure is."

"Aunt Gene said the visit went really well at their place?" Beth takes a bite of steak, looks at Luke and me.

"Yeah, helped Uncle Al mend some fence. Moved some cattle. Uncle Al has slowed down quite a bit."

"That's what Gene said. Past six months, he's been having some back trouble," James says.

"They think about selling the place?" Luke looks at his mother.

Beth shrugs. "I'm not sure. Guess when you've done something one way for so long and grown accustomed to it, change isn't something you're interested in."

"Gene also said you gave her and Uncle Al a lot of money," Beth says.

"I did. Hope they'll sell the damn place and slow down."

"You going somewhere or something, son?" James asks and takes a bite of his chicken. Chews. Watches Luke.

Do they not know he's sick?

My hands grow sweaty, and my stomach turns into a fit of knots. They lost Ella, and now, they're losing Luke. *Surely, Luke will tell them?*

Luke pulls out a white envelope from his back pocket. This one though is different. It's thicker. Much thicker than the others.

"What's that?" James asks, wiping his mouth with his napkin.

Luke takes a small bite of chicken, and I look down at his plate. He's barely eaten anything.

"Stuff," Luke answers.

James's eyebrows rise, and I think he knows something is up, but I don't think he's prepared for the story.

I reach under the table and gently place my hand on Luke's thigh.

"I made peach cobbler. I'll go grab it," Beth says.

"I'll help," I say and stand and follow Beth to the kitchen.

What I love about Luke's family, no matter what part of the country you're in, the dinner table is always set, and we always gather at the table to eat a meal together. There's always a pitcher of lemonade or iced tea or water. There's always three to four courses for every meal, and there's always dessert.

As Beth grabs the cobbler from the oven, she says, "Honey, will you get the ice cream from the freezer? The vanilla."

I open the freezer and find it full of meat and ice cream of four different flavors.

"James loves his ice cream at night." She shakes her head and smiles as she gets four bowls and four spoons.

I set the vanilla ice cream down next to the scoop that's already on the counter.

She adds the cobbler, and I add the ice cream.

I feel as though I'm carrying a secret. A secret that I wish I didn't know. A secret I wish weren't true.

"Since Luke was just a boy, he's always carried around this sense of needing to take care of others." Beth smiles. Scoops the cobbler.

I listen. Sometimes, I feel like I'm in the right place at the right time just to listen. And I'm not sure how this happens, but I always have a sense of knowing when it does happen.

"He's always felt like he has a sense of responsibility to others," Beth sighs. "I'm not sure where he got it from, but it's magical."

"We learn a lot by watching others," comes out of me, and I surprise myself by my own words.

Beth thinks on it. Smiles. "I suppose."

"And sometimes, they astonish us by what they overcome."

This time, Beth looks at me, cocks her head.

"For the time I've known Luke, I know that he has two amazing parents, and he's extremely proud of both of you. And you both raised an incredible man."

"That boy has a heart of gold. And that didn't come from us. He doesn't have to tell me that he's in love with you because it's quite obvious." She stops talking for a moment. "Good love is worth the argument; great love is worth fighting for."

I scoop the last of the ice cream into the fourth bowl of peach cobbler and stop. Stare back at her.

Mother fought until she couldn't fight for love anymore. Until it came time to protect her children. One of which she couldn't. My childhood and my adult life collide together. My past and my present. What Mother was doing all along. I blink several times, unable to speak.

"Are you all right, Catherine?" Beth asks, touching my elbow.

"Y-yeah. Just … your words hit me."

I take a minute, and Beth sees this.

She switches gears. "Have you met Fiona?"

"Yes. She seems just like her dad."

Beth smiles, nods. "She is." Looks out the kitchen window and then back to me. "I'm not too sure what your prison time was all about, but you don't seem like a lawbreaker." Her eyebrows rise as the corners of her mouth turn upward.

"We learn a lot by watching others," I say again, not wanting to delve into my past or explain myself, and I don't think those were two things on Beth's agenda.

It's quiet between the two of us, except for the birds chirping outside the kitchen window.

She grabs two bowls of cobbler, and I grab two bowls of cobbler. We walk back into the dining room and eat our dessert with the men.

James Taylor, Led Zeppelin, Jimi Hendrix, The Beatles, and Eddie Van Halen cover the walls of Luke's old room along with a Christie Brinkley poster.

"Not a bad choice." I walk around the room and stop at the poster of Christie Brinkley.

Luke throws himself on his old queen-size bed. "To be a seventeen-year-old boy again."

I turn to him, cross my arms, smile. "Would you go back to being seventeen if you could?"

"No. You?"

I shake my head. "Nope."

"How about your twenties?" he asks. "Shit. Sorry."

I was in prison then, and it's not something I want to go back to.

A guitar sits in the corner of his room. An old Zenith television sits against the wall on the dresser. It's a turn-knob television and no remote in sight and two antennas in the back.

"This thing still work?" I ask.

"I think so." Luke gets up from the bed, walks over across the room, and twists the knob on the front. The television sparks to life. He smiles at me. "That's the thing about Kentucky; we're about twenty years behind technology, which could be a blessing and a curse."

It's a rerun of *The Andy Griffith Show.*

"It's been years since I've seen this show," I say and sit down on the bed and face the television.

Ingrid and I would wake up early before school and watch one and a half episodes before we had to get ready for school.

Luke walks back across the room to sit next to me on the bed.

We watch blankly. Allow the world to settle at our feet, pushing reality at bay for as long as we can. The reality, the responsibilities, the decisions.

"Do your parents know?" I ask.

"No."

"Why?"

"It's all in the white envelope."

"Why can't you tell them—like, in person? Face-to-face?"

"I'm afraid to."

I think on this. Tuck my hands underneath my thighs. Stare at the television. "Is it as scary as losing your sister?"

There's a long, empty silence between us.

"You're the one leaving, Luke," I barely whisper.

"I guess that's just it. I know this will break their hearts—and I'm terrified of doing that."

"If Fiona had cancer, how would you like the news to be delivered?" I ask.

He doesn't answer.

"I don't know what's worse—losing someone you love quickly or losing someone you love slowly. I guess there's two sides to every coin."

"I had more clarity when Ella died," he finally says. "When she had the cancer, we talked a lot of about forgiveness and how she felt. How I felt. How Mom and Dad felt, you know?"

I nod, not because I know, but because I don't know, so I take in the newfound knowledge.

"I want to be cremated, just so you know."

I watch Andy walk into the police station and make a joke about the doughnuts.

I wasn't ready to hear that. I'm not sure why he chose to tell me, but I put my hand in his as a burning sensation starts in my chest. "You should tell them, Luke."

Luke looks at me. "I'm not sure I'm ready to bear that cross."

"What if they open the envelope?"

"They won't."

"How do you know?"

Luke smiles, laughs. "I guess I don't know for sure."

"What's your plan if they open it?"

"I don't have one."

Fear can be fickle.

I feel his hand sliding down my belly, and it takes me a moment to get my bearings. I'm on my back, and Luke is facing me, on his side. His hand moves down my thigh, between my legs, and back up to my stomach.

After our talk, I showered and slipped into a T-shirt and panties.

I pull my legs apart, and he scoots closer. I see his silhouette. Make out the outline of his hair.

He puts his lips to mine as his hand makes its way down my stomach once more and dips below my panties. I push my bottom up off the mattress because he feels good. He slides his finger between my folds, and the room grows even darker.

I feel him harden next to me.

He applies pressure to my knot and then pushes a finger inside me.

Quietly, I gasp.

He adjusts me so that my back is to him, and he puts me in just the right spot, so he can put himself inside me. When he does, we both whimper out of love, out of spite, out of selfishness, and we allow ourselves to get lost in each other.

He pushes.

I pull.

It's quick.

We break.

When we both come, we lie here, entangled in each other until we fall asleep.

I hear Luke get up. It's still dark out.

"Luke"—I turn to him—"where are you going?"

"Helping Dad outside this morning." He's slipping underwear on.

"But it's dark out. How will you see anything?"

"Best time of day to work."

He puts on his jeans, watching me. Pulls a T-shirt on over his head, and I can't help but feel grateful that I'm the only woman who gets to share his body with him. I'm the only woman who gets to touch his abs, his chest, his arms. I'm the only woman who gets his mouth in ways that others dream of. But more importantly, I have his heart.

"Come here," I tell him and pat the spot next to me, exposing my breasts only a little.

Luke notices as he lies down, fully clothed, next to me.

Aware of what I'm doing and what I'm setting my own body up for, I zip down his zipper to his jeans, and Luke groans quietly.

"What are you doing to me, Cat?" His head falls softly against the backboard of the bed.

"Returning the favor."

He's hard almost immediately as I take him in my mouth and slide past the ripples of his sex.

"Oh, God." Luke's hands tighten around me.

I look up at Luke as my head moves.

His eyes are closed, and one hand is on my head.

I tighten my lips around him, and I hear him sigh.

I go until he's undone.

He lies in bed, trying to collect himself as I get out of bed, allowing my breasts to brush across his T-shirt.

But he catches my hips in his hands right above him and takes my mouth for his own keeping, kissing me hard.

When I pull away, he says, "These are my lips, understand?"

"Yes."

"My hips, my breasts, my everything."

I smile and allow my body to linger over his, only for a few seconds before I put my clothes on.

Luke stands and helps me step into my panties, T-shirt, and jeans.

"Why are you getting up so early?" he asks.

I stand and put my hands on my hips. "I thought you said it was the best time of day?"

"It is."

"Okay then, I'm ready to get started."

Luke smiles, kisses my forehead, and says, "Okay."

Beth, James, Luke, and I are out on the back deck, looking at their land. It's the afternoon, and we've sat down for a break.

The white envelope, as Luke predicted, still sits on the dining room table, unopened.

Luke's eyes look a lot like James's. The only difference is, James wears glasses. And I can't help but wonder if Luke would look like James at his age. Even though they're not related by blood, the resemblance is astounding.

James and Luke discuss the possible purchase of fifty more head of cattle from the Dentons. Whoever they are.

"This place never gets old," Beth says, taking a sip of her freshly poured lemonade.

"It's beautiful."

"What was it like, growing up in Beverly Hills?" she asks.

I take a sip of my lemonade. Set it down on the wrought iron table. "Like you're constantly looking for ways to improve. Because you're never quite up to standards."

Beth nods, closes her eyes as she looks up toward the sky. "I see. What was it like in prison?" She still looks up toward the heavens, waiting for my answer.

"Like a slow drip of water being given to a thirsty man."

She listens, and I continue, "Time passes slowly while you're there, I guess, but when your time is up, you look back and realize how quickly it went."

"Did you do it?" And she asks this in the sincerest way.

I understand why. If my son were engaged to a woman who had been in prison for thirteen years on a murder conviction, I'd have questions, too.

But I give her the answer I gave Luke. Not the story I told the court or the story I try to tell myself in an effort to rationalize that what I'd needed to do was just fit the mold.

"No."

Beth sits, the same cool, calm face. She's now looking over their land as the sun slowly makes it descent over the rolling hills of bluegrass.

"You know what I think?" she asks, looking over at me only momentarily.

"I don't."

"I think that you made a decision based on love, and that is a selfless decision in my book, Catherine."

I take in her words, run them through my brain like a copy machine. I don't overthink them. I just sit with them and watch them disappear from my mind.

"I can bet that prison is similar to grief, too?" she asks, looking at me.

I've experienced both.

Beth looks out across the land again. "Every night, I used to sit in Ella's room after she died, trying to make sense of it all. Boy"—she shakes her head—"God took the brunt of that one. For years, I slept in her room. Stayed in her room for hours during the day. Reorganizing her room, moving furniture, only to move it in the exact way she'd had it before. Then, one day, a loud voice said, 'Deal with it, Mom. Then, move on.' " Beth smiles through her pain of loss, a smile that exists somewhere between relief and sadness.

Prison is a lot like grief. I can metaphorically move furniture around, my thoughts, my feelings. I can organize myself, try to compartmentalize where I stand, but until I deal with the weight, the gravity of what happened—deal with *it*—I can't move on. Or I can just push it away like I've always done, organizing and moving shit around.

"So, I dealt with it. I looked at myself, looked at the grief, meshed it together, and felt my way through it."

Beth looks at me keenly and then back to the land. In this moment right now, I realize that it doesn't matter if James and Beth know about Luke's cancer; they will move on—eventually. It will hurt, and Beth will most likely retreat to the safety of Luke's bedroom once he's gone, but someday, she will get back on her two feet to live another day.

"Talked to God a hell of a lot. But I stopped asking God why because Nancy Durell down the road said, 'Honey, God's grieving with you.' Hit me like a ton of bricks when I realized Nancy was right." Beth looks at Luke. "Everyone grieves in their own way. Some have to leave because the pain of where they're at, both emotionally and physically, is just too much. But others like to stay put in it. I have no idea why all this is coming out, Catherine, but you really make a good listener. Thank you." Beth winks at me.

But I'm absorbing more than she knows.

"Well, shall we go in and get supper ready?" Beth asks as she stands.

"Right behind you," I say, following her lead.

"You boys stay out of trouble. We're going to go get supper ready."

James and Luke are still in deep conversation about the cattle.

I walk over to Luke and kiss him on the cheek. "I love you," I whisper and soak up the feeling these words give me.

He leans into me, closes his eyes, and then whispers, "I love you always."

If only we had always.

"We looked great on the outside. But not on the inside," I say about my family to Luke as we lie in bed.

He lightly drags his fingers across my bicep.

"We didn't talk about anything. Not like your family. Everything was pushed under the rug in a nice, neat pile, and Ingrid and I were asked not to say a word, and if we did, lying would be better."

Luke's breaths are measured, and his heart has the same rhythm I fell in love with.

What if Luke breaks me? What if I snap? What if my grief makes me crazy like it did Mother?

"My mother is in a home. Can't feed herself—or won't feed herself. Won't take care of herself. She hasn't spoken a word since that night everything happened." Things he already knows.

"Do you know why?" Luke asks.

"A wise woman once told me that everyone processes grief a little differently. My guess is, she can't. She's living on the outside but dying on the inside."

"Have you told her that?"

"No." My answer catches me off guard because it comes out so quickly. Disbelief sits on the edge of my shoulder, wondering why he would ask such a question. And in the same token, why haven't I told her that? When you're raised a certain way for so long, the coping, the learned skills become who you are—even when you don't know it.

Maybe I should tell Mother that.

"I don't want to be stuck, Luke." I run my fingers through his chest hair. "After you die"—my feelings get caught in my throat—"I don't want to be stuck."

"You won't, Cat."

"How do you know?"

"Because you know better."

Luke kisses the top of my head, still running his finger along my bicep. I still play with the tuft of hair on his chest.

Something I'd rather say internally, I say out loud, "Sometimes, I'd rather not have moments like these, the ones where I'm so comfortable with you, so peaceful, only because it would be easier when you're gone."

"If that were the case, there'd be no living proof that we fell in love. Make a trail, Cat. Let others know our story. Through sadness, we can find truth and love and all things go—" But before Luke can finish, he starts to cough.

I jump up from the bed, grab a roll of toilet paper, and go back into the bedroom. Luke is sitting up now, coughing harder.

I roll some of the toilet paper in my hand and push it to his mouth.

Press my hand to his back as I wish he didn't have to feel through this.

After some time, the coughing has ceased, and I take the used toilet paper and flush it down the toilet.

We spend three days with Beth and James.

Eating dinner at their table in their dining room.

Laughing.

Discussing the world.

Talking about life.

Sleeping in Luke's childhood room at night.

Making love at night—quietly.

Making biscuits.

Working on the ranch.

We ride horses, which I've only done twice before in my life.

Father's career allowed us to do a lot, Ingrid and me. But what it didn't do was allow for the simple things in life to be enjoyable, like sitting and talking and being present for one another.

What a day of rest and relaxation would do for one at the McCays' wouldn't fly at the Clemens'. Ingrid and I would spend all day wondering if we'd done everything correctly.

Perhaps it's my childhood perception. Perhaps it's just my childhood feelings, but everything about the McCay house is so much simpler, so much more real and happier.

James and Beth are on the porch as Luke and I are walking out to an old tree across the land. We're holding hands and laughing about a meme we saw about cats versus dogs.

All of a sudden, Luke picks me up and throws me over his shoulder, and he's running to the tree. We're laughing and breathing hard, and somehow, I can't stop smiling.

I have no power.

No control.

I'm in an awkward spot, and I'm pretty sure my ass is in Luke's face.

And yet, I'm beaming with gratitude.

"Put me down!" I laugh. "I'm going to break your shoulder!"

Luke laughs. "It's going to take a lot more than a hundred pounds to break my shoulder!"

He picks up speed and I have no idea how he's doing this, but for once in my life, I don't feel unsafe or unloved or not good enough.

I feel free.

We reach the tree, and Luke gently sets me down right in front of him. He gazes into my eyes and pushes my long hair back, taking my cheeks in his hands.

We both continue to laugh until we can't. Until we allow our reality to fall back in line.

Luke stares at me and begins to quietly sing.

The first time I met you,
I tried to fight it,
That we couldn't work,
'Cause my time was limited.

THE LIGHT WE SEE

Tried to convince myself you were perfect when
Nobody is perfect.
But then you smiled,
And I smiled,
And we laughed,
And love came sneaking up on us.

I held you in my arms,
Willing you to believe
Everything was okay.

The light we see,
Meant for you and me.
Pieces of me you put together,
Made me stronger,
Us stronger,
We were made for one another.

Life in the moment,
That's how we'll live
Until I take my last breath,
Until I can't feel you beneath my skin.
That's how we'll stay.

Your last memory of me,
Hold it with clarity.
Keep it alive,
And every time you remember it,
Know I'm with you.

The light we see,
Meant for you and me.
Pieces of me you put together,
Made me stronger,
Us stronger,
We were made for one another.

Catherine. Oh, Catherine.
Things don't just happen.
We'll love until we can't.

Tears stream down my cheeks.

"You're not supposed to cry, Cat," Luke whispers and wipes them with his finger.

I don't have any words for him. I can't answer him because somehow, the words are lodged between the tears.

"When you can't feel me anymore, know that I am with you, and I'll make sure you love again."

"I-I don't want to," I barely choke out.

"Yes, you do. It's just hard to see your life with anyone else but me. Give yourself time, Cat. But for right now, I'm here and you're here and we're together."

I wrap my arms around his middle, rest my ear against his chest, and try to memorize the rhythm of his heart.

This needs to be enough for this moment.

CHAPTER 38

Mother taught us not to speak when we're bothered, but rather, just keep moving, so when I see on Luke's phone, *Missed Call—Wife*, I want to throw up.

I want to run.

Surely though, there has to be an explanation, right?

Luke asked me to marry him.

He can't be a husband to two women.

My thoughts start to spin and build on themselves and twist and turn my mind into something it's not. Maybe. Or something it is.

How come no one said anything?

Wife continues to flash across his phone screen.

Luke opens the car door and sits back down in the passenger seat.

My head spins.

I stare down at my ring, the one Luke gave me. The only piece of jewelry I wear.

"Gas is expensive but not as bad as California," he says. Looks at me.

I'm not sure what to say. What to do. *Is this whole trip a facade?*

What is happening?

How did I miss this in my Google search? He's been connected with Hollywood actresses and non-actresses, but nothing serious. And also, how could I have been so stupid, so naive to believe that a guy like Luke wouldn't have women on the side?

"Catherine!" I hear his voice.

"What?" I ask, trying to pretend the last thirty seconds wasn't me drifting in and out of fear.

"What's wrong?"

I can feel him staring at my profile.

"Nothing." My voice is weak, and I had intentions of it being strong, of brushing off my own insecurities.

I bet his wife is as beautiful as he is.

How come Uncle Al and Aunt Gene acted like I wasn't the other woman?

How come James and Beth never said anything, especially after they saw the ring?

How come nobody said a fucking thing?

How come my thoughts are so loud?

How come the fear and anger are screaming at me?

I attempt to start the car, but Luke pulls out the keys.

"Catherine, fucking talk to me. What is wrong?" he asks, holding the keys in his hand.

Keep moving forward, I tell myself.

Luke still has the keys, but I can't be in this moment with Luke. It hurts too much.

I get out of the car and slam the door and start to walk.

I hear a car door shut behind me.

He doesn't say my name, but I know he's behind me.

Keep moving forward.

"Catherine."

Keep walking. I don't know where I'm headed, and there's traffic and it's difficult to navigate and I just need out.

"Catherine!" he says again. "Stop."

His hands reach around my shoulders, and he tries to stop me.

"Let go," I tell him.

He lets go, and I keep walking.

"Catherine. Please, if you don't stop, I can't help fix whatever is wrong." He reaches for my hand.

I continue to make my way down the busy road.

"*Good love is worth the argument; great love is worth fighting for.*" Beth's advice is clear.

But it's when he grabs my shoulders and doesn't let go.

Turning into his pull, I say, "Why the hell is your wife calling your cell phone?"

He freezes. His eyes wide, his face stoic, he doesn't know what to say. He's caught off guard.

I hold up my hands. "Come on; you want to talk about it, right?"

My breathing is staggered, and my eyes search for a simple explanation in his eyes, but Luke, he doesn't have one.

"Why is your wife calling your cell phone, Luke? I hate talking about shit. I hate it. And I'm not good at it because I never had to do it as a kid. I'm shitty at it, and running is easier."

I stand on the side of the busy road, and Luke is rendered speechless.

The dark circles under his eyes are more pronounced, more noticeable, and I try not to give in to his sullen look.

Fight for your rights. He owes you an explanation. I hear Ingrid's voice. *And listen to it.*

"What do you have to say for yourself, Luke?"

God. I put my hands on my head in my own stupidity. "I made love to you, Luke." My voice begins to break, but I swallow through it. I don't care who hears us.

He stands there like a school-age boy and takes my words. All of them.

"How can you possibly get yourself out of this one?" I ask breathlessly as I take off the ring he gave me. I put the nail in the coffin. "Is this hers, too, or did you get a two-for-one special?" I grab his hand and put the ring back in his palm. "Don't follow me, Luke. I need some space."

I turn on my heel and walk toward a stoplight, crossing the street. Surely, this ought to be easier than dealing with the situation at hand. Besides, how can you outtalk this one? How can you possibly outsmart the situation?

He's caught.

I'm furious, which isn't in my genetic makeup. I'm not sure how to deal with this. I think I'm angrier with myself for allowing myself to fall in love with him.

I don't hear my name, nor do I look back. I keep walking toward the lights, praying I'll find a hotel room or something.

Shit. My wallet, my phone, everything is in the car. I can't go back.

I need a phone to call Eddie. He can charge a hotel room, and we can count it against the house sale.

Pay phones don't exist anymore, but after a mile and a half or so, I find a Holiday Inn Express. I walk in, shaking.

"Can I use your phone?" I ask the man behind the desk without a name tag. "I lost my purse."

He puts the black phone on the counter, and I walk to it, realizing I don't have Eddie's number memorized.

Shit.

"Catherine." I hear Luke say from behind me. He touches my shoulder. "At least give me a chance to explain. Give me that. Please."

Every muscle and every bone in my body wants to say no, but my heart refuses to accept no as an answer.

"Good love is worth the argument; great love is worth fighting for."

I look at the man across the counter, the nice gentleman who allowed me to use the phone. His eyes move from me to Luke and back to me. If he asks Luke if he's Dylan Klein, I'll scream.

Instead, he leans forward and whispers, "I'd let him explain."

Even if you drove more than halfway through the United States, thinking he didn't have a wife?

"Two rooms, please. Nonsmoking." Luke cautiously walks up to the counter and looks at the man and then to me.

"I'll get two rooms, and if you don't want to stay with me after you know the full story, you'll have your own room to go to. Deal?"

The anger I felt just moments ago has somehow faded somewhat. The pace of my heart has slowed.

Let him explain, a voice says in my head.

The man from behind the counter takes Luke's card and runs it.

Nervously, I tap my foot, wait for the transaction to clear, and think of all the possible ways Luke could make this right, redeem himself, and I also think about all the ways this could blow up in my face.

Before I turn to go with Luke to get our stuff, I look at the man across the counter. "If this goes all wrong, it's your fault."

He nods. As if we were best friends and he'd just given me advice at a time I needed it most.

"Something tells me it won't," he says. Smiles with his eyes.

"You got a backup plan? Because I don't. I'm all out of plans."

He shakes his head. "You won't need one."

"What's your name?" I ask.

"Mick." He extends his hand.

"Catherine." I curiously eye him.

He's not tall and not short, somewhere in the middle. He wears a maroon bow tie with a white button-up shirt. A stud in his nose with bright blue eyes.

"Thank you, Mick. I really hope you're right."

He nods. Mick leans over to look at Luke. "Dude, don't fuck this up, okay?"

Luke almost laughs, but I can tell he's heartbroken, too. I can tell because when he smiles, it isn't from his heart; it's a mask that he wears to hide things he doesn't want others to see. I just have to have enough trust to take the chance.

Mick grabs two cards from underneath the counter. "Room 201 and 202." He hands them to Luke.

"Thank you," Luke says.

We walk toward the door, and Luke holds it open for me. His car is parked just off the hotel lobby. We grab our things and quietly make it up to the second floor on the outside of the hotel, as all the doors face the middle with outside access.

Luke unlocks the door with the slide of the key. He pushes and opens it. "After you."

I walk through, carrying my overnight bag, and Luke follows me in, shutting the door behind us.

He sets his bag down. Takes mine from me and sets it down. Runs his hands through his hair. Takes in a big, deep breath. "This is not how I planned on telling you, Cat." His voice is quiet. I can tell that he's tired. "Julie is my wife. We've been married since 1995, and for a long time, we worked. We worked well together."

He sits down on the bed, but I stand. I don't move. I just watch him.

"But sometimes, things happen and don't happen. Feelings and love and all that shit that makes love move forward suddenly goes away, and you're left with nothing but open wounds that can't be fixed. And there's no way you can fix them because you didn't do anything wrong." His voice is full of pain. "Life happened."

I sit down on the opposite bed, let my bag slide down to the floor.

"We tried to have a baby. We tried for a long time. And somehow, in all that work, Julie lost herself. I lost myself, trying to find her. She left, and I was left, trying to pick up the pieces of my life, our life."

Luke puts his hands just above his knees and stares at me dead in the eyes. "I should have told you this part sooner, too. And I'm sorry I didn't. I saw Ingrid watching Julie and your father. She'd received random calls in the middle of the night with excuses like wrong number, a sales call—all shit I didn't believe, and I think she knew it, too. But that's the thing about love. We believe what our heart wants to see, not the reality of the situation until it's blindly held in our face. I saw your father with my wife. We knew. We all knew in that moment that their relationship wasn't platonic. But I tried to make it work, you know? She was my wife, and we'd made a promise." His voice dies off.

"I remember," I whisper.

I remember that day so vividly—when Ingrid's words came to life.

"I saw Father with another woman."

It wasn't that I didn't believe Ingrid. I did. But I had to see it for myself.

"There's a reason we keep running into each other, Cat," he says in the most needful way.

"Julie needed a baby, and she was willing to do anything to get it. I was just a person to fit the bill for her heart when she needed me." He takes a big breath in and lets it out. "We haven't spoken in over five years. I-I never filed divorce papers because I didn't plan on getting married again. Not until you. And this is where the story gets better, I promise." Luke reaches over and lightly touches my knee for a moment. "I never forgot about you. Your face. Your eyes, the way they told stories to keep your innermost secrets at bay. I knew if it was fate and if we were meant to be, you and I would meet again. Because I learned through love and loss that, most times, we just need to show up for life."

He smiles at me, the real, genuine one, as he reaches up and touches my cheek with the back of his thumb. "Then, I showed up as guy number seven."

I try to smile through my heartache.

"And then you showed up at my house three weeks ago, and I knew." He pauses. "I called my attorney and had him draw up the divorce papers, and that's probably Julie calling to cuss me out or ask me *what for* because she received them." He shrugs. "But I won't call her back if you don't want me to."

My mouth falls open. "You have to. You need closure, Luke."

He nods. "I have closure. You are my closure. And I think our lives fell into place."

I shake my head, trying to wrap my head around all these thoughts that keep running through my brain.

"What I realized is that we have people we're supposed to love along the way. Fall in love with. People that we're supposed to love even if it isn't for forever. Jules was one of those. And you, you're something different. Something I've never experienced before, Cat. I'd still like to marry you if you'll have me."

There are no second thoughts with Luke. Ever. I didn't know our time would be limited, but even still, it's all worth it. All of it.

I'm driving through New York, and we're laughing. I don't remember why we started laughing in the first place, but Luke is laughing, and it's the most beautiful thing to my ears.

He's paler now. His coughing fits are more pronounced and more often.

He's growing sicker, and we both know it.

But we're laughing, and everything is right with the world just for a moment.

He's talked me out of the hospital too many times to count.

When fear lumped in my throat and I didn't know what to do, he just said, "Stay with me."

The fear passed, and he eventually rode out the temporary.

But now, looking at this man that God gave me, I'm not sure what's worse—laughing or crying.

Luke's smile fades, and I notice his lips have lost their redness. They're almost match his skin tone. The dark circles under his eyes have become permanent.

"I'm ready to go home now, Cat."

I don't want to ask if he means home as in Carpinteria or home as in heaven. I'm too scared to ask. So, instead, I just nod as tears fill my eyes, and I say, "Okay."

My engagement ring catches the glint of the rising sun. We left early because neither of us could sleep, and I was worried for Luke. Sometimes, his breathing becomes labored.

I make a mental note to call Fiona when we get to where we're going.

She needs to know.

Above everyone else, including me, she needs to know, so she has time to say good-bye.

"You're an excellent father, Luke, you know that?"

He doesn't answer.

"Luke? Are you okay?" I've started to do this recently, check on him, scared that he somehow stopped breathing or his heart stopped or something else completely irrational.

"I'm with you," he says weakly, and it gives me peace.

He grabs the Starbursts from the dashboard, picks an orange one, and hands it to me. He takes a yellow one for himself.

"Are … are Starbursts good for you?" I ask.

Luke turns to look at me. His smile starts first, and then he starts to giggle and then laugh.

Then, I start to laugh.

"I'm a dying man, Cat. I'm not too concerned."

Then, we both start laughing, and tears start to roll down my cheeks. I'm not sure if it's because it's the first time he's said he's dying or his laughter that affects me so deeply.

I wipe my tears and will myself to believe it's Luke's laughter just so it's easier to cope.

"Cat?" Luke's looking out the window now.

"Yeah?"

"Don't call anyone, okay? After I'm gone?"

I swallow, and my throat feels rough, like sandpaper. I don't answer him.

If you had asked me in the beginning of this trip, I would have said *okay* without any other questions. But now, I've seen Luke with the people he loves most.

And I'm not sure if it's the cancer talking or him, but I say, "What about Fiona?"

"I don't want her last memory of her father to be a broken one."

"You aren't broken, Luke; you're sick. There's a big difference." I pause for a moment. "I used to think that was right. To hang on to the good memories of life, but it isn't the good memories that build us; it's the ones we don't want to see, don't want to remember, don't want to feel." I think about my own past. "You taught me that, Luke."

Luke doesn't say anything more.

I break the silence by asking him about what his perfect world looks like because as we approach Upstate New York, I see the worry that he carries in his eyes.

He reaches over and puts his hand on my shoulder, giving it a squeeze. "We'd get married in a small ceremony, close to where your mother is. Fiona would be my best man." He smiles. "We'd have a place in Myers Flat to escape to, to see the big trees. We'd have a kid, name him James, after my dad. We'd make love under the stars in the summer and by the fire during the winter. We'd have the family over for holidays and keep it as low-key as possible. We'd go for walks in the evening, and I'd teach James to play the guitar. But wherever you chose for us to live, I'd hope it was close to the ocean," he sighs. "This is hard."

I don't ask why because I know why. We won't get this future together.

"But we have today, Luke."

Because Luke taught me to stay in the present moment. To breathe it in. When I am weak, he is strong. And when he is weak, I need to be his strength.

"Our son, James, will learn to play the guitar. I'll find our place in Myers Flat. I'll be sure Fiona knows her little brother. I'll have a place by the ocean, so we're closer to you."

I look over, and I see a single tear slip down Luke's cheek.

"Are you scared?" I ask, pulling strength from within me that I know I'll need. I reach my hand around his neck, feeling the warmth of his skin.

"No, I'm not scared to die. I'm scared you won't live your life."

A groan escapes my throat, and deep inside me, I'm scared he's right. I feel the tears threaten to fall. I swallow them.

I wait one moment before I speak, praying my voice doesn't crack, "I promise you, I will live." Right now, I'm not sure I trust my own words, but I'd never lie to Luke. I just hope I can do it.

"They talk about a man's dying wish. I have one wish." Luke looks out the windshield now.

"What's that?" I whisper.

"That you and Fiona each find a person who loves you just as much as I do." He pauses. "It will be different, the love, but the amount of love is the same. And don't settle, Cat. Don't settle for someone just because you want your heart to stop aching. Don't settle for anything less than you're worth. Find someone who takes your breath away. Find someone who will make you laugh. Find someone who takes care of you, and most importantly, find someone who loves you when you don't feel lovable. When you're broken, make sure they don't fix you but help you through it, okay? Find someone like that because that is what you deserve.

"You don't deserve guys one, two, three, four, five, six, eight, and nine. You deserve guy number seven because he will always remember you. He'll hold your heart in the most delicate way possible, but give you the truth when you need it. And don't compare my love to anyone else's. It will be different. But give different the benefit of the doubt. Give it a chance."

The sunlight shines down between the clouds.

"The light we see isn't because it's there; it's because we took the time to notice it," Luke whispers. "I spent my life going a hundred miles an hour. If it wasn't construction, it was projects at home. If it wasn't filming, it was doing interviews. I never gave the people I loved the most my time. So, when my time was called short here on this earth, I began to reflect on all the time I didn't spend doing what I wanted to do or what I should have done. Don't make that same mistake. Give yourself the gift of time because we never know when it will be cut short."

The envelopes.

The time we spent with his family, his friends.

This was Luke's amends.

He stopped his time in Southern California to slow down. To give his time to the people he loves most in this world. He gave them what he couldn't for many years. This trip was about a dying man's wish to be with the love of his life.

"The envelopes," I say.

He nods. "The envelopes were letters to some, money for others." Luke reaches into his back pocket, pulls out another white envelope, and puts it on the dashboard. "Don't open this until I'm gone, okay?"

I look forward, willing myself to keep driving and not fall apart. I hold my breath, keeping the sob in my throat. I finally swallow. My eyes burn, and I bite the side of my tongue, so my tears won't fall.

When I've gathered enough courage, I say, "I will always remember the way you love me, Luke, and know that I am worthy of that kind of love again. I can't—I can't guarantee I'll find it, but I'll be open to it."

New York passes by us as we make our way down the stretch of road.

The fall colors, the life sits and waits for us as Luke directs me where to go.

Off the beaten path. Behind a grove of trees are black wrought iron gates.

"This place is beautiful," I say.

The man in the booth just off the gates greets us with a tip of his hat. "Mr. McCay, I assume."

"Rodney, good to meet you. Thank you."

Rodney doesn't give off the fact that Luke looks significantly different.

"Ma'am," he says to me.

"This is my soon-to-be wife, Catherine." Luke smiles a goofy smile that makes me laugh.

I put my hand through the window, and we exchange a handshake. "Hello, Rodney."

"Indeed," he says. "The house is ready for you, and Dr. Brinkman arrived yesterday along with two nurses. And your publicist."

My stomach begins to twist and turn at the thought that Luke will need a doctor and two nurses because that means we're another step closer to his departure.

"Thank you, Rodney."

He tips his hat again, and I drive forward. The road weaves through black spruce and eastern hemlock and then opens up to a two-story brown palace with green ivy growing up the face of it. In some ways, it reminds me of home. Its size, its circular driveway, but that's it. I hope the memories inside are better.

"This is beautiful, Luke. How long have you had this?"

Luke looks up through the front windshield as we drive up to the house. "Escrow closed two weeks ago."

I ease the brakes, and the car comes to a stop. I look at him. "You've never been here before?"

"Nope."

"You-you just bought a house that you've never been to? Never stepped foot in?" I turn off the engine.

"I did."

"Why?"

"Why not?" Luke shrugs. "It's just a house, Cat."

"So, you didn't know Rodney?"

Luke smiles. "No, first time I've met him. We've had a few discussions on the phone."

I admire Luke's ability to be spontaneous.

"Come on." He reaches up and touches my face. "Let's go check out our house."

Our house.

Our home.

After a trip across the country, we're finally at a place where we can call home. Whether it's home really or not, I'm not sure, but I do know Luke is home for me, so wherever he is—is my home.

The front double doors are magnificent. Hand-carved brown mahogany. They must be twenty feet tall.

Luke looks at me, and I look at him, our bags in hand.

He leans in and kisses me on the mouth. "I love you," he whispers when he pulls away.

He smells like mint, and if cool water had a smell, it would smell like Luke.

"I love you, too." My fingers feel their way to his, and I take his hand as he opens the front door.

His steps are slower now. His movements less calculated. I feel as though I need to stand behind him and make sure he makes it to where he's going.

We come into a grand entryway. The dark brown mahogany floor matches the front doors.

To the left, the house opens up to a wall of windows that overlooks a valley of trees. The living room has couches and pillows and a massive stone fireplace. To the right is the kitchen with mahogany cabinets and cement countertops.

The fire is going. It's warm but not too warm.

A second story sits upstairs that we haven't gotten to yet.

"It's prettier in person," Luke says, grabbing the wall to steady himself.

"I hear a Mr. Luke McCay in the house," a singsong voice sounds from out of the blue.

And the voice comes into view. She's tall with long red hair that is pulled back. A black pencil skirt with a white blouse and very cute heels. They click down the hallway as she approaches us. A laptop in one hand.

"Catherine Clemens, my name is Pearl Glenwood, and I'm Luke's publicist. It's so nice to finally meet you." She extends her hand to me, and I, her. Pearl seems to be in her mid-forties, I'd say, but I've never been any good at guessing people's ages, so she could be much older or much younger.

"Nice to meet you, Pearl."

Luke's hand moves to my lower back.

"What the hell is on your hand?" she says to me.

"Luke, fucking seriously, you have to tell me about this shit before it happens."

Luke looks at Pearl, and in his calm, cool demeanor, he says, "Pearl, I'm a dying man. I can do whatever the hell I want."

But Pearl doesn't miss a beat, and I see when Luke says the word *dying*, that it makes her feel uncomfortable. Her quick wit, in my opinion, makes her good at this job. "And it is my job to make you look good until your dying day. So, tell me shit. 'K?"

Luke laughs, and I laugh.

Pearl looks down at her phone, which is now buzzing. "I've got to take this."

"Dr. Brinkman, Luke's here," she calls and clicks back down the hallway in the way she came.

A tall, thin man comes from the other direction. A thin nose with black wire-rimmed glasses.

"Great to see you again, Doc."

Luke and Dr. Brinkman shake hands.

"This is my fiancée, Catherine." Luke grins. "I'll never get tired of saying that," he whispers in my ear.

We exchange pleasantries.

Dr. Brinkman eyes Luke in an investigative way. "Come on, Luke," the doctor says. "Let's get your vitals and run some tests."

Stay in the moment, I remind myself. I take a big breath in, but I'm reluctant to let go of Luke's hand that I've just taken for my own safekeeping.

He looks back. "Are you okay?" Looks at my hand that won't let go.

"Yeah," I lie to make things easier for him. I drop his hand as if it were an afterthought.

Luke stares at me hard. He knows I'm lying. I know I'm lying. I say, "I'm going to find a bedroom to put my things in."

And somehow prepare to lose you.

"Okay." He pauses. "This shouldn't take long."

I nod, turn, and walk down a hallway.

"Our bedroom is upstairs, I think. Though I'm not sure where." He grins. "But wherever you find is where I'll sleep," he calls again.

Tears start to burn my eyes, but I push them away.

I walk up the spiral staircase just off the living room to another floor with doors. Thankfully, they're all open, so I won't intrude on anyone.

My phone rings, and it says *Mr. Jenkins.*

I answer, "Hello, Mr. Jenkins."

"How are things, Ms. Clemens?"

They're fucking falling apart. I am falling apart. "They're well."

"Good, good. I've received your emails. And it looks like you'll be wrapping up the trip soon?"

"Yes," I lie because I'm not sure what else to do.

I can't tell Mr. Jenkins that Luke has cancer and it's terminal. And that I've fallen in love with the subject. And that I'm not going to write the story. And that I'll return the money he's paid me as soon as our family home sells. But it's just too much right now.

"Check in next week, will you?" he asks.

I oblige.

"See you," he says and hangs up.

The chef, Dante, cooks dinner for Luke, me, Dr. Brinkman, Abby and Tanner—the nurses—Pearl, and Rodney.

Luke insisted Rodney come in and eat some food during shift. His job, my understanding, is to keep the media out just in case someone gets wind of our situation.

This was Pearl's idea. Pearl said she would have five security guards out front, but Luke said one would suffice. He's "not Steph Curry or the president"—Luke's words, not mine.

Luke barely eats. I know this part because I've watched it over the last several days.

When we're done, I do the dishes.

Luke tells me it's okay, that I don't have to, but I need to do something with my hands because they won't stop fidgeting, and my mind won't stop spinning.

I feel Luke enter the room.

It's just us in the kitchen.

The light over the island is the only light on.

And I ask the only question that's been burning a hole in my heart, "Did you come here to die?"

"Yes."

I close my eyes and feel his answer in my soul. Anger sits and waits for me to do something, anything, than just accept his answer.

"Have you tried any sort of treatment?" My heart begins the grieving process.

"It's terminal, Cat."

I know this, and it seems like he still has to remind me of this.

I drop the handful of silverware. "You say that, but have you exhausted all avenues? Have you looked into treatment at all? You could try to fight this, Luke."

I hear Luke take a few steps closer.

"I'm angry, Luke. I'm angry you brought me here, angry that you're not fighting for your own fucking life."

"You're angry because you're sad. You're fearful, and you're not quite sure how to let go of me."

"I don't need your analytical shit, Luke. I just need you better."

"Let's say I did try treatment. What would that do to our quality time left? If I had tried the treatment like my doctors suggested, even though it wouldn't have saved my life, just prolonged the inevitable, I sure as hell wouldn't have had this trip with you because I'd have been too sick. I sure as hell wouldn't have gotten to feel you from the inside because I would have felt shitty. I wouldn't have fallen in love because I would have missed all these moments with you, so focused on trying to feel better." He stops.

I'm leaning against the sink, sitting in a pool of self-pity.

"Sometimes, it comes down to the time we have left," he whispers. "I wanted quality, not quantity. I wanted to say good-bye to the ones I love, and in that process, I had an opportunity to love again. Fall in love with the most beautiful woman I've ever seen in my life."

I feel him right behind me now.

I need time. I need time to process this. "I'm going to sleep in another bedroom tonight."

"Okay," he says, and when he takes a step closer, I leave the kitchen.

It's two in the morning, and I can't sleep. I can't sleep without Luke and the comforts of his body around mine, and I feel as though I'm missing memories that I can keep in my heart once he's gone.

I don't want his time spent here on this earth wanting me. I want him to take in each moment, so when it's time and he's hurting, he can cling to those, and I can cling to mine.

I throw on my robe over my sleep shirt and tiptoe down to his room so as not to wake the doctor and the two nurses and the publicist.

Quietly, I open the door to his bedroom and see him fast asleep on his back, hands crossed over his chest.

My heart tells me to curl up next to him, allow my body to finally rest.

I sit in the big, comfortable chair next to the bed and watch him sleep. I take in the way his chest moves up and down, the peaceful look on his face, and inside, I feel like his time here on this earth is coming to an end, and as much as I want to fight him and the situation and the awful disease, I know I'm powerless.

I don't touch him, afraid I'll interrupt the peace.

I see a book on his nightstand called *The Seven Stages of Grief.* I pick up the book and read the back.

Is Luke reading this book for me, to understand where I'm coming from?

The book stares back at me as if it knows something I don't. As if it has knowledge that it's keeping from me.

I grab Luke's phone from the nightstand and scroll through his Contacts to find Fiona's name. I hit Share Contact. I scroll through for my name, but it isn't under Catherine. I scroll until I come across the name My Light. I hit the Contact, and my number appears. Smiling, I look back at Luke, who's still asleep, and send myself the contact info.

Quietly, I tiptoe out of the room to make the call that I don't want to make to Fiona. I know Luke is running short on time, and his daughter needs to know even if it will break her heart.

Two Days Later

Fiona has just arrived, and I get her set up in a bedroom.

Pearl comes clicking down the hallway. "Fiona? I didn't know you were coming." Pearl eyes me dangerously.

"I called her. She needs to be with her father, Pearl."

"Fuck me. Did you say anything to anyone, Fiona? We weren't supposed to call you."

I glare at Pearl. "It's her father, Pearl. Who the hell cares? She can do what she wants with the information."

"It's my job, Catherine, to keep everyone quiet, so Luke isn't hounded by the media."

"And it's my job, Pearl, as Luke's fiancée, to make decisions based on matters of the heart. He needs his daughter, and his daughter needs him." Quickly, I cover my mouth after saying the words I always wanted, always felt in my heart, but never spoke.

Pearl glares at me and turns on a dime, clicking down the hallway.

Fiona looks at me, her eyes wide with fear.

"Don't worry about her. I'll take care of her. Your father is this way."

Luke has been confined to our bed. Dr. Brinkman says it's unsafe for him to walk anymore, for fear he might fall.

And Luke's response, "I'm a dying man, Doc. What's it going to do, kill me?"

We're just outside the door, and Fiona can't open it.

"What are you afraid of?"

Fiona is looking down at her feet. Shakes her head. Looks up at me. "That I'll see what I envision in my head. That my daddy isn't who he was." Her eyes fill with tears.

I take her shoulders and pull her to me. "He's still got the same heart, Fiona. A heart that loves you more than anything in this world."

She starts to cry as her arms slowly ease around me.

Once she's done, she lets go and wipes her eyes. "I'm sorry."

"You don't need to be sorry, Fiona." I pat her back. "Come on," I say and open up the door.

Luke is lying there, reading a book, and when he sees his daughter, he looks at me and back to her and back to me and back to her. "Baby," he says breathlessly as if it is just what he needed when he needed it. As if this is his only heart's worry. "I'm so glad you're here."

He didn't know she was coming.

"I'll leave you two alone." When I shut the door behind me, I gently fall against it, cover my mouth, and let the tears fall.

Watching someone die isn't easy. It isn't for the faint of heart.

Letting go of Ingrid was the hardest of all.

But she appears in front of me. She's beautiful in her purple dress. Holding hydrangeas. She wasn't mine to hang on to, and I think the reason she's hung around so long is because she knew I couldn't let go.

"I'm selling the house," I say to her.

"I know," she says. "It's time for me to go, sister."

"I know," I say. "But how will I survive without you guys?"

"A day at a time," she says.

That night, that awful night, when I ran upstairs, Ingrid was already gone. A puddle of blood around her, pouring from her abdomen. Memories I'd rather not have.

Mother couldn't save her.

I was too late.

But maybe redemption for that guilt is being here with Luke.

There are two sides to every coin. On one side, a father had fired the shot that killed his daughter.

On the other side, a father whose biggest heartbreak is not being there for his daughter when his time runs out.

"Don't worry; I'll be there to greet Luke when he gets to where he's going," Ingrid whispers.

My eyes fill with tears. So badly, I want to reach out and hold her, feel her against me again. "I'm going to miss you."

She nods. "I'll always be with you. When you see hydrangeas, know that I'm with you."

And I feel the warmth on my hand when she touches it.

"Time for me to go."

"I love you, Ingrid, and I'm so sorry I couldn't save you."

She shakes her head. "It wasn't your job to save me, sister; it was your job to love me."

And with that, Ingrid walks down the long, dark hallway and fades into nothing.

"Ms. Clemens?" Dr. Brinkman asks. "May I speak to you for a moment?"

"Of course." I'm in the great room, looking out the window.

Dr. Brinkman walks to me. Stares out the same window.

"Luke put something in guest bedroom one. He said he'd like you to put it on and meet him outside by the old grove of trees."

I'm caught off guard. "Of course."

Hope gathers inside me. Maybe, somehow, Dr. Brinkman has figured out how to save Luke. Maybe his body is healing.

Dr. Brinkman nods, and I make my way to guest bedroom one.

Once inside, I find a beautiful lace wedding gown hanging from the window. The pearls that stream down the dress look like fallen raindrops. It's absolutely beautiful.

I walk to the dress and gently run my fingers down the short train.

A note sits next to it.

Put me on.

I smile and take my clothes off. Slide the dress on that somehow fits perfectly. There's no need to zip or button anything, and I think Luke knew this when he picked the dress.

I look in the mirror and loosely braid my hair and make my way out of the room and downstairs to the old grove of trees.

In a wheelchair, my mother sits with Pamela, who is sitting next to Beth and James. Fiona stands next to Luke, helping to hold him up to an arbor.

Dr. Brinkman hands me a bouquet of hydrangeas, and I know without a doubt that Ingrid is with us.

"Thank you, Dr. Brinkman."

He nods.

"Fading Away" starts to play.

And tears start to stream down my face. I look at Mother, whose tears are falling like found dreams. Found moments. The good ones. The ones we don't walk away from.

I walk down the aisle to Luke and Fiona.

The minister says, "Who gives this woman to marry this man?"

I hear Mother's broken words. "I … do."

I cover my mouth and choke back a sob and will Mother to feel my love.

Fiona reaches up and wipes her eye.

I look into Luke's eyes, and I'm home. Everything around us fades, and it's just Luke and me and all the miles we spent together, learning to love and give love and forgive ourselves.

Fate isn't for the faint of heart. It's having faith, knowing our hearts will change and grow and hurt, trusting that, no matter what, we're better people for having experienced love.

"I love you, Cat."

"I love you, too. Did you arrange all of this?"

"With the help of Fiona," he says weakly.

The minister starts. "We are gathered here today ..."

CHAPTER 41

Luke died a day later with Fiona, Beth and James, and me gathered around him.

We're leaving the house and everything in it. After all, it is just a house.

I am the last one to leave.

But before I shut the door, I know I have to make one last call, my best attempt at closure of it all.

I make a call to Mr. Jenkins.

"Hello, Catherine. Are you ready to send the story?"

I take a big, deep breath in and feel Luke. "That's the thing, Mr. Jenkins. There isn't a story. I've sent the money back to you, plus additional funds for any trouble I have caused."

He raises his voice. "WHAT?"

"Luke died. While I won't go into the details, know that Luke was an amazing man with a great story to tell. It's just not my story to tell." There's a pause. "Thank you, Mr. Jenkins, for giving me a chance, for believing in me. But know my motives are in the right place."

"Eddie said you were a woman of integrity. A woman who always stuck by her word. While I don't know the story or understand any of this, I trust you. I can't believe I'm going to say this, but if you want the job as a staff writer, I'll have one waiting for you."

"Thank you, Mr. Jenkins."

We hang up, and I grab my purse and my backpack and walk to the front door and let myself out. I climb into Luke's car and drive away, leaving the past behind me.

The Last White Envelope

Dear Catherine,

Sometimes, I wish this hadn't worked out, the falling-in-love part. Not for me, but for you. I wish your heart didn't ache, and I know it does right now. Your grief will be heavy, I know.

I feel like we're all on a journey, every human on this earth. Our starting points are the same—birth—and our ending points—death—are the same. But it's the journey within us, the journey we choose to take.

And shit happens to us.

It happens to everyone.

It isn't about what we don't do; it's about what we do with the information we know.

I chose this journey with you. From the second I saw you when you were a teenager to when I was guy number seven, I knew you were the one. You just weren't ready, and I wasn't either. But when you showed up at my house in Carpinteria to do your story, I knew it was fate that had brought us back together at the right time.

Also, I believe that our hearts aren't destined to fall in love with one person. I believe I was in love with Julie. I believe that situations can push people apart. And we forget that love is a verb, not a noun. Right love takes action. Good love takes lots of action. And great love is a never-ending story, being built and fixed every single day.

But with you, it's just different. My heart is content; it beats differently when I'm with you. You make me want to live longer, be a better person, love deeper, give often, and be true to who I am. With you, it doesn't matter who I am; you found something inside me, the same thing I found in you, and in that, we found us.

I will always love you, Catherine. I will love you even when the tomorrows are gone, and all we have left are memories. I will love you when my time has run out. I will love you even when my body is in ashes. Our bodies only keep us here, but our spirits set us free.

People don't make us whole; we make ourselves whole, but I don't think we can do that until we learn to love ourselves, our past, and where we came from.

When you see orange Starbursts, think of me. When you see the light through the clouds, think of me.

Andrew Wyman, my attorney, has an account set aside for you to do with as you wish.

In Myers Flat, you'll find a cabin I purchased on the Eel River for you to go to when you need time to slow down, to take a breather and remember what life is really all about.

Also, he has all the arrangements about what I want after I'm gone.

No funeral.

Just ashes.

The car is yours.

I gave Julie the house in Carpinteria to do with as she wanted. I'm sure she'll have some grieving to do there, too.

You are my light. I hope you always feel that, Cat.

Go be bold.

Move mountains.

Find love, the kind that you can't fall out of.

Yours forever,

Luke

I close the letter and carefully place it back into its envelope, barely able to see because of the tears. My face feels swollen from crying, and I'm lonely inside, but I know in my heart that this feeling is temporary—though the *temporary* might last years. I look over at the passenger seat with Luke's ashes, and a wave of grief comes over me.

I turn to the back seat to grab my purse and see a medium-sized canvas bag.

Who in the hell put that there?

I reach in the back seat and pull the canvas bag to the front seat, putting it on my lap. I pull the drawstring, and all I see are orange Starbursts.

I laugh out loud, dropping my head back.

Then, the tears come and go, and come and go.

Another wave of grief passes over me.

If my heart didn't ache so much, it would mean I hadn't had the opportunity to love the way we did.

EPILOGUE

Six Years Later
August 2020

"Mommy, I wish Daddy were here to walk me in," little James says in his sweet tiny voice, holding my hand as we both stare from the walkway of Mrs. Love's kindergarten classroom.

I decided to name our little boy after Luke's father, James. I know he would have wanted it that way.

Fiona leans down. "That's why you have a big sister. Unfortunately, Dad couldn't take me to my first day of kindergarten either. But, James, I know he's here with us in spirit; I feel it. Come on; I'll walk you in."

Fiona looks at me. I can't help the tears as they begin to fall. For my little James, for Fiona, and for us, Luke and me.

"Thank you," I whisper.

Fiona nods. Smiles. She's twenty-six now, and everything she does reminds me of her father. She moved out to California to be closer to us, to teach at James's school. Her heart is her father's. And I can't help but love this beautiful young lady just as much as I love little James.

Fiona met a man named, of all the names in the world, Luke. Can you believe it?

He's a nice man, and he'd have met all of Luke's expectations. I know it. He plays the guitar and surfs. And I don't question any of it anymore.

As for me and little James, I don't know where we're headed, but I see as far as today, and that's okay.

Before Fiona walks James in, he spots an orange Starburst on the ground. "Mommy! Look, it's Daddy!"

Sometimes, it's the light within the storm that saves us even if we think we don't need saving.

The End

ACKNOWLEDGMENTS

Hang Le, my cover designer—You have a way of taking what I have in my head and putting it into a beautiful picture that encapsulates my stories. I adore you.

Jovana Shirley, my editor and formatter—You are extremely great at what you do. You take my books and make the words find their place. I'm so honored we get to work together.

Julie Deaton, my proofreader—Thank you for putting the finishing touches on my books, and your attention to detail blows my mind. I'm so thankful you're in my corner.

Jessica Estep, my publicist, the other half of my brain—You are a dream. I don't know what I'd do without you.

Book bloggers—You promote our books for fun and for free. We can't do what we do without you. Know that all your hard work doesn't go unnoticed. Thank you for taking the time with mine.

My readers—Oh goodness. Thank you for embarking on this journey with me. Thank you for believing in me.

The Bailey Bunch, my reader group—Together, we are strong. Thank you for your grace, your strength, and for pushing me to finish the next book. I'm so lucky to have you ladies.

Brandon, Teyler, and Kate—You are the greatest gift of all. Thank you for being my soft place to land.

A NOTE TO THE READER

THANK YOU FOR READING *THE LIGHT WE SEE.*

If you enjoyed the book, please consider leaving an honest review on the website you purchased the book from. By leaving a review, it makes the book more visible to more readers. The more reviews, the better promotional opportunities for the author.

Get the latest information on book releases, sales, and more.

Sign up for J. Lynn Bailey's newsletter at http://bit.ly/2VVmqna to get sneak peeks, early excerpts, and free books.

Have you joined my reading group *The Bailey Bunch*? Join below for behind the scenes book information, giveaways, and top-secret book information. Learn about the inter-workings of my writing process, and my crazy ideas.

The Bailey Bunch: http://bit.ly/2EscfjT

Connect with J. Lynn Online:

www.facebook.com/AuthorJLynnBailey

www.instagram.com/jlynnbaileybooks/

https://twitter.com/authorJLynn

www.jlynnbaileybooks.com

ABOUT THE AUTHOR

J. LYNN BAILEY is a best-selling and award-winning author who has loved to write since she learned to read, around the second grade. She's earned a bachelor's degree and master's degree from Humboldt State University.

When she isn't running her children to their next sporting event, watching *North Woods Law*, or on the hunt for her next Laffy Taffy joke, you can probably find her holed up in her writing room, feverishly working on her next book. She lives in Northern California with her family.

OTHER BOOKS WRITTEN BY J. LYNN BAILEY

The Granite Harbor Series

Peony Red

Violet Ugly

Magnolia Road

Lilies On Main

Black Five

Standing Sideways

THE DILLON CREEK SERIES (COMING IN 2020)

Made in the USA
Lexington, KY
23 November 2019